"Don't you think you could add a new lesson or two to their day?"

"Papa! She did already. We're going to start reading lessons soon," Polly said.

"Hmm, I'm not sure that's enough."

Georgia loved seeing him tease his daughters like this, but she didn't like her reaction at his innocent wink at all. She was sure he had no idea how it affected her and she wasn't sure at all why it had. Except that he was even handsomer than usual when he was in a playful mood like now.

"Oh, Papa, you're teasing, isn't he, Miss Georgia?" Lilly asked.

"Oh, I don't know…" She played along with Sir Tyler.

"Miss Georgia!"

"In fact, now that you girls are through with your breakfast, I need to talk to Miss Geo… Miss Marshall about your lessons. So if it's all right with her, perhaps you could go out into the garden while we have our talk."

Georgia turned, finding Sir Tyler watching her, and something in his expression sent her pulse on a collision course straight to her heart.

Janet Lee Barton loves researching and writing heartwarming romances about faith, family, friends and love. She's written both historical and contemporary novels, and loves writing for Love Inspired Historical. She and her husband live in Oklahoma and have recently downsized to a condo, which they love. When Janet isn't writing or reading, she loves to cook for family, work in her small garden, travel and sew. You can visit Janet at janetleebarton.com.

Books by Janet Lee Barton

Love Inspired Historical

Boardinghouse Betrothals

Somewhere to Call Home
A Place of Refuge
A Home for Her Heart
A Daughter's Return
The Mistletoe Kiss
A Nanny for Keeps

JANET LEE BARTON

A Nanny for Keeps

HARLEQUIN® LOVE INSPIRED® HISTORICAL

Recycling programs
for this product may
not exist in your area.

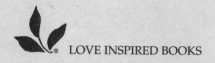

LOVE INSPIRED BOOKS

ISBN-13: 978-0-373-28365-1

A Nanny for Keeps

Copyright © 2016 by Janet Lee Barton

www.Harlequin.com

Printed in U.S.A.

And again, I will put my trust in him.
And again, Behold I and the children
which God had given me.
—*Hebrews* 2:13

To my editor, Giselle Regus,
for always being willing to brainstorm ideas with me.

To my readers who look forward to each new story.

To my husband, Dan,
and my family for always supporting me.

And most of all, as always and forever,
to my Lord and Savior for showing me the way.

Chapter One

New York City
Spring 1898

Georgia Marshall stepped off the trolley and headed down the sidewalk toward Gramercy Park and Heaton House. The spring day was beautiful with clear blue skies and sunshine, along with trees and flowers beginning to bud, but she was preoccupied and barely noticed. After her interview with the school superintendent, it appeared she must give up on finding a teaching position until the next term, which meant she needed to find employment as soon as possible.

Thankfully, she had some money saved from her teaching days in Virginia. And when she arrived in New York City, Mrs. Heaton had refused to charge her rent until she found suitable employment. She'd insisted Georgia was a family friend and she didn't want her to feel pressured. Because of her charitableness, Georgia hadn't needed to dig into her savings.

However, she couldn't take advantage of Mrs. Heaton's kindness any longer. She would find employment, even if it wasn't in her preferred field. She refused to return home. There was nothing for her there. She'd pour over the classifieds again later that evening in hopes of finding something she might be qualified for.

Just walking up the steps to Heaton House comforted her. Georgia had felt at home from the very first, and the warm and welcoming feeling always seemed to lift her spirits. She let herself in, surprised to hear a man's voice in the parlor at teatime. It was unusual for any of the male boarders to be home at this time of day.

She peeked inside to see Mrs. Heaton speaking to her new neighbor from England, if his accent was any indication.

"Georgia, dear! Come in and join us. I believe you might have met at Matt and Millicent's wedding last month, but if not, let me introduce you to Sir Tyler Walker. Sir Tyler, Miss Marshall is a family friend and boarder here."

Georgia caught her breath as the tall, broad-shouldered man, who'd stood and started toward her the moment she entered the room, took her hand in his and bowed over it. "I don't believe we did. But, Miss Marshall, it's a pleasure to meet you now."

She knew he was a baronet, but this wasn't England and she didn't know whether to curtsy or not. She knew nothing of the hierarchy in England, so she dipped her head instead. Still, she wasn't sure how to address him. "A pleasure to meet you, too, Sir…Walker?"

"I'd be called Sir Tyler in England, but I'm making my home here now, so perhaps Mr. Walker will do?"

"That might make it easier." Georgia tried to ignore the fluttery feeling in the vicinity of her heart and slipped her hand from his. She smiled and took a seat beside her landlady, who held a cup of tea for her. "Thank you, Mrs. Heaton. This is just what I need."

The baronet took his seat across from Mrs. Heaton once again and let her freshen his tea.

Georgia hoped no one noticed that her fingers trembled as she raised her cup to her mouth. She remembered seeing Sir—Mr. Walker and his daughters at the wedding, but not up this close. He was the most handsome man she'd ever met, with his almost black hair and ocean-blue eyes.

"Mr. Walker has come asking for help in finding someone to act as a nanny to his young daughters, until he can find a permanent one," Mrs. Heaton explained.

"Oh? I thought you'd brought your help over with you?" Mr. Walker and his entourage had been quite a topic of conversation at the dinner table for several nights not long after he'd moved in next door.

"Yes, well, the nanny became homesick and wanted to go back to England. I'd promised I would pay her way back home and had to keep my word. But the one I hired to replace her didn't last but two weeks. And neither did the next."

"I'm so sorry," Georgia said. He did have a dilemma on his hands, but her heart went out to his two young girls. They'd lost their mother and were bound to still be missing her.

"Yes, so am I." Mr. Walker released a deep sigh

before continuing in his charming English accent. "It appears my daughters might be trying to run off the help. The maid is watching them now, but she isn't happy about it. She doesn't want to be their nanny and I can't say I blame her. The girls are a bit incorrigible at times."

"And quite adorable," Mrs. Heaton added.

Mr. Walker smiled and shook his head. "I'm not sure what to do. I know they miss their mother, and moving away from their familiar surroundings might not have been for the best, although I could no longer—" He cut off what he'd been about to say and cleared his throat.

The sorrow in his expression was unmistakable and Georgia's heart flooded with sympathy for him. His wife had been gone just over a year, and trying to raise his young daughters without her must be terribly difficult.

"I'll get in touch with any friends I believe might be able to help and let you know what I find out as soon as I can," Mrs. Heaton said.

"Thank you, Mrs. Heaton. I appreciate your willingness to assist me." Mr. Walker took a sip of tea and then placed it back on the saucer and stood. "I suppose I should get back. No telling what those two might be up to. I can't let the maid up and leave, too. I've begun to think that my mother was right. I should have brought some of her household staff with me."

Mrs. Heaton accompanied him to the door and Georgia heard him say, "It's good to have a neighbor one can come to for advice. Thank you for tea."

"You're quite welcome anytime, Sir Tyler. I'll be in touch soon."

"I look forward to hearing from you."

Mrs. Heaton came back into the room and refreshed both hers and Georgia's tea. "Poor man. It's got to be so distressing to move away from all that's familiar after losing one's spouse. And even more so while trying to hold his family together and comfort his children."

"I agree. After all, our culture is a bit different here than in England."

"Yes, it is. Not so much at his level as at ours, but he seems to want to embrace the American way of life. His wife was from here and he wants his girls to grow up in this country."

"He must have loved her very much."

"I'm sure he did. Perhaps he'll find a suitable wife before long—one who will love him and his children."

"He's a handsome man," Georgia said. "I'm sure that once the daughters of the wealthy in this city are introduced to him, he'll have his choice of women."

"Oh, but not all of those young debutantes will be interested in marrying a man with children. It may be more difficult than we think. In the meantime, I hope we can find someone to help out."

"You mean until he finds a mate?"

"Yes, or a permanent nanny. I'm not sure he's ready to find a wife just yet. I'll think on things. But for now, I'd best go see how our dinner is coming along." She gathered up the tea tray and started toward the door before turning back to Georgia. "If you come up with any ideas, I'd love to hear them."

"I'll think on it."

Mrs. Heaton turned just before she left the room. "I'm sorry, Georgia. I didn't have a chance to ask if you had any good news about procuring a teaching position anywhere."

"No, ma'am. I believe I'm going to have to find a position of some kind but it won't be teaching, at least not until the new term in the fall. My timing seems to be awful. I'd put my name in at several schools when I first came, but they have a long list of those looking for positions and I'm far down on it."

"Perhaps you should try something else," Mrs. Heaton suggested.

"I believe I'm going to have to."

"You know, Georgia...I'm sure Sir Walker will pay very well and you want a job. Would *you* consider filling in for a short time?"

Only now did Georgia realize the same thought had been forming at the back of her mind, but she didn't think she was qualified. "I don't know. I've never been a nanny for anyone."

"But you've taught young children, haven't you?"

"I have." And she was quite good at it, from what her letter of reference said.

"Oh, his little girls are so sweet," Mrs. Heaton said. "I hear them outside playing on warm days. It's so sad that they don't have a mother."

"It is," Georgia said. "I'm sure that losing the nanny who'd always taken care of them must be almost as hard as losing their mother. Perhaps I should consider it. I don't have anything else to do right now and—"

"You'd be doing a great favor for Sir Tyler. He has such sadness in his eyes."

Yes, he did. And that sadness and worry about the care for his daughters had touched Georgia's heart and made her wish she could help—even though she'd never thought about being a nanny. "But doesn't a nanny live in? I don't think I'd want to do that."

"I'm sure you could come to an agreement. It would be temporary, after all. Perhaps you could offer to be there to get them up and dressed and stay until they ate dinner or were put to bed. And surely you could ask for some free time on weekends."

"I suppose I could think about it…" Georgia said.

"It might be an answered prayer for you both," Mrs. Heaton said. "But I must check on dinner now. I appreciate your giving thought to it."

She hurried away and Georgia headed up to her room. Mrs. Heaton took helping others very seriously and Georgia knew she wouldn't rest until Mr. Walker had what—or who—he needed. Perhaps this was an opportunity for her to have work and assist a neighbor in need at the same time. She'd have to pray about it.

Tyler took his leave, glad he'd gone to ask Mrs. Heaton for guidance. She was a kind woman and he felt sure she would do what she could to try to find someone to fill in as nanny.

And although he hadn't been formally introduced to Georgia Marshall at the wedding he and his daughters had been invited to not long after they'd moved in, he remembered seeing her there. Since then he'd caught a glimpse or two of her going in and out of Heaton House.

One couldn't help but notice her. She was lovely, with her dark brown hair and deep green eyes. But he hadn't expected his reaction to being near to her.

Her smile had warmed his heart and made his chest tighten in a way it hadn't since his wife passed away.

And because of that reaction, Tyler quickly forced Miss Marshall out of his mind. He wasn't looking for love or a wife. Not now and not in the future. All he needed at the moment was someone to take care of his daughters.

His butler opened the door the moment his foot touched the top step. What would he do without Mr. Tate? Thankfully, the man had no plans of desertion, at least not that he'd voiced to Tyler.

"How did it go, sir? Did Mrs. Heaton have any ideas about replacing the nanny?"

His butler was the one person Tyler felt he could confide in here in his new home. "Not right away, but she's going to see if she can find someone to help. I'm glad I thought to go to her, since it's obvious that the service I've gone through hasn't worked."

"Much as I dislike saying so, I believe that is true, Sir Tyler. And I hate to be the bearer of bad news, but I feel I must tell you that the cook is making noises about leaving again."

"Oh, dear, what have the girls done now?"

"It's not Miss Polly or Miss Lilly, sir. They've done nothing to cause this. Mrs. Biddle just doesn't like it here very much. Or so she says."

Tyler sighed. He'd felt better after speaking with Mrs. Heaton, but he wasn't confident even she could find anyone to help him. And now this. "I'll speak to her."

"That might help. It certainly can't hurt at this point."

Dear Lord, please help me. Now I might need a

cook, too. I should have brought over a housekeeper to deal with some of these problems. Did I make the wrong decision in coming here? And what made me believe I could do this? I felt it was the answer, but perhaps I was wrong.

"Where are the girls now?"

"The maid gave them a snack earlier and they were in the playroom when I checked on them a few minutes ago."

"Thank you, Tate. I can't tell you how much your presence here is helping with this move. You aren't thinking of leaving us, are you?"

"No, sir. It is a change to be sure, but my loyalties are with you and your family, Sir Tyler. I wish to work for no one else."

"That puts my mind at ease. I'll check on the girls and then go speak to Mrs. Biddle."

"Very good, sir."

Tyler gave his butler a nod and headed upstairs to his daughters' playroom. The designer he'd hired on recommendation from his in-laws had done a wonderful job. The room was bright and sunny, decorated in blue and white. The girls were busy playing with their three-story dollhouse and talking for the dolls. He loved watching them and stood quietly at the door until they noticed him.

"Papa!" Polly jumped up and ran to him with her younger sister, Lilly, right behind her.

"We missed you, Papa!" Lilly said, kissing him on the cheek as he gathered them both up, one in each arm.

"We truly did," Polly agreed, giving him a kiss on the other cheek.

He took them to the settee and sat down, one on each side of him.

"I went to Mrs. Heaton's to ask—"

"Without us? Oh, Papa, we love taking tea at Mrs. Heaton's!" Lilly exclaimed.

They'd gone only once to have tea with Mrs. Heaton and her daughter and granddaughter. But they'd taken a liking to their neighbor right away. "We'll go another time, I'm sure, Lilly. But today I needed to ask her assistance in finding someone to help out—at least until I can find a permanent nanny."

"Oh, Papa," Polly said, "we don't want any mean old nanny. Why couldn't Mary stay?"

"Why did she have to leave us?" Lilly asked in an overly dramatic tone.

"She got homesick for England and I'd promised I'd send her home if she didn't want to stay."

"Why wouldn't she want to stay with us?" Polly asked, her eyes filling with tears. "She's been with us since we were born and after Mama passed away, too."

"You know Nanny loved you both. It was hard for her to leave you. But she missed her family and she doesn't like cities."

"Oh," Lilly said, a tear plopping out of her eye. "But we miss her."

"I know you do. And I'm sure she misses the two of you, too."

Mary had been a good nanny and the girls did love her. She'd cried when he took her to the ship to leave, telling him she knew how much he and his girls had already lost and that she felt as if she was deserting them. Which was exactly how Tyler felt, too.

He'd heard Mary was thinking of leaving from Tate and Mrs. Biddle, but she'd kept it from him and the girls as long as she could. But she had been miserable. In the end, she missed her own family too much to stay, and Tyler felt he had no choice but to let her go back.

"Well, I hope you'll like the next nanny better than the one I hired to replace Mary and then the next one. You weren't very nice to her, you know."

"She wasn't nice to us when you weren't around, Papa," Polly said.

"I'm sorry. You should have told me, instead of trying to run her away."

"We weren't exactly trying to do that, Papa. We were kind of..." Lilly looked over at Polly.

"If she wasn't going to stay, we wanted her to leave as soon as possible," his older daughter stated matter-of-factly. "If they don't want to be nanny to us, we don't want them to be."

Tyler sighed and pulled his daughters closer, kissing them each on the top of the head. He didn't know what to say. He understood their reasoning, but he felt terribly inept at figuring out what to do in this situation. It seemed he questioned every decision he'd made since Ivy had passed away.

All he really could do was pray for the Lord to help him talk Mrs. Biddle into staying, and for Mrs. Heaton to come up with someone to help out as soon as possible. He'd never thought the move to America would be such a huge adjustment for them all. And that might have been the root of the problem. He hadn't thought things through at all.

* * *

Sir Walker's dilemma had been on Georgia's mind ever since he'd left Heaton House. She'd heard his daughters playing in their courtyard from time to time when she'd been out in Mrs. Heaton's small garden reading. They were pretty little girls and she hated that not only did they have to adjust to a new country without their mother, but they also didn't have a nanny to care for them in her place. She'd mulled over Mrs. Heaton's suggestion and prayed about it and thought she'd come to a decision.

She dressed for dinner in a pink silk damask-and-satin dress trimmed with cream lace and silk braid. Then she went through the bathroom she shared with one of the new boarders, a seamstress named Betsy Thomas, and knocked on the door to her room.

"Georgia, come in. I was just about to go down to dinner. That pink looks lovely on you."

"Thank you. You look very nice, too." Betsy was quite pretty with dark, almost black, hair and blue eyes. She was dressed in a silk gown almost the same shade as her eyes. "We'll go down together."

"I appreciate that. It still feels a little awkward entering the parlor alone. I don't know why, when everyone has been so kind to me."

"You've only been here a few days. By next week, you'll be breezing in without even thinking about it."

"I hope so."

Mrs. Heaton had put out her sign the week before. Her boarders seemed to have a propensity to fall in love while living at Heaton House, and she had to keep putting out a sign to fill the boardinghouse once

more. But it never took more than a few days to ac-
complish that.

Georgia loved living here and getting to know the
other boarders. They were a tight-knit group who enjoyed spending time with each other—even after they
married. They enjoyed going on all kinds of outings
together. And one of the best times was having dinner together.

With Mrs. Heaton at the helm, it was a time to
share how their days had gone and to either commis-
erate or rejoice with each other, depending on what
had happened.

She and Betsy joined the others in the parlor. Julia,
the boarder who'd been there the longest, and Emily,
who was fairly new, were there with Stephen and
Joe—they'd moved in at the same time Emily had.
Then there was Samuel and Dave, who'd joined the
mix a few days ago at the same time as Betsy. The
men dipped their heads to Georgia and Betsy as they
entered, just as Mrs. Heaton announced dinner was
ready.

It was customary for the men to escort the ladies
to the table, and tonight it was Stephen who crooked
his arm for her. But as he pulled out her chair, it was
Emily he had his eyes on. Samuel beat him to her
this evening and Georgia could tell Stephen wasn't
at all happy about it.

It was such fun wondering who might be the next
couple to come out of Heaton House. Georgia knew for
sure that she would not be part of one. She was barely
over being rejected by the one man she'd thought to
marry until he'd become her brother-in-law. Since then
she'd vowed she would never give her heart to another.

Mrs. Heaton brought Georgia's attention back to the present as she asked Stephen to say the blessing. Then Gretchen and Maida, Mrs. Heaton's household help, brought in dinner and began to serve. As dishes were passed around the table, their landlady asked about their day. That conversation didn't take long tonight, as nothing out of the ordinary seemed to have happened in anyone's workday.

She turned to Georgia. "Have you had time to think about helping Sir Tyler out?"

"I've prayed about it and I believe it might be the thing to do, at least for a bit, although I really don't know anything about being a nanny."

"Why don't I telephone Sir Tyler and speak to him about it? I'll stress that it will only be temporary until he can find a permanent nanny and see what he thinks?"

Georgia released a sigh of relief. She wasn't sure how to even approach the man about helping out. "That might be the best."

"I'll telephone him after dinner and let you know what he says. Then you can decide for sure if it's something you might want to do."

Mrs. Heaton was a dear. Georgia knew the woman would want to assure herself that everything would be on the up-and-up if she took the position. After all, they didn't know Sir Tyler all that well and Mrs. Heaton would want to make certain Georgia would be treated well. Of that she had no doubt.

And deep inside she was sure Sir…Mr. Walker… No, Sir Tyler? Oh! What was she to call the man?

Whatever she settled on, she felt sure he was an

honorable man. Which only created another problem—Georgia wasn't certain her instincts where men were concerned could ever be trusted again.

Chapter Two

The next morning after breakfast, Georgia hurried upstairs to neaten her hair and put on a hat before she and Mrs. Heaton went to meet with Sir Tyler Walker.

"He sounded so relieved, Georgia. I'm sure you'll be able to find Sir Tyler willing to work any schedule you please. He seems desperate and is now afraid he might lose his cook," Mrs. Heaton had said after speaking with him the evening before.

"Oh, the poor man," Georgia had answered. It seemed as if he had more than his share of problems at the moment.

Now, as Georgia came back downstairs and entered the parlor to wait for Mrs. Heaton, she told herself to relax. She'd not agreed to anything yet and she didn't have to take the position. Still, the thought of those little girls being left with no mother—and now no nanny—twisted Georgia's heart, and the nurturer in her wanted to help them. And besides, she truly needed a paying position.

Mrs. Heaton entered the parlor and smiled. "You

look lovely this morning, Georgia. Don't be nervous and please do not feel you have to take this position, if you don't think it right for you. Also remember, Sir Tyler may be a baronet in England, but he lives here now and we are not English citizens. Even with pay, you'll be doing the man a great favor if you accept the position and he should treat you accordingly."

"Thank you for that reminder, Mrs. Heaton. I'm glad you're going with me. I'm feeling a little jittery."

"There's no need to be. But let's be on our way. You'll feel much better once you've spoken with him and made a decision."

They headed out the door and were on the steps of Walker House, as they called it, in just over a minute.

Mrs. Heaton rang the bell and a man Georgia assumed to be the butler opened the door instantly.

"Mrs. Heaton, and Miss Marshall, I presume?"

At Georgia's nod, he said, "Do come in. Sir Tyler is waiting for you in his study. Please follow me."

They fell into step behind him and Georgia couldn't help but notice how tastefully decorated the home was. Had Sir Tyler hired a decorator or—

"Mrs. Heaton and Miss Marshall have arrived, sir," the butler said.

"Very good, Tate. Would you bring us some tea?"

"Certainly, sir."

He seemed to disappear as his employer crossed the room to greet them.

"Welcome to my home, ladies," Sir Tyler said, motioning them to have a seat.

Georgia knew he'd said "Mr. Walker" would be fine, but it was hard to think of him as that, knowing he was part of the gentry in England. He might not be royalty, but still…

"Thank you, Sir Tyler," Mrs. Heaton said, seeming to have no problem addressing him as they did in England.

"Yes—thank you." Georgia joined her landlady on a comfortable couch across from two chairs and a round table. Sir Walker—Tyler—took one of the chairs. The room was warm and masculine, with book-filled shelves lining the walls. It reminded her of Mrs. Heaton's study, only it was larger.

"I can't tell you how relieved I was when Mrs. Heaton telephoned last evening," he said. "Even more this morning, as my cook still hasn't assured me she will stay, and I might be needing to find a new one any day now."

"Oh, you have had your share of bad news, haven't you?" Mrs. Heaton asked.

"It certainly seems that way to me," the baronet said before turning to Georgia. "Miss Marshall, Mrs. Heaton has told me that you are a teacher by trade?"

"I am."

"Would you mind adding some lessons to the duties of being a nanny?"

"Of course not, if we come to an agreement. What exactly would my duties be?"

"Well, mostly making sure my daughters are cared for, eat proper meals, have a schedule of sorts." He shrugged and looked her in the eye. "To be quite truthful, I'm not totally sure. My wife handled everything like that and then I just let the nanny carry on as she always had, until she left."

"I understand," Georgia said. Only she really didn't.

Her mother had a cook and maid to help out from time to time, but she'd raised her children without the help of a nanny. And now Sir Tyler looked so forlorn she couldn't tell him that his explanation gave her no idea of what would really be expected of her.

"Mrs. Heaton and I spoke last evening and, well, I wonder… Would you be willing to come in of a morning and get them dressed, see that they have breakfast and lunch and decide what their activities of the day might be? Then making sure they have dinner and baths at night and perhaps staying to put them to bed before you leave? Would that work for you?"

He didn't put his own children to bed? Or eat with them? Oh, this might be more difficult than she'd first thought. And she didn't want to upset him by asking.

"I realize it's a very long day, but I'm willing to pay quite well." He named an amount that left Georgia speechless for the moment, and she was glad when he continued speaking. "And my staff and I will manage on the weekends."

"So this is from Monday morning until Friday evening? And I'll still be living at Heaton House?"

"If that is what you want. Mrs. Heaton has explained that would be better, as you aren't in service to me, only stepping in until I can find someone more permanent. Is this agreeable to you?"

"I— Could I meet with your daughters first? They might not take to me and I don't want to upset their world any more than it's already been."

There was a look in his eyes she couldn't quite read, but it made her wish she hadn't reminded him of his loss. "I'm sorry. I—"

"No." He shook his head and cleared his throat before continuing, "Thank you for your thoughtfulness, Miss Marshall. I should have thought of that myself. Of course you may meet them."

Tate returned with tea just then, and after serving them, he turned to Sir Tyler. "Will that be all, sir?"

"Please have the maid bring Lilly and Polly down, Tate. Miss Marshall would like to meet them."

"Yes, sir." With that, the butler exited the room.

"How old are your daughters, Sir Tyler?" Mrs. Heaton asked. "I know they're near my granddaughter Jenny's age."

"Yes, they are. Polly is five and Lilly is four. They like Jenny very much. And they like you, too, Mrs. Heaton. In fact, they were quite upset with me for going to see you at teatime without them yesterday."

"Oh, please bring them over soon for tea. I'd love to have them."

"That's very kind of you. Perhaps Miss Marshall might do so—if she agrees to step in. My daughters mean everything to me. I pray I haven't done the wrong thing by uprooting them and moving them away from all they know best. But they do seem to like it here. Or perhaps they don't want to let me know that they don't."

Georgia's heart softened toward the man who seemed so concerned about his daughters' well-being. And yet he didn't appear to know much about their daily routines or how they felt about the move. How could that be?

Suddenly she heard footsteps running down stairs and the sound of the sweet voices she'd heard from Mrs. Heaton's garden. But they quieted just before they entered the room, appearing quite serious when they did. Though upon recognizing Mrs. Heaton, the corners of their mouths turned up in sweet smiles.

"Papa, Mr. Tate said you wanted to see us," one of Sir Tyler's daughters said. Georgia assumed she was the oldest, as she was about an inch taller than the sister who stood beside her.

"Yes. Mrs. Heaton has brought Miss Marshall to meet you. Miss Marshall, these are my daughters, Polly, the oldest and tallest, and Lilly."

"I'm pleased to meet you both," Georgia said as the blond-haired, blue-eyed girls smiled in her direction.

"Miss Marshall is considering helping out with you two until we can find a new nanny. But she wanted to know what you both think of the idea."

"We've seen you coming in and out of Mrs. Heaton's house," Polly said.

"Yes, and we've peeked through the hedge and seen you in her garden, too," Lilly added.

"I thought I'd heard you over there." Georgia smiled to show she wasn't upset that they'd been looking through the boxwoods.

"Would you live here?" Polly asked.

"No. I'll still live at Heaton House. But I'll be here first thing in the morning and until bedtime on the days I work."

"You won't watch us every day?" Lilly asked.

"No," her father answered. "Miss Marshall isn't a nanny, but a teacher here in America. She's looking for a permanent teaching position while we're looking for a permanent nanny. It is nice of her to offer to help us out, isn't it?"

Both girls nodded, but Georgia couldn't tell if they

were happy or disappointed that she wouldn't be living with them.

"But what if we need something in the night?" Lilly asked.

"You'll come to me," Sir Tyler answered. "I'm just across the hall."

"You won't mind?" Polly asked.

Sir Tyler's brow furrowed as if he was surprised at the question. "Of course not."

Georgia couldn't quite grasp that his daughters might think he would be upset if they woke him during the night. Had they called only the nanny?

"Well, then, I think it might work out," Polly said, sounding as grown up as a five-year-old could, and as much as the child she was could muster.

In that moment, Georgia knew she'd be taking this position if they agreed.

"What about you, Lilly?" her father asked. "Do you want Miss Marshall to help us out?"

Lilly looked from him to Georgia and then to her sister. Georgia saw the older sister give a little nod and Lilly smiled. "Yes, I think I do."

"But you must mind her as you would your nanny. You understand that, don't you?"

"Yes, Papa, we do," Polly answered for the two of them. "May we have tea with you and Mrs. Heaton and Miss Marshall?"

Sir Tyler smiled. "I suppose, since you didn't get to go with me yesterday, I can only say, yes, you may. Mrs. Heaton, would you mind pouring them a cup?"

"I'd be delighted." Georgia watched as her landlady poured for the little girls and they took their first sip of tea.

"And, girls, be sure to mind your manners," their papa said. "Miss Marshall hasn't agreed to help us out yet."

"Oh, please say yes, Miss Marshall!" Lilly said.

"Oh, yes, please do!" Polly added.

Georgia felt a tug in her heart at their pleas. She glanced at their papa and thought she saw hope in his eyes until he looked away. This family needed help and Sir Tyler was going to pay well. She needed work. There was only one answer she could give. "Yes. I'll be here first thing Monday morning."

The relief in Sir Tyler's eyes and the smiles on his daughters' faces made her feel she'd done the right thing. Now she could only pray that she had.

Promising to check on his daughters after the maid, Amelia, gave them their baths and got them ready for bed, Tyler headed out the door for a walk. He needed some fresh air. He'd been pouring over American law books in order to take the New York bar exam and it wasn't an easy task, but this was to be his home now and where he did business. He had no choice but to learn the differences and make note of them. He didn't want his clients complaining that he'd made any kind of mistake because of subtle variations.

Now he took a deep breath of the evening air and released a huge sigh of relief. The girls seemed happy that Miss Marshall had agreed to take care of them until he could find someone suitable, and he was quite pleased himself. Or perhaps *relieved* was a better word.

That Mrs. Heaton had known Miss Marshall all her life and recommended her highly, thinking so much of her that she wanted to make sure the young woman's reputation would be protected under his care, said all he'd needed to know about her.

Georgia Marshall seemed to relate to his daughters on some level he didn't really understand. They'd chattered away as if they'd known her all their lives after she'd said she would help out, and he'd been surprised at how well they'd minded their manners.

Making the move to America hadn't been an easy decision for him, but his wife's family had holdings here and they wanted him to look after them for their granddaughters' sake.

As the middle son, he'd had no real reason to stay in England. His older brother would inherit the land and all there. However, Tyler wasn't penniless, as his grandfather had bequeathed him a very nice sum on his death. Tyler had gone to school and become an attorney and could easily set up practice here—once he passed that exam.

Most important in his decision to make the move was that he'd be raising his daughters in their mother's country, as she'd wished before she passed away. He felt that was the very least he could do for the woman he'd loved dearly.

Had it been just over a year since Ivy had passed away? Sometimes it felt like a lifetime and other times only as if it was yesterday. But always, there seemed to be an empty spot in his heart, and tonight was no different. Especially now, as he neared his home from his walk around Gramercy Park and heard people laughing as they approached from the opposite direction.

Somehow it didn't surprise him to see a group

of Mrs. Heaton's boarders coming back from one of their outings. It was a mix of men and women, and he wondered if one of the ladies might be Miss Marshall.

He didn't have to wonder long as they all reached their destinations at the same time. One of the women broke away from the group and he was taken by surprise as his chest tightened when he recognized her under the streetlamp.

"Sir Tyler?"

"Yes. Miss Marshall, how are you this evening?"

"I'm fine. We've all been to the soda shop for ice cream. It's getting warm enough now to enjoy it."

"I took the girls there a few days ago and they loved it. I've been out for a walk while they are being put to bed." He'd been introduced to some of Mrs. Heaton's boarders at the wedding reception he'd attended, but there appeared to be new people in the group heading into Heaton House.

"Good evening, Sir Tyler," the one he knew as Joe said.

"Good evening. It's a nice night for ice cream, isn't it?"

"It is. Georgia, are you coming in?"

"Yes, of course." She turned to Tyler. "Good night."

"Good night."

She turned to where Joe was waiting for her and then back to Tyler. "Have a good evening."

"You, too." He tipped his hat as she hurried up the steps to Heaton House. Then she disappeared inside, leaving Tyler suddenly feeling lonelier than ever.

Tate opened the door as soon as Tyler's foot hit the top step. "Good evening, sir. Did you have a nice walk?"

"I did, Tate. Thank you. I'm going up to look in on the girls. I'll be back down in a few minutes. Would you bring me some coffee?"

"Certainly."

Tyler headed upstairs, wondering if Joe was Miss Marshall's beau. He'd seemed quite protective of her, but then, so did Mrs. Heaton. The thought that Miss Marshall might have a suitor didn't sit well with him and that unsettled Tyler. He shouldn't even be wondering about her personal life. It was none of his business. She'd agreed to help him out and for that he was very thankful. As long as his girls were taken care of, that was all that mattered. He had no business even wondering about Miss Marshall's social life—none at all.

Tyler slipped into the room his daughters shared, even though there were plenty of rooms and each one could have had their own. However, since their mother's death, they'd wanted to be together at night. He kissed them each on the forehead, softly so as not to wake them. Oh, how he loved them.

Tyler hoped all would go well with Miss Marshall until he could find a permanent nanny—and that the girls didn't try to run her away as they had the last one. But they knew Miss Marshall was only temporary, so surely they wouldn't.

Tyler slipped out of the room, leaving the door cracked open so he could hear them if they called out in the night, and went down to his study to find Tate just pouring his coffee. The butler must have waited until he heard his footsteps.

He sat down in his favorite chair and took the cup Tate handed him.

"Cook sent you a piece of cake, sir. She seems much better after you spoke to her."

Tyler wasn't all that hungry but he wasn't about to hurt his cook's feelings, especially when he was trying to keep her on. He took the dessert plate from Tate. "I'm glad to hear it. I hope she's changed her mind about staying."

"It appears so, at least for the moment."

"I suppose we'll have to be happy with that. Thank her for the cake, will you?"

"I will, sir." Tate gave a nod and quietly took his leave.

Tyler finished the dessert he really didn't want and took a sip of coffee, and then he leaned his head back against his chair. This time of night was never easy for him. It'd always been the time that he and Ivy had enjoyed together, talking over their day after the girls had been put to bed. She'd tell him funny stories about the things Polly and Lilly had said and done that day, and then she'd update him on their upcoming social engagements and family commitments.

It hadn't taken Ivy long to win over his parents. A second or third cousin to one of his best friends, she'd come to visit her relatives and they'd fallen in love. At first Tyler's family had voiced disapproval, but as he wasn't the heir apparent of their estate, he was more able to obtain their blessing than his older brother would have been.

That Ivy came with a substantial wealth of her own certainly helped, although it'd had nothing to do with how he felt about her. He would have loved her had she been a pauper.

But tonight his thoughts weren't just on Ivy. Instead

they were also on Georgia Marshall. He wondered if hiring her was the right thing for his daughters. What if they became too attached to her before he found someone permanent?

And he really didn't know anything about her personal life. What if she did have a beau who wouldn't like her spending so much time here? Tyler hoped that wasn't the case—for he had no idea what to do if she changed her mind. Something about her calmed him, made him believe that his girls would be fine in her care. They liked her and had talked of little else all afternoon.

She was quite appealing, of that there was no doubt. Her smile was contagious and he'd actually been aware of smiling that morning, seeing Polly and Lilly's excitement about her coming to help out. Had it been that long since he'd smiled—that he'd noticed he was?

Did the girls see him as serious all the time? Now that he thought about it, the times he heard them laugh and saw them smile were mostly when they were alone together playing, talking, just being with each other. Oh, they smiled at him when he came into a room, and occasionally giggled, but—

Dear Lord, please help me. I don't want to be an unsmiling, unhappy father to them. I want them to be untroubled and to know how much I love them. Please show me how to bring those grins about that Miss Marshall seems to do so effortlessly. And if hiring her was not best for my daughters, for Miss Marshall, for all of us, please help me to know.

"Papa! Papa! Wake up, please! Lilly's crying again!" Tyler pulled himself out of a deep, depressing sleep to find his oldest daughter tugging on his pajama sleeve.

"What? What is it? Lilly is crying?"

"Yes, Papa. Hurry!" With that, Polly ran out of the room.

Tyler threw on his robe and rushed across the hall to the girls' bedroom. Soft sobs drew him to Lilly's bed, where Polly was trying to comfort her.

"Lilly? Sweetheart, what's wrong?" He sat down on the bed and pulled the tiny figure up and onto his lap. Her sobs didn't stop. "Lilly, it's Papa. Tell me why you're crying."

"I m-miss Mama!" She sniffed and hiccuped before the sobs started again. Tyler rocked her back and forth, trying to hold back his own tears. Did she do this often? If so, why hadn't the nanny awakened him?

He looked at Polly, but found she was sniffling, too. He held out an arm to her and pulled her up close, glad it was dark so that they couldn't see the tears he was trying to hold back.

"I wish I could bring her back for you both. I know you miss her very much. So do I. But we have each other and always will. You know Mama wouldn't want you crying, don't you? She loved you with all her heart and wanted you to be happy."

They both nodded as the sobs began again. Tyler had no idea what to do or say next. *Dear Lord, I feel so out of my depth here. What kind of father am I that I don't know how to comfort my girls?*

He began to hum a nursery rhyme he didn't remember the words to as he held his girls close. Suddenly Georgia Marshall came to mind. Maybe he could change the subject. "Miss Marshall begins work on Monday. Are you sure you want her to come to work here?"

Both girls nodded.

"Well, Monday will be here before you know it. That's something to look forward to, isn't it?"

"Yes, Papa," they said at the same time.

The sobs had stopped, and he breathed a sigh of relief as he hummed another song. Soon Lilly slumped against him and he could tell she'd fallen back asleep.

"Let me lay Lilly down and then I'll put you back to bed," he whispered to Polly. She scooted to the end of her sister's bed to give him room and he gently laid Lilly down and covered her up. Tyler kissed her on the forehead and then picked up Polly and carried her to her bed.

"Thank you for coming, Papa. I never know what to do when Lilly sobs like that."

"You did fine, Polly. You're a very good big sister."

"And you're not mad because I woke you?"

"Oh, sweet child, of course not. Why did Nanny never awaken me when either of you were crying?"

"I don't know. She just said we weren't 'posed to."

"Well, from now on, we'll make sure that any nanny we hire knows to awaken me, all right?"

"Yes, Papa. Thank you." She hugged his neck tight.

"Will you be all right? Or do you want me to sit with you awhile?"

"I'm sleepy now. You can go back to bed."

She sounded too grown up for a child her age. How long had she been dealing with this kind of thing on her own?

"And be sure to come get me or call out if you need me."

"It's truly all right?"

"It truly is." He hugged his oldest daughter, who was too young to be taking so much on her shoulders. Then he pulled up the covers over her and kissed her on the forehead. "Sweet dreams."

"Night, Papa. I love you."

"I love you, too."

Tyler turned and went back out, leaving the door open in case he was needed again. For the first time since Ivy had passed away, he felt he'd given his daughters a measure of comfort—if only in letting them know they could call on him when they were sad.

But how awful for them, that they were just now finding that out. *Oh, dear Lord, please help me to be more attuned to their needs. I know that back home, nannies are the ones who take care of many of our children's needs, but I never want my girls to fear coming to me for any reason.*

Ivy had been much more attentive than most of the mothers in their group, and he knew she would not want him to leave everything to a nanny. But how was he to know what to do—or when to do it?

Tyler's ego deflated like a punctured balloon. He had no idea.

Chapter Three

On Monday morning, Georgia got up and hurried
to the bathroom she shared with Betsy. It was still
quiet and she took care not to make any more noise
than necessary before going back to her room and
dressing in a dark green skirt and green-and-white-
striped shirtwaist.

She hurried downstairs and helped herself to a
light breakfast at the sideboard. Gretchen came in
and poured her some coffee and Georgia had just
finished when Mrs. Heaton came in.

"I wanted to see you off on your first day. I do hope
you and the girls have a good one."

"Thank you, Mrs. Heaton. I want to be there before
the girls begin to stir." She'd asked Mr. Tate what time
that might be when she'd seen him out the day before.
He'd told her they usually stayed in bed until the nanny
told them they could get up, but that they usually were
up and dressed and taking breakfast by eight.

"I understand that. I'm sure they're excited about
you coming this morning," Mrs. Heaton said.

"I hope so. And I hope I don't disappoint them. I'm still not sure exactly what is expected of me, but Sir Tyler seems willing to let me find my own way. Truthfully, I believe Mr. Tate might be my best source of help."

"You'll figure it all out. I look forward to hearing how your day goes."

"Thank you." Georgia took one more sip of coffee and stood. "I'll see you this evening."

Several of the other boarders came in just then and wished her well as she headed to the foyer.

Mr. Tate had informed her that he'd let her in through the front door, since she wasn't actually a servant, or she could come in through the kitchen entry downstairs. But as Georgia let herself out of Heaton House, she decided to use the kitchen door. She didn't want anyone believing she thought herself better than them, and besides, ringing the bell might awaken the girls before she could get to them.

Sir Tyler and his daughters had sat a few pews behind the Heaton House group at church the day before, and they'd seemed quite glad to see her when she'd gone back down the aisle after the service.

The girls had looked neat and tidy, although Georgia noticed that their dresses appeared a bit short and her heart went out to both them and their father. He probably hadn't paid that much attention to their hemlines and neither had they. She'd take stock of his daughters' clothing that week, and then, if need be, she'd broach the topic of getting new ones to Sir Tyler.

He had asked her if she'd mind coming over that Sunday afternoon so he could give her a key and make sure she knew her way around before starting work the next morning. Of course she'd agreed, and she was glad she had. It was much larger than Heaton House, but at least she now knew just where to go once she was inside. She used the key to unlock the kitchen door and Mrs. Biddle seemed a bit surprised to see her, but approving that she'd used this entrance.

"Good morning, Miss Marshall. Would you like some coffee or tea before you go up?"

"No, thank you. I had some at Heaton House. I think I'll go check on the girls now."

"I'll have breakfast ready around eight—that's when they normally come down."

"I'll go up now, then. Thank you, Mrs. Biddle."

"You're welcome, dear." The woman actually smiled at her and Georgia hoped they would have a good relationship.

She hurried up the back stairs to the girls' room and opened the door as softly as she could, only to find the two little girls in their nightclothes, looking out their window that faced the street. "She's not coming," Lilly said.

"Oh, I'm sure she is. She'll be here any minute now. If she wasn't coming, Maid would have already been up here to tell us," Polly said.

Lilly put her hands on her hips and glared at her sister. "Maid wouldn't know yet!"

"Good morning, girls! Am I late?"

They turned to her with such relief on their faces, she wanted to rush to them and hug them. But she let them decide how they wanted to greet her.

For a moment they stood there just staring at her. Then Lilly grinned from ear to ear. "You came!"

"Of course I did. I told you I'd be here and I keep

my word. We'd better get you both dressed for breakfast. Cook said it'd be ready soon. Show me your wardrobe and we'll choose something for you to wear."

They led her to their wardrobe and with their help she was able to find them something she hoped was suitable. The girls pulled out matching plaid dresses in different colors. Polly's was in blue and green and Lilly's was in pink and yellow. The skirts were a bit shorter than she thought they should be, just as the ones they'd worn to church had been, and Georgia feared everything in their wardrobe was a little outdated.

It appeared she would need to speak to their father about their clothing soon. She really did need to talk to Elizabeth and get her help on how children of the wealthy dressed. Her friend came from a rich family although she wasn't part of that lifestyle any longer. But perhaps she would remember how she was treated as the child of wealthy parents.

She could also speak to Betsy about the styles for children now.

"Are we ready?" Georgia asked, after tying their hair up with ribbons that matched the dresses they had on.

"Yes!" they said in unison as they hurried out the door and to the stairs. As she followed her charges, they looked quite good to her, but she wasn't sure if what they had on was appropriate for breakfast. Still, all she could do for now was hope that no one in the house had anything bad to say about how they were dressed.

There seemed to be a lot of whispering going on between the girls as they made their way to the breakfast room, but Georgia couldn't make out what they were saying. She thought it sweet that they were so close, but of course they would be after losing their mother.

She followed them into the room and Mrs. Biddle brought in their breakfast as soon as they sat down at the table. The round table was just the right size for four to six people. It appeared to have had the leaves taken out and was nowhere near as large as the one in the dining room.

It was set for only three, and as Georgia had told Cook that she'd eaten already, she thought Sir Tyler would be coming.

But Mrs. Biddle took away the third place setting and asked, "Did you want coffee or tea now, Miss Marshall?"

"Oh, Sir Tyler doesn't have his breakfast with the girls?"

"Oh, no. He has his in the dining room, but he'll most likely look in on them before they're through eating."

He ate alone at that long table? Just him in that room? Georgia didn't think she'd ever understand the ways of English gentry. "I'll have some tea, then, please."

Mrs. Biddle hurried to the kitchen and brought back a small pot that held at least two cups, then poured Georgia a cup and set the pot down beside it.

"Thank you," Georgia said in example to the girls. She had no idea how they'd been trained, but she knew manners mattered. And just because someone was in service didn't mean one shouldn't show appreciation for what they did.

Georgia waited until the cook left the room and

said, "I'll say the blessing." She waited until the girls bowed their heads and then she began, "Dear Lord, we thank You for this day and ask that You guide us through it. We ask You to bless this food and the cook who prepared it for us. Thank You for our many blessings. In Jesus's name, amen."

She smiled when both girls added their *amen* to hers. "What do you think you two would like to do today? Would you like to go to the bookstore so we can order you some books? Your papa would like me to start your lessons. Is there anything specific you'd like to learn more about?"

"I want to learn more about America because Mama lived here when she was young, too," Polly said.

"Me, too," Lilly said. "Let's learn about 'merica!"

"Then that will go to the top of the list."

Georgia had just taken a sip of tea when Lilly looked up and grinned at something behind her. She turned to see Sir Tyler leaning against the door frame just as Lilly said, "Papa!"

"Good morning, Papa! Miss Marshall did come, just as you and she said she would!" Polly said.

"Good morning. Of course she came." He smiled at Georgia and something in her chest quickened as he pushed away from the door frame and came around and kissed each of his daughters on the top of the head. "You both look very nice today. Have you made any plans?"

"We're just starting to," Georgia said as he took a seat across from her and between his girls.

Mrs. Biddle must have heard his voice from the

kitchen, for she hurried in with a cup of coffee for him, gave a small curtsy and left the room.

"We're going to get some books to have lessons with, Papa," Lilly said.

"Yes, on America," Polly added.

"That's good," their papa said as he took a seat at the table. "Your mama would be happy that you'll be learning about this country."

They both nodded as they continued with their breakfast and Sir Tyler turned his attention to Georgia. "What else were you thinking of doing today?"

"Well, if it's all right with you, I thought we'd go get the books we need and then perhaps we might call on Mrs. Heaton's daughter, Rebecca, and her daughter, Jenny, for a bit if they're home."

"Oh, yes, please say it's all right, Papa," Polly said.

"Of course it is. Miss Marshall has my permission to plan your days just as Nanny did."

"The old one or the new one that left? She didn't plan much of anything," Polly said.

"I'm sure Miss Marshall will come up with all kinds of things for you to do. She is a teacher, after all."

That seemed to satisfy the girls for the moment, but Georgia knew she had much to learn about them before she could plan each day adequately.

"I've got a busy day ahead, so I'll leave you to yours. I think it might be more enjoyable than mine. I'm still trying to find an office space."

"You could come with us," Lilly said a bit shyly.

Georgia waited for his answer. As far as she could tell, he worked a lot from home and his hours were his own. He could go with them, but she—

"Not today, dear. But you have fun and I'll see you later." Sir Tyler turned to Georgia. "And thank you again for coming to our aid, Miss Marshall. I appreciate it more than I can say."

"You're welcome." She looked to see that the girls had finished their breakfast and couldn't help being a little disappointed in their father's response to his daughter's plea. She really didn't know what else to say as Sir Tyler took a last sip of his coffee then stood and left the room.

But his daughters didn't give her time to dwell on him, as they were excited to get the day started.

"Are we really going to go see Jenny, Miss Marshall?"

"We are if it's convenient for them. I'll telephone before we go to the bookstore to place our order. Did your other nanny teach you to read or write anything?"

"Not the last one, but Nanny from England had started to. We have papers."

"Well, let's go see where you're at and I might let you practice your letters for a while. While you're doing that, I'll come back down and telephone to see if we can go visit later today."

The girls fairly flew up the stairs, but as Georgia met Mr. Tate at the bottom of the staircase, she asked him to show her where the telephone was.

"There is one in the kitchen downstairs and Mrs. Biddle will be glad to show you where it is. The others are in Sir Tyler's study and in his bedroom."

"Thank you, Mr. Tate."

"You're quite welcome, Miss Marshall."

Georgia hurried back up to her charges, who had

pulled out their latest papers for her. Their English nanny had started them out well. It was a pity she hadn't stayed on.

Tyler left the breakfast room certain that his girls were in good hands. When he'd heard the conversation going on from his seat in the dining room, he hadn't been able to resist peeking in a bit earlier than usual.

He'd told himself it was because he wanted to let Miss Marshall know he was pleased she'd taken the position and that was true, but in truth he'd been looking forward to her arrival almost as much as his girls were. Tate had told him she was there, of course, but that wasn't the same as seeing her in his home with his daughters.

They'd been very animated, talking about what they'd like to read as he'd stood in the doorway before Lilly noticed him, and he couldn't resist sitting at the table with them for a few minutes before he headed out.

He'd enjoyed the brief time, although it'd been hard to keep from glancing at Georgia Marshall. She'd looked quite lovely, dressed in green to match her eyes. But his mission wasn't to think about how pretty the woman who'd stepped in to help him out was. It was to find out how the girls were taking to Miss Marshall, for they would be spending most of their time with her.

Tyler went to his study to finish off a letter to his family and one to his in-laws before grabbing his satchel for a meeting with Michael Heaton. He'd spoken to Mrs. Heaton's son after church the day before to ask about leasing office space in his building. Michael had said he did have two offices available and would be glad to show them to him that morning.

Tate was waiting at the front door for him—the man seemed to know exactly when to be there every time Tyler came or went. "Have a good morning, sir."

"You, too, Tate. I think Miss Marshall and the girls are going to get along fine. Please get these in the mail today." Tyler handed the letters to his butler. "And tell Cook I should be home for luncheon. If I see I won't be, I'll telephone."

"I'll let her know, sir."

"Very good." Tyler hurried down the steps, and as it was such a nice day, he decided to walk to Michael's office. It wasn't too far away. He and his girls liked the Gramercy Park neighborhood a great deal, especially the park in the center of it that only residents had keys to. And now that things were beginning to bloom, they liked it even better. But Central Park was their favorite.

He hoped Miss Marshall would get them out of the house so they could get used to the city better. Nanny had been a little apprehensive about taking them out and about because she didn't know her way around. At least that was the excuse she'd given, and he hadn't really trusted the new nanny enough to give her permission to take them anywhere but to Gramercy Park.

The relief he felt that they had someone who had come so highly recommended was immense. He was sure Mrs. Heaton was a woman of high regard and had thought so since the first time he'd met her.

As he reached the office building on Third Avenue, he was impressed with the architecture and interior. Any client he had would be happy to come to an office here.

Michael had given him directions to his office and Tyler took the elevator to the top floor. Once there, a middle-aged receptionist showed him into Michael's inner office. He stood up from his desk and held out his hand. "Sir Tyler, it's good to see you again."

Tyler shook his hand. "Mr. Heaton, thank you and the same to you."

"Please call me Michael. Why don't I show you the offices I have in mind for you and then we can come back and discuss the details, or talk about them over lunch, if you like it?"

"That sounds fine with me." Actually, he'd like to get to know Michael Heaton better. If he was anything like his mother, Tyler would be glad to have him as a friend.

Michael led the way out of his office and took Tyler to a nice-sized office across the hall from his. It had a reception room and an office similar to Michael's, but with only one window looking out instead of two corner windows. The size would work well, though.

"Of course, you'd be responsible for the furnishings," Michael said. "I've found everyone has their own tastes in the matter of decoration."

"Yes, well, I suppose that is true and I'd be glad to furnish it. From what I saw in yours, I think our tastes are quite alike."

"Then I can tell you where to go to find similar items."

They went to the next office space that had a larger window looking out onto Third Avenue. Tyler liked it a lot. "I like them both. But I think I'd like to take this one."

"You're sure?"

"I am ready to sign a lease on it."

"Well, then, let me treat you to lunch and we'll talk over the terms."

"Might I borrow your telephone to call home and let them know I won't be there for lunch?"

"Of course." Michael pointed to the telephone on his desk. "I'll go tell my receptionist we'll be out for a while."

Tyler picked up the receiver and asked the operator to connect him to his home. Tate answered the telephone, of course, and informed Tyler that he'd let Mrs. Biddle know, and that Miss Marshall and his daughters would be having lunch with Mrs. Heaton's daughter.

"Oh, well, I hope Cook hasn't gone to too much trouble just for me."

"It will be fine, Sir Tyler. Don't worry."

"Thank you, Tate. I'll see you later."

Tyler hung up the receiver feeling a bit unsettled. But there was no reason to. He'd told Miss Marshall that she could plan their days. If having lunch with a friend was something she thought the girls might enjoy, there was no reason he should be concerned in any way.

Chapter Four

Tyler went out to the reception area, where Michael Heaton was waiting for him, and they took the elevator downstairs and then strode out onto the street. Tyler had found that New York City traffic was every bit as bad as London's was, but he was beginning to learn his way around.

"I thought we'd walk to the restaurant I have in mind. It caters mostly to businessmen, and don't tell the ladies, but I've found it's nice to talk business there." Michael grinned at him.

Tyler laughed. "I understand."

They arrived at the restaurant and in a matter of minutes were seated and had their orders taken.

"Mother told me that Georgia Marshall was stepping in to help you out for a while," Michael said.

"Yes, she is. You know her?"

"Oh, yes. Besides being a boarder at Heaton House, our families have been friends for a long time. Georgia will do her best for you."

Tyler could feel himself relax at Michael's words.

"I believe she will. This transition hasn't been easy on any of us and I can't begin to tell you how much I appreciate your mother's help. The fact that she highly recommended Miss Marshall put my mind at ease. But still, I am concerned a bit. My girls ran the last nanny off with their pranks, and while I believe it was because they are still missing their mother and the nanny who went back to England, I'm not sure what I'll do if they do the same to Miss Marshall."

"I can't imagine what you've been through. I am sorry for the loss of your wife. I'm sure Georgia will do her best to help your daughters. I wouldn't be too concerned about them running her off. She's taught school for several years now, and from what I've heard, she is very good with children."

"Do you know why she came to New York?" Tyler hoped Michael wouldn't think him too nosy, but he was curious.

"I don't know for sure. My wife thinks it was from a broken heart."

"Was she engaged?"

"No. But we all thought she'd marry her next-door neighbor. But he surprised us all—Georgia more than anyone, we suspect—and asked her sister to marry him instead. Georgia stayed in Ashland until after the wedding but, well, you can imagine how difficult it must have been for her."

"Oh, yes, I can," Tyler said. He was a bit surprised by the anger he felt toward Miss Marshall's neighbor, realizing that he was now her brother-in-law. How painful that must have been for her. "I am sorry for the heartbreak she might be going through, but I must admit I'm glad to have her free to help us."

And to know that she didn't have a beau who might have demands on her time.

"I think helping you out will be good for her, too," Michael said.

"I hope so."

Their meal came and the conversation turned to business.

"So you want the larger office next to mine?"

"Yes."

"It needs a fresh coat of paint and, of course, I'll have that done. When would you want to move in?" Michael asked.

"How about the first of June? That will give me time to choose the furnishings, take the bar exam and see how things are going with the girls and Miss Marshall."

"Sounds good to me. I'm glad to have you as a tenant, Sir Tyler."

"And I'm glad you had space available. I'll pay the rent starting now, of course."

Michael shook his head. "There's no need for that. We'll have a contract drawn up to start in June. Until then, feel free to come by and take measurements or whatever you need to do. I'll not be leasing it to anyone else."

By the time Tyler left the restaurant, he felt he'd made a new friend and at least begun the tedious task of setting up office. He'd go look for furnishings at the shops Michael had recommended over the next few weeks.

For now, though, he looked forward to getting home and seeing the girls and Miss Marshall. But when he arrived back home, it was to find that Miss Marshall and his daughters weren't back yet, and disappointment that he had no one but Tate to share his news with washed over him.

He made his way down to the kitchen to make sure Mrs. Biddle wasn't upset that her lunch plans had to be changed. She seemed quite surprised to see him in the kitchen. "Sir Tyler, is there anything I can get for you?"

"No, thank you, Mrs. Biddle. I hope that Miss Marshall and I didn't put you out too much with our change in lunch plans. She gave you plenty of notice, didn't she?" Although he wasn't so sure *he'd* given her enough.

"Oh, yes, she did, Sir Tyler. And Miss Polly and Miss Lilly were ever so thrilled about going."

"Very good." He made his way back to his study, glad Mrs. Biddle wasn't upset. And he was happy his daughters had been excited about the day's plans. Still, the house seemed much too quiet and he had a feeling he wouldn't settle down to work until his girls were back home.

By the time Georgia put the girls down to nap, she was feeling better about accepting the position as their nanny. She'd been very pleased with how well behaved they were at Rebecca's. And she was happy that they got along so well with Jenny. The girls had played outdoors while she and Rebecca caught up with each other. Their families had been friends for a very long time back in Virginia, and Georgia felt blessed that she'd been able to reunite with Mrs. Heaton's family when she'd moved to the city.

"How do you think you're going to like being a

nanny?" Rebecca had asked as she'd poured them some tea.

"I don't know just yet, but I'm going to try to do well at it. The girls have had so much to deal with—I believe they're still grieving the loss of their mother and missing the nanny who'd cared for them since they were born. I pray I can help them adjust to living in America."

"I'm sure you will, Georgia. You've always had a way with children."

"I hope I can live up to your expectations, Rebecca," Georgia said. "I would like to be able to help them and their papa."

"He's very handsome, isn't he?"

"Yes, he is," Georgia said. Much too handsome, in her opinion. And she was more than a little disturbed by the amount of time she'd spent thinking about him. She'd become adept at pushing thoughts of men—especially handsome ones—out of her mind. She did not intend to give her heart to another. Not after Phillip Wilson. The one man she'd loved—her best friend from childhood, no less—gave her the impression from an early age they would one day be married and then had asked her sister to become his wife!

After that, Georgia had come to the conclusion there wasn't one trustworthy man out there—not with her heart, anyway. No matter how handsome he might be. "I'm sure he'll have his choice of wealthy young women once they realize he's here."

"Perhaps," Rebecca had said. "But he might not be interested in them."

"I suppose only time will tell." And she really

didn't want to think about that possibility. His daughters had enough to adjust to as things were.

She'd been relieved when Rebecca had changed the subject and suggested they take the girls on an outing. They made plans to take them to Central Park, and after they'd told the girls, that was all Polly and Lilly could talk about on the way home.

"Nanny never wanted to take us to the big park," Lilly had said. "We asked, but she just was too afraid."

"Well, there's nothing to be afraid of. Perhaps she was a little nervous being in a new country and all," Georgia said.

"But we aren't nervous. Papa said America was a wonderful place and where Mama was born. What is there to be frightened of?" Polly asked.

Oh, the innocence of a child. "One should always be cautious when going out, but when people are in a place they've never been before, it isn't uncommon for some to be quite apprehensive. Your English nanny was raised in a smaller place than New York City. So was I, and it takes getting used to going out and about in a place this large," Georgia said.

If it hadn't been for living at Heaton House and going in and out with the other boarders, she would have been quite fearful. It hadn't taken long to understand why Mrs. Heaton always insisted her female boarders had male escorts, or went in a group if they went out of an evening. But Polly and Lilly were too young to understand that now. And there was no need to make them fearful. "But I soon got used to it and I'm sure your nanny would have, too, had she stayed long enough."

"I miss her," Polly said, "but I'm glad we have you."

"Thank you, Miss Polly. I appreciate you saying so. Now rest a bit before you see your papa. He'll want to know about your day when you see him."

"Yes, ma'am," Polly said, then yawned.

They'd played hard with Jenny, and Lilly's eyes were closing as Georgia pulled a light cover over her. She pulled the shades on the windows and went downstairs to ask Mrs. Biddle for a cup of tea.

She wasn't expecting to run into Sir Tyler in the foyer. "Miss Marshall. You're back. I was just going to see if Tate had seen you come in."

"Oh, we've been back awhile. I'm sorry—did you need me or the girls?"

"No, I was a little surprised that you weren't here for lunch—"

"Oh! Should I have asked if it was all right to—"

"No, I gave you freedom to plan their days. And it's fine. I wasn't actually here at noon, either. I had lunch with Michael Heaton. I've decided to lease an office in his building, but maybe I should have waited a while longer. Do you think it will be too hard for them to have me working away from home with all the changes I've put them through?"

"I don't know. Are they used to having time with you during the day? And how far is the office from here?"

"The office is on Third Avenue in Michael Heaton's building. I usually see my daughters in the morning and check in on them at lunchtime. Then, of course, there is teatime, when Nanny brought them in. And I... Things have been different since their

mother passed away and we don't really have a schedule. I've been hoping you'd help with that."

"I can try. And if the girls aren't used to spending a lot of time with you during the day, I doubt that
setting up your office a few blocks away will upset
them too much. If you were needed, you'd be able
to get home quickly. I suppose we'll just have to see
how it goes."

He visibly relaxed and Georgia breathed a sigh of
relief. Sir Tyler wasn't angry with her. He seemed to
be trying to find his way through the painful adjustment of raising his daughters without his wife. And
as Georgia's heart melted in compassion for the man,
she prayed she'd be able to help him.

By the end of the first week, Georgia felt as if she
might be able to handle the nanny position. The girls
seemed to like her and they were well behaved—at
least so far.

They were very close and whispered between themselves quite often, and they seemed to get along with
each other exceptionally well. Of course, that was most
likely due to the loss they shared. Her heart hurt for
them each time she thought about how much they'd
been through.

But she was still having a hard time adjusting with
the way Sir Tyler parented. Evidently wealthy English
parents didn't spend quite as much time with their
children as American ones did. Or maybe that wasn't
quite fair. It could be that the wealthy of both coun-
tries did things differently. Even among her friends
in Ashland, not all of them had parents like hers.

Still, she knew Sir Tyler loved his girls. He'd made

that very plain from the beginning. She could see it in his eyes when he watched them together. But he just didn't seem to have any idea how to really interact with them.

She almost hated to leave them on Friday evening, but she'd promised Polly and Lilly that she'd be there early Monday morning and that seemed to satisfy them.

Georgia headed downstairs to let Sir Tyler know they were ready for him to listen to their prayers. It was something she'd begun to do each evening, hoping to give them a bit more time with him.

Mr. Tate was at the bottom of the stairs and must have been waiting for her, for he nodded and said, "Sir Tyler asked me to tell you he is in his study, Miss Marshall."

"Thank you, Mr. Tate." He led the way and Georgia was left to follow.

"Miss Marshall, Sir Tyler."

"Please come in," Sir Tyler said, getting up from his chair and motioning to a chair adjacent to his. "Would you like some tea before you leave?"

"No, thank you."

Georgia took the seat as he turned to his butler. "Thank you, Tate. That will be all for now."

He then sat back down. "I suppose my girls are ready for me to come up and hear their prayers."

"They are. They were giggling with each other before I got out of the room."

"I can't tell you how that warms my heart. They've always gotten along well, but I haven't heard many giggles lately—not until you came to us. I wanted to be sure and let you know how much I appreciate whatever it is you've done to bring that about."

"Oh, I'm not sure I can take credit for that, Sir Tyler. I—"

The expression in Sir Tyler's eyes when he shook his head and smiled at her had her heart skittering in her chest.

"Oh, I believe you can. At any rate, thank you." He slipped his hand into the pocket of his jacket and pulled out an envelope. "This is your first week's pay."

"Oh, I wasn't expecting to get paid so quickly. Thank you." She took the envelope from him and their fingers brushed, making her catch her breath. She hoped he couldn't tell how flustered she felt.

"You're welcome." He stood and so did she. "I suppose I'd best go listen to those prayers. They already pray for you, you know."

"How sweet," Georgia said as they walked out into the foyer. "I pray for them as well. I'll see you all on Monday or at church on Sunday, I suppose."

"You will. Have a good weekend, Miss Marshall."

"You, too, Sir Tyler."

He gave another smile and turned to the stairs while Mr. Tate showed her out.

"Good night, Miss Marshall," the butler said.

"Good night, Mr. Tate."

She heard the door shut behind her and hurried over to the steps of Heaton House. Happy as she was to have the weekend off, she felt a little guilty for leaving Sir Tyler and Mr. Tate.

Then she scolded herself. She wasn't indispensable, after all! She heard the boarders in the parlor as soon as she opened the door and hurried inside to join them.

"Georgia! How nice it is to have you home for more than a few hours!" Julia exclaimed.

"Oh, it is!" Emily added.

"I'm glad to be here. I've missed evenings at Heaton House. What have you got planned for the weekend?"

"Your favorite meal, for one," Mrs. Heaton said from behind her. "It's good to know we have you for the whole weekend."

"Mostly we're going to enjoy spending time with you," Julia said. "But remember, Matt and Millicent's housewarming is next Saturday."

"Oh! I'd forgotten about that. Are we going in together on a gift?"

"We were just talking about that. Mrs. Heaton suggested we get a brass bowl similar to what we got for the other couples. We can go down tomorrow morning and pick one out together, if you'd all like," Julia said.

"Oh, I'd love to help." And hopefully it would take her mind off of Sir Tyler and his daughters. The girls should be asleep by now, but what was he doing? She always wondered about that once she left. The first night, she'd stopped at the window of the upstairs hall that looked out on Mrs. Heaton's garden. She'd seen a glow of lamplight on the courtyard next door and thought it must be coming from Sir Tyler's study window.

And as she went up for the night with the others tonight, she was drawn to that window once more after the other girls went to their rooms. Sure enough, a splash of light shone on the yard. She hoped Sir Tyler was working, for the thought of him just sitting all by himself in his study late at night saddened her deeply.

Dear Lord, please help them to have a good weekend. I do feel so bad about leaving them. And yet the girls are asleep and Sir Tyler is doing whatever it is he does of an evening. I'm sure he has his own routine, and besides, it's none of my business at all! I must stop thinking of him so much. Please help me to put him out of my mind and remember that my job is to see that his daughters are well taken care of in my charge. And that is all. In Jesus's name, I pray. Amen.

Chapter Five

The weekend passed quite pleasantly for Georgia. She'd gone with Julia and Betsy to Macy's to look for the brass bowl for Matt and Millicent on Saturday morning, and then the group went to the ice-cream parlor for sodas that evening after dinner. She did get to see Polly and Lilly the next day at church and they seemed as glad to see her as she was to see them, as they ran up to her as soon as the service was over.

She also remembered to broach the subject of their wardrobes to Sir Tyler once the girls ran off to talk to Jenny. "I did want to speak to you about something and I kept forgetting last week—"

"You aren't going to give notice, are you?" he asked.

The concern in his eyes had her rushing to reassure him. "Oh, no! I'm sorry to have given you any cause to worry. No, it's about the girls' wardrobes. I think they might need some new things and—"

His laughter was a sound she hadn't heard before and it warmed her heart to know she'd evidently relieved his mind.

"Their wardrobe? Of course. I'm glad you brought it to my attention. We'll decide what to do tomorrow."

"Thank you. That sounds good. I know you want them to—"

"Look like proper young ladies. And you're right about that. In fact, their nanny mentioned something about it when I took her to the ship, but I was so upset about her leaving, I'm afraid I didn't pay much attention."

"That's understandable. We'll take care of it."

"We will. I'm sure they could use a few new things," Sir Tyler said.

They needed more than a few items, but she'd wait until the next day to go into detail about all that.

As the girls had waved goodbye to her, Georgia had almost wished she was going with them. She feared she'd become attached to them much too quickly, but how did one keep from doing so when they had no mother to turn to?

Still, she had to remind herself that she was only their acting nanny and that she would be replaced one day. She couldn't let herself become too fond of them— or their papa.

He'd been very kind to her, but she really knew little about him other than he was part of English gentry and had been married to a wealthy American, according to Mrs. Heaton. Besides, she just could not trust her instincts where men were concerned. Otherwise she wouldn't have believed that she would marry Phillip for all those years. She still thought he'd led her on. But at the same time, Georgia felt she should have seen the truth. It was her sister that Phillip was truly interested in and he was only using Georgia as a reason to visit and see Meredith.

Georgia still felt a little pang remembering the day they'd announced their engagement. It'd been all she could do to stay in the room and congratulate them instead of running up to her bedroom to sob as she'd done later that night.

If she couldn't trust her intuition with someone she'd known all her life, how could she ever trust it with a man she barely knew? And why was she even thinking about any of this anyway? She believed Sir Tyler was still mourning his loss. And even if he wasn't, she'd vowed never to lose her heart to another man. No matter how kind and handsome he was.

Now, on Monday morning, as she let herself into the Walker home and greeted Mrs. Biddle, she shored up her resolve and turned her attention to the job she'd been hired to do.

She hurried upstairs to find the girls still asleep, which surprised her, for they'd been up waiting for her all last week. It looked as if they might be hiding under the covers and she grinned. They probably thought they'd jump out and give her a scare when she approached. "Polly? Lilly? Are you being sleepy-heads today?"

She gave the small mound in Polly's bed a little shake, but it felt very soft, and when she pulled off the covers it was to find only a pillow all punched up.

The mound in Lilly's bed looked suspiciously the same and Georgia didn't bother with a nudge. Instead she threw the covers off to find the younger girl's pillow pretending to be her.

Maybe they were in their bathroom hiding from

her. She hurried across the floor and knocked on the door. When there was no answer, she threw it open only to find it empty. Her stomach felt as if she'd just swallowed a heavy rock as she hurried to the playroom. Surely they were there. Only they weren't.

Where could they be? And why would they be hiding from her? She hurried back downstairs, heart pounding, praying that they were just pulling some kind of prank and hadn't run off.

She stopped in the morning room and looked out into the yard, but they weren't there. Then she heard a little giggle and then another. She followed the sound into the breakfast room, where they were sitting at the table, all dressed—if not properly—and grinning from ear to ear as she entered.

"Surprise!" Polly said. She was smiling but Georgia could tell she was a little apprehensive about her reaction.

She tried to keep her voice normal and not give away how concerned she was at their actions. It didn't seem like them at all, but then, she'd known them only a week. "Girls, you know you're supposed to wait until I get here and help you get dressed to come down to breakfast. Mrs. Biddle hasn't begun yours yet. Let's go up and get you dressed in something a little more becoming before your papa sees you. Unless you want him to fire me?"

"Oh, no, Miss Georgia!" Polly said. "We don't want that!" She jumped up from her chair. "Come on, Lilly, hurry. We don't want to get Miss Georgia in trouble."

"But I thought you—"

Georgia saw Polly shake her head at her younger sister. "Hurry, before Papa or Mr. Tate see us!"

Georgia hurried behind them and let go of a relieved sigh when they made it back to the girls' room without being detected. Something was going on here, but she didn't know what it was, at least not yet. However, now was not the time to question them—they needed to get back downstairs. But she had to find out what caused the girls to act in such a way.

She quickly got them changed into something more presentable and brushed their blond hair up and tied it with ribbons that matched their dresses. Then they headed back downstairs, the girls whispering in front of her.

They slipped into their chairs just before Mrs. Biddle brought in their breakfast and Georgia could see the relief in their eyes. Evidently they knew she was disturbed by their actions, for they were more subdued than usual.

"My goodness, it's quiet in here this morning," Sir Tyler said from the doorway. "Are you all feeling all right?"

"Good morning, Papa!" both girls said in unison. But they flashed Georgia a look as if begging her not to tell their father of their actions.

"I believe we're all well, Sir Tyler," Georgia said. "But they do seem a bit quiet this morning—did you overdo things at the park yesterday?"

"I don't think so. Do I need to summon a doctor?"

"No, Papa," Polly said. "We're fine."

"I believe it's taking them a bit of time to fully wake up this morning."

"Hmm, Lilly didn't have a bad night, did she?" Sir Tyler asked Polly. "You promised to call me if she does."

"I slept good last night, Papa," Lilly said.

"I'm glad."

Georgia didn't realize that Lilly sometimes had trouble sleeping. Perhaps she should ask Sir Tyler about that when they were alone. She needed to speak to him about their wardrobes anyway.

As if he read her thoughts, Sir Tyler turned to her. "Miss Marshall, could you come to the study once you get the girls settled down after breakfast? There's something I'd like to speak to you about."

"I'd be glad to, Sir Tyler."

"I'll see you then. Girls, you mind Miss Marshall and don't give her any trouble, you hear?"

"We won't, Papa," Polly said.

"We will, Papa," Lilly said. "Will mind, of course."

Did he know about their trick this morning? Georgia didn't know how he could have—unless the maid or Mr. Tate saw something. With Sir Tyler's invitation, it appeared she'd soon find out.

With pleas not to tell their papa of their mischievous behavior that morning still ringing in her ears, Georgia headed down to Sir Tyler's study. She'd promised the girls that she wouldn't tattle on them, but if their papa asked, she'd have to tell the truth.

She left them with the assignments she'd given them and was sure they'd do their very best. They'd apologized several times and she'd accepted, but when she asked why they'd pulled such a prank, they clammed up.

Mr. Tate seemed to know the minute she came downstairs and was there when her foot hit the last step.

"Miss Marshall, Sir Tyler said he was expecting you. Come along and I'll let him know you're here."

"Thank you, Mr. Tate." She followed him to the study, although she could have got there on her own. But Mr. Tate truly did seem to run this household and she wondered again if he knew about the girls coming down early.

"Sir Tyler, Miss Marshall is here," he said.

"Please show her in, Tate."

The butler motioned her in and then seemed to disappear, although Georgia had a feeling he was camped just outside the door.

Sir Tyler had stood when she entered and motioned her to take a seat in one of the chairs flanking the fireplace. When she sat down, he took the other. "Now, before we get to the subject of the girls' wardrobes, I must ask you something. Have my girls been giving you any trouble? Tate seems to think they were up to some mischief this morning."

Georgia's promise to his daughters was fresh in her mind and she wasn't sure how to answer. She didn't want to get Polly and Lilly in trouble. She wanted to help them—and their father.

"They haven't really—"

"Miss Marshall, did they send you hunting for them today?"

At his point-blank question, she could answer only one way. "They did. But I believe they thought I might think it was funny."

"Are you sure? I doubt it was fun trying to find them."

Mr. Tate must have seen much more than she thought he had. "It wasn't. But they didn't seem themselves this morning and I wondered… Did anything happen this weekend that I should know about?"

She felt impertinent even asking and waited for Sir Tyler to put her in her place, but instead he let out a sigh.

"No, not that I know of. But my daughters don't always confide in me. It's something I'd like to change but I'm not sure how to." He seemed to think he'd said too much as he stopped and shook his head.

"They seemed fine this whole weekend and were looking forward to seeing you today," he continued. "They were a little upset I hadn't asked you over yesterday afternoon, though. I suppose they thought that since you came over the Sunday before, you'd come again. But I explained that you had things you needed to do on weekends. They seemed to understand, but then, I sometimes wonder if I expect too much comprehension from them."

"Perhaps. They're still very young. I hope you won't punish them for this morning. They begged me not to tell you and I know they don't want to upset you."

Sir Tyler rubbed a hand over his chin and shook his head once more before smiling at her. "I agree not to mention it, if you promise to tell me if they pull any more shenanigans. And please, if they do tell you why they hid from you today, let me know."

"Of course I will."

"Good. Now, about their wardrobes. What is it they need?"

"Well, I'm afraid it's more than just a few things. They've outgrown many of their outfits and the styles are always changing. I'm not sure how you expect them to look."

"Why, like other young girls their age, I suppose."

"Sir Tyler, there are those who set style in this city and those who try to get as close to it as they can. But the very wealthy do often have more and better clothing than others."

"I see. I think. But I admit to not knowing much about feminine attire. Or what is in style at any given time. I want them to look well dressed, but not necessarily on the same scale as royalty in England or those in league with the Vanderbilts and the Astors. While my daughters will inherit some wealth, it will not be on that scale."

Georgia understood what he was saying, but there were many degrees of wealth and most tried to keep up with the style of the very wealthy. Even the middle classes tried to dress in style, even if not having custom clothing made for them.

"Perhaps I can get Elizabeth Talbot to help me find the right things. She came from a fairly wealthy family, but not the…"

Sir Tyler chuckled at her hesitation. "But not to the degree of the Vanderbilts?"

"Exactly."

"Then I leave things in your capable hands. Besides, you always look quite fashionable to me. I'm sure you'll do a fine job."

Georgia felt her face flush at his compliment and she wasn't sure what to say next.

"Will we need to acquire a seamstress? Or are there shops where you can take Polly and Lilly to find what they need?"

"There are shops, of course, or seamstresses. In fact, Betsy Thomas, a new boarder at Heaton House, is a very good seamstress. I might be able to find out more about what is in fashion for girls Polly's and Lilly's ages from her. And Michael Heaton's wife, Violet, used to work for Butterick as a seamstress. I could ask her opinion, too. And Elizabeth Talbot might know of some of the better shops, if you'd prefer to go that way. Whatever you'd like me to do."

Sir Tyler's chuckle seemed to come from deep within his chest. "I'm afraid you are a much better judge of what to do than I am, Miss Marshall. Truly, I do trust your judgment on this. Just let me know what you decide and I'll see that you have the funds to take care of it."

"But I don't know—will they need some outfits for parties or…? Sir Tyler, I don't know what their social life consists of."

"They don't have one at this point, Miss Marshall. They are very young and would not be going to most gatherings I might be invited to at this point. But I've not delved into the social scene here yet, and to be quite honest, I'm not really looking forward to doing so."

Georgia tried not to show her surprise at his statement. It caught her off guard, and at the same time, her respect for him grew.

"And my in-laws are out of the country for now," he continued. "Once they return my social life might change a bit, but not much if I have anything to do with it. My wife and I socialized when we had to back in England, but both of us were much happier to spend our evenings at home."

He looked away for a moment, and when he glanced back at her, his eyes seemed to be so full of sadness, she wanted to cry for him. How hard it must be for him to face the future without the woman he loved. She could relate even if she'd never been married to Phillip. But she'd loved him for a long time, and once he'd married her sister, she had no choice but to face the future alone.

At least Sir Tyler had his daughters, but to have to raise them by himself had to be a dauntingly lonely task.

"So, just go ahead and do what you think best," Sir Tyler said, his voice bringing her out of her thoughts and back to the now they both faced.

"Yes, sir. I will. I'll speak to my friends and see what we can come up with."

"Thank you, Miss Marshall. I don't know what we'd do without you right now." With that, he stood and Georgia did the same, feeling she was being dismissed.

She turned to go. "I should be going to check on your daughters now."

"And remember—if they pull any more pranks on you, I want to know. They do have their ornery sides from time to time."

"I will. But I'm not too worried about it right now. And I do have experience with childhood pranks. A teacher's first year is full of them."

"Still, I expect to know."

"Yes, sir. You will. I didn't know Lilly had a problem sleeping at night." She hoped he didn't think she was overstepping her bounds, but she felt she needed to know as much as she could about his daughters if they were in her charge.

"Neither did I until recently. She is still missing

her mother. Both girls do, of course, but Lilly wakes up crying sometimes. And evidently it didn't seem to be something my former nannies thought they should tell me."

"I'm sorry they didn't. That is something you should have been told from the beginning."

"Yes, I think so, too. And I trust that you will tell me anything you think I should know about them in the future. Not just pranks, but whatever you feel needs brought to my attention, good or bad."

"I will." Georgia gave her word. "I suppose I should go check on them now."

"Probably. No telling what they might decide to pull on you next."

Tyler watched Miss Marshall walk out of the room. He had to give it to her—she wasn't going to try to get his daughters in trouble, which must mean that she already cared about them.

He'd been quite worried when Tate told him what he'd seen. Evidently the girls had come down a bit early, dressed, but not very well, giggling and whispering. They'd stopped when they reached the foyer and looked around, probably to make sure Tate didn't see them. Then they'd headed to the breakfast room, just as Miss Marshall entered the foyer. She went upstairs only to run back down minutes later.

Tate had stood in the hallway long enough to know she had things under control as she marched them back upstairs. They came back down neat and tidy, and it was then that Tate had come into the dining room, where he was having his breakfast, to tell him what had happened.

For the life of him, Tyler couldn't understand why they'd pulled such a prank, trying to frighten Georgia. She must have been appalled at their actions, and yet she seemed to be taking his girls' actions in stride. Perhaps better than he was.

Tyler sighed and prayed they wouldn't be up to any more mischief. The last thing he needed was for Miss Marshall to up and quit. Had they done something similar with the other nannies?

But had his daughters been up to mischief, surely Tate or one of the other servants would have seen something and let him know, like Tate did today. Still, it was obvious that he needed to pay more attention to what his girls were up to. He couldn't have them running off all the help.

Tyler was just about to leave to go see if the painters were through painting his new office when his butler entered the room.

"Sir, I was wondering what you've decided about the housewarming invitation you received several weeks ago—the Sterlings, remember? You attended their wedding not long after we moved in."

It had completely slipped his mind. "I'm afraid I forgot. When is it?"

"This coming Saturday, sir. I wondered if you need me to pick up a gift?"

Tyler sat back in his chair. "I suppose I should go. The girls were invited, too, weren't they?"

"Yes, they were."

"Well, it would certainly be something to entertain them this weekend."

"It would at that."

"Then yes, please, pick up something appropriate

for me, Tate. And thank you for telling me about the girls' prank this morning. I've asked Miss Marshall to let me know if they do anything like that again, but I'd like you to do the same, if you see anything out of the ordinary going on."

Tate nodded. "Of course, Sir Tyler. For what it's worth, I believe Miss Marshall handled the situation quite well."

That was high praise coming from Tate. High praise indeed. And that his butler seemed to hold Miss Marshall in high esteem put Tyler's mind at ease. He was sure his daughters couldn't be in better hands. "Yes, so do I."

Chapter Six

Polly and Lilly were on their best behavior after hiding from her on Monday, and by midweek, Georgia was hopeful that there'd be no more pranks.

She and Rebecca were taking the girls to Central Park that day and she'd asked Mrs. Biddle to make a picnic lunch for them. They were beyond excited when their papa looked in as they finished breakfast.

"What's all the excitement about? I can hear you giggling all over the house," he said in a teasing manner.

"We're going to the park today, Papa! And eating there, too," Lilly said.

"I know. I hope you have a wonderful time and remember to thank Miss Marshall, as this was her idea."

"Yes, but you gave them permission. Would you like to join us for lunch?"

"Oh, yes, Papa! I'm sure Mrs. Biddle would pack enough for you, too," Polly said. "Jenny and her mama are coming!"

He chuckled, but shook his head. "It sounds like

fun, but not today. I have a lunch meeting with your grandparents' land manager to talk over some changes they want to make."

At the disappointment on his girls' faces, Georgia rushed to smooth things out. "Oh, I'm sure the girls understand. We'll plan another ahead of time so that you can go with us."

"Thank you, Miss Marshall. I would like that a lot and I'm very sorry I can't make it today. You will ask me another time, won't you, girls?"

Polly let out a long-suffering sigh. "Of course we will, Papa. Maybe we should plan it now so you can put it on your calendar?"

"That's a good idea, Polly," Georgia said. "Why don't we let your papa look at his calendar and find a day he can go with us? After all, he does have to work and our schedules are a bit more flexible."

"Will you find a day soon, Papa?" Lilly asked, a pleading look in her eyes.

"I will go find one now. Miss Marshall, after you have the girls settled down with their lessons, please come down to my study and we'll get that date settled."

"Yes, sir. I'll get them started and be right down."

"I'll see you soon, then." He gave each girl a kiss on the cheek. "I look forward to hearing all about your day."

"We'll tell you all about it, Papa!" Lilly said, scampering down from her chair. "Come on, Polly!"

The two girls hurried out of the room. "I think they're ready to get started. I told them they had to finish their work before we go."

"Very good idea, Miss Marshall. I'll go look at my calendar now."

Georgia hurried up to get the girls started on their numbers and then came back down to the study.

"How about next Friday?" Sir Tyler asked as she entered the room. "I'll block out the whole afternoon."

"They will love that! Would you like to take them alone?"

"Oh, no. They'll enjoy it more if you're there, too."

"Well, if you're sure."

"I am. We've gone a few times, but not for long and I could see there was much more to it than what we saw. We didn't really do too much but the girls seemed happy just riding through."

Georgia's heart sank. They just rode through? She'd make sure they did something fun to tell their papa about today, and when he went with them, she'd try to have a list of things he might enjoy doing with them, too. This man needed to spend more time with his girls. And Georgia believed he needed it as much as they did!

"I'll try to show them around a bit more. It's fairly new to me, too, as I haven't lived here all that long. But the boarders have a lot of outings there and Rebecca takes Jenny quite often. I'm sure Polly and Lilly will have a good time."

"I've no doubt about it. I know they'll enjoy playing with Jenny."

"Yes, they will. But they'll enjoy going with you more. I'll go tell them your plans. They'll be very happy to have it to look forward to."

"I'm finding it's always good to give them something to look forward to, especially in the coming week. I think it makes the weekend pass faster for them."

"Are they having a hard time on weekends?"

"Not really. Although they do say they miss you. But they'll get used to it in time."

"I hope so."

But as she hurried up to check on the girls, she couldn't help but wonder if she should split up the days off so it didn't seem so long for them. She'd have to do some thinking and praying about it. She wanted to be there for them, but she worried about them becoming too attached to her—as she was already feeling toward them.

After all, she wouldn't be there forever. Sir Tyler was a very handsome man, and her heart still did some funny kind of flip when he smiled at her, and that was something she must guard against.

He'd be marrying again one day and it wouldn't be to a nanny—or a teacher, either, for that matter. No, he'd married a woman far above Georgia's standing the first time and she was sure he'd do the same the next time. And even if— No! There could be no *even ifs*! What was she thinking? She'd decided she'd never trust her heart to any man again, much less one belonging to the English gentry. Why, she knew nothing of how those people did anything, and she was certain his family would never approve of a—a commoner! For that was surely how they would look at a mere schoolteacher and temporary nanny.

Georgia couldn't let herself start daydreaming about the handsome baronet. Not now. Not ever.

* * *

The picnic with Rebecca and Jenny had been quite fun and the girls were full of ideas for the outing with their papa the next week. They pulled no pranks and even told Georgia to have a nice weekend when she hugged them good-night on Friday evening.

She'd been praying about whether to change her days off, but so far had no clear insight into what the Lord thought she should do. All she really did know was that those two little girls had quickly worked their way into her heart and she feared their papa might do the same if she let her guard down.

Perhaps she *should* resign. And not let herself get too emotionally entangled. But then she remembered the expression in Sir Tyler's eyes when he'd asked if she was giving notice. Even if she felt she should quit now, before it became even more difficult to, how could she do that to him and his girls?

Besides, she needed this job and it felt good to be able to finally pay her rent. She wasn't going to take advantage of Mrs. Heaton's generosity in letting her stay there for free any longer and there'd be no openings for teachers until the next term. Even if something came open, there were many ahead of her who had applied for a position. So, she'd have to stay put for now. She had no choice.

But it was almost a relief to let herself into Heaton House and know that she had a few days to shore up her determination to keep her attraction to Sir Tyler from growing. Surely once he began spending most of his days at the new office, it would be easier not to think about him!

She'd telephoned Elizabeth and Violet earlier that

day and found that they both thought Betsy would be a wonderful choice to help with Polly's and Lilly's wardrobes. She joined the others in the parlor, and when she broached the subject with Betsy, the woman seemed delighted.

"Oh, Georgia, the timing is perfect. I've just finished up with one of my most demanding customers and working on little girls' clothing will be a wonderful change. I have a lot of fashion plates we can look over and I've an idea what they might need at that age."

"I'm so glad you're able to take the time for this now. The girls aren't out and about much, but still, they do come from a wealthy family and I want to be sure they dress as one of their social station would. Only I don't really know exactly what that is, and it appears Sir Tyler isn't all that concerned except that they look like proper young ladies."

"How about we take a trip to the Ladies' Mile with the girls next week and see what colors and styles they're drawn to that would be appropriate for them? Macy's will probably have a great selection, but with all the other dress shops around, I'm sure we'll come away with a good idea about what things to add to their wardrobe."

"That's a wonderful idea, Betsy! Polly and Lilly will love it. I doubt they've ever been shopping there." She couldn't wait to tell them. Maybe they could have lunch downtown, too. She'd be sure to speak to Sir Tyler about it on Monday.

For now, she was going to enjoy her weekend. Everyone was looking forward to Matt and Millicent's housewarming and she was no exception. It'd be good to spend time with the other boarders, past and present.

As Julia began to play the piano and Georgia joined the others in song, she had to fight thinking about Sir Tyler. She wondered if he was having dinner at that long table all by himself. She pushed the thought out of her mind. He might not feel lonely at all and there was nothing she could do about it even if he did.

Oh, yes, she needed the weekend and the time away from Walker House and the very handsome father of her charges.

Tyler smiled as his daughters entered his study on Saturday afternoon. They were very excited about going to Matt and Millicent Sterling's housewarming with him. He'd told them the night before when he'd gone to hear their prayers and tuck them in.

"Oh, Papa! Jenny is going to be there and was so excited about it. She asked if we might be there, but I didn't know we'd been invited! She'll be so happy to see us," Polly had said, while Lilly nodded and clapped.

He totally enjoyed that time with his girls now and he had Miss Marshall to thank for it. Why had he not thought of tucking them in before? He did check on them before he went to bed and would continue to do so, but to hear their sweet prayers and kiss them good-night had begun to make his evenings better, for at least he felt as if he was being there for them in a way he never had before.

They seemed to look forward to their time with him each night, too, and he hoped they did, for it made his day. Ivy must have listened to their prayers before she passed away, but they were younger then, so he didn't know. But why hadn't she included him or even mentioned it to him?

Come to think of it, he couldn't remember his parents coming up to tuck him and his brother in and hear their prayers. But just because they hadn't didn't mean he couldn't, even though he continued to feel adrift on a ship somewhere when it came to knowing how to be the father he wanted to be to his daughters.

"Are you *sure* you don't mind giving up a trip to Central Park?" he teased now.

"Oh, Papa, no! We just went with Miss Georgia and Jenny and her mother, and besides, you're going with us next week. We'd rather go to the housewarming," Polly said.

Tyler wondered if Miss Marshall would be there. Polly and Lilly were dreading the *whole weekend without her*, as they'd told him before he'd let them know about the party.

As they stood there for his inspection now, he couldn't help but smile at the anticipation shining in their eyes. "You both look very nice."

"We look better when Miss Marshall dresses us, but Amelia did her best." Lilly sighed.

"I'm sure she did," Tyler said. He'd have to remember to add a bit to the maid's pay, for she truly didn't want to be a nanny.

Tate had gone out that morning and bought a gift for the Sterlings, and he handed it to Tyler as they headed out the door. A hack was waiting to take them to the housewarming, and as it made its way through the city streets, the girls took turns holding the gift.

The hack stopped on a side street of one of the busiest areas in the city and Tyler paid the driver before helping his girls out of the vehicle. Then they hurried down the walk to a shop that bore a sign proclaiming Photography by Millicent, with a smaller sign hanging underneath that read Matthew Sterling, Architect.

Matt and Millicent lived on the top two floors and Tyler thought it a great idea for a couple with such talent. They could see others milling around as they entered the building and his daughters were immediately greeted by Mrs. Heaton's granddaughter, Jenny.

"Polly and Lilly! I'm so glad you're here!" the young girl exclaimed. "Mama is watching Mrs. Sterling take photos. I just had mine taken and I'm sure she'll want to take one of you two!"

Jenny took the hand of each and then looked at Tyler. "May they come with me, Sir Tyler? You can come, too."

Tyler didn't know what to say at first, but agreed. "Yes, they may. I'm right behind you." He recognized other boarders from Mrs. Heaton's, who greeted him, and some of the married couples he'd met at the wedding, but he didn't see Miss Marshall.

He was just behind his girls, about to enter what he supposed was Millicent Sterling's photography studio, when Matt stopped and welcomed him.

"Sir Tyler. I'm so honored you and your daughters could make it. It's a little chaotic at the moment, but we're about to all go upstairs to let everyone see our home and have some refreshments."

"I'm honored to be invited. I—"

A burst of soft laughter that he now recognized as Miss Marshall's caught his attention and he turned to find her coming out of the studio with his girls and Jenny right behind her.

"Papa, Jenny wants to show us around. Is it all right?" Lilly asked him.

"Well, I suppose. Just don't go upstairs until we're called to do so, and then come find me."

"Yes, sir," Polly said, and the three girls hurried off.

"I hope I did the right thing," Tyler said.

"They'll be fine. Jenny is a very good little girl. She won't lead them astray," Miss Marshall said.

She smiled and his chest tightened in a way it hadn't done in a very long time. Deep down, he knew he was more than a little attracted to this woman and that just wouldn't do. He had no intention of losing his heart to anyone—not after losing his wife. He never wanted to go through that kind of heartache again. Ever.

"Miss Marshall, I can see my daughters were delighted to see you. They've been moaning that they had to wait until Monday to do so."

"I'm glad to see them, and you, too. I didn't know you'd be here."

"I'd forgotten about it until Tate reminded me. I didn't know who would be in attendance, but it's good to see people I know." Especially Georgia Marshall. And he suddenly realized that it was the possibility of seeing her that had made up his mind for him. He might be in real trouble here.

"I hope you're having a good weekend?" Sir Tyler asked.

"I am." Georgia's heart began doing some kind of fluttery thing as she looked into Sir Tyler's deep blue eyes. He truly was a handsome man. She hadn't been expecting him, but he might as well be here, because she'd had no success at keeping thoughts of him at bay. Even today, she'd wondered what he and the girls were doing. It seemed hard to break eye contact with him and she forced herself to turn and point to the room she'd come out of. "Have you seen Millicent's studio yet? Or Matt's office?"

"No, I haven't had a chance," he said.

"Well, come on and I'll show you around. I love how they've fit in both their businesses and private life into one building. They have a wonderful place to live, too."

"You've seen the upstairs?"

"Oh, yes. Several times, while helping them to get settled." She led him into the photography studio, where it looked as if Millicent was just finishing taking photos.

She grinned at the two of them. "Sir Tyler! I'm glad to see you here. Thank you so much for coming. I took a couple of sweet shots of your daughters and I'll get them to you as soon as possible."

"Thank you, Mrs. Sterling. I look forward to seeing them."

"Have you had a chance to see the downstairs?"

"Miss Marshall is showing me around now. Jenny is showing my girls around. I hope that's all right."

"Of course it is. I'm about to let Matt know we're ready to head upstairs, so I'll leave you in Georgia's hands. She knows the way up."

"Yes, I do. And I'll get him there shortly. I want him to see Matt's office first," Georgia said.

"I'll see you upstairs, then."

Millicent hurried out of the room and Georgia

turned to Sir Tyler. "What do you think of her studio?"

"It's quite nice and much larger than I expected."

"They took out a wall and enlarged it. I love that she has several backgrounds to choose from and she has all kinds of props she can bring in."

"I like the one with the fireplace the best," Tyler said. "Does she only take photographs here?"

"Oh, no. She'll go to homes, parks, wherever her clients want her to take their photographs."

"I expect she's in demand with the photos she's taken of the Park Row going up."

"I believe her business is growing by leaps and bounds because of her skill. And Matt's business is taking off, too. I'm very happy for them."

"It seems they've both made a good match."

Georgia chuckled. "It took them long enough to realize they loved each other. Everyone at Heaton House sensed it long before they did and—"

"Gather around, everyone." Matt's voice called them into the reception area, where he and Millicent were standing several steps up on the staircase. "Please join us in the house part of our building and help us warm our home."

Sir Tyler's daughters and Jenny ran up to them. "Papa, may we go on ahead?"

Sir Tyler looked at Georgia. "What do you think?"

"I think they'll be fine. I see Rebecca at the top of the stairs. She'll make sure they are."

"Go ahead, then," he said.

The girls ran off and Georgia and Tyler followed at a slower pace. He placed a light grip on her elbow as they headed upstairs with the others and Georgia's pulse seemed to take off like a horse hearing the gun-shot at the start of a race. She couldn't deny she was glad to see him, although she hadn't even known he was invited. She'd just been wondering what he and the girls were doing when Polly and Lilly had come into the studio with Jenny.

"Did the girls mind putting off your Saturday outing with you?" she asked as they reached the landing of the staircase.

"Not at all. They were thrilled at the chance to see Jenny again and I'm sure they hoped that you'd be here, too."

"I'm glad I got to see them. I was feeling a bit guilty for taking the weekend off, but they seem to be all right."

"Of course they are."

"Oh! I'm sorry—I didn't mean to sound as if they might not be or that they wouldn't be happy being with you."

Sir Tyler pulled her aside to let others behind them enter the foyer of the Sterling home. "There's no need to apologize, Miss Marshall. You didn't offend me. Nor is there any reason for you to feel guilty. My daughters will be fine through the weekend, but they did miss you this morning. And they are looking forward to you coming back on Monday."

"I'm looking forward to it, too." She did hope he was enjoying the extra time he'd been spending with them, even though she knew it must be a very big change for him. But he smiled at her just then and she felt relieved that she hadn't upset him by her careless remark.

But he had graciously put her in her place. She wasn't indispensable. He'd already replaced two nannies. Polly and Lilly would be fine until Monday and she'd probably see them at church the next day. As for him, Sir Tyler was only her employer, after all, and she'd spent way too much time worrying about him, too. He'd be fine also. It was time she relaxed and enjoyed her weekend.

She turned to go, but she couldn't leave him to his own devices now. He didn't know the others all that well. "Let me show you around."

"Thank you. I'd appreciate that very much, Miss Marshall."

They entered the foyer, where Matt and Millicent greeted them. "Feel free to wander around and have some refreshments. Everything's set up in the dining room," Millicent said.

"Come this way, Sir Tyler," Georgia said. "I'll show you the parlor first." It wasn't as grand as his house, but still, she loved Matt and Millicent's home. It was very warm and inviting and full of sunshine from the windows facing the street. They then went back into the hall and Georgia showed him the study in back of the parlor, then across the hall to the kitchen. Both rooms had sunny windows at the back, overlooking a small courtyard. It was into the dining room next, where they decided to go see the upstairs, hoping the crowd around the table would soon clear away a bit.

It was upstairs that they found Polly, Lilly and Jenny. They were with Rebecca and her husband, Ben, and heading back down.

"We're going for refreshments now, Papa," Lilly told her father.

"Well, there was quite a crowd down there just now. Try to save something for us, all right?"

"We will," Polly said.

It didn't take long for them to look at the bath and bedrooms upstairs. They were furnished beautifully and Georgia couldn't be happier for her friends. As they came back down, she caught a glimpse of Matt and Millicent. He had an arm around his wife as they stood speaking to Mrs. Heaton, and it was then that a flood of longing washed over her, taking her breath away. Georgia raised a hand over her suddenly aching heart, almost stumbling on the stairs in the process.

Sir Tyler grasped her elbow a little tighter. "Are you all right?"

"Yes. I'm sorry. I must have lost my footing."

Only she really wasn't fine. She wanted…something she'd never have. Others at Heaton House had found people to trust with their hearts, but Georgia didn't know how she ever would. Not after this past year. And longing for something she was certain she'd never find wasn't the answer to her problem. Only accepting it was.

Chapter Seven

Sunday's lesson was about putting the past behind you and going forward, but Georgia wasn't sure how to go about it when she was still hurting after finding out Phillip loved her sister and not her. How could she have been so blind?

And because she was, how could she forget the lesson she'd learned from it? However, she did know that she needed to forgive Phillip—and she would try to get there for the sake of her sister and her family. She did love them.

But, oh, how glad she was that she didn't have to watch them start their life together each and every day. Perhaps by the time she saw them again, she could be genuinely happy for them, if not for herself.

Still, she had many blessings to count, and after the last song and the closing prayer, she saw two of them heading down the aisle toward her.

"Miss Georgia!" Lilly said as she barreled toward her, stopping just short of knocking her down, and would have, if Georgia hadn't caught her.

"How are you this morning?"

"I'm good. I had such fun at the housewarming yesterday, and tomorrow is Monday and you'll be back, won't you?"

"I will. And I have a surprise of sorts for you and Polly."

"You do?" Polly said from behind her sister.

"I do. I think you'll like it."

"I can't wait!" Lilly said.

"Neither can I!" Polly said.

"What's this all about?" Sir Tyler asked as he reached his runaway daughters.

"I told them I have a surprise for them tomorrow."

"Oh?" He smiled at her, but his raised eyebrow seemed to be asking if she was going to let him know what it was.

"I think you'll approve," Georgia said. "But I can't tell you without giving it away, so—"

"So you can give me the details when you come to work in the morning, before you go upstairs."

"I'll be happy to." Surely he wouldn't be opposed to her plans. It seemed he'd already given her carte blanche in regard to their new wardrobes.

As they walked out the door of the church together, she found Mrs. Heaton was waiting for them.

"Sir Tyler, I realize this is late notice and I do apologize for it, but I wonder if you and your daughters might like to come to Sunday night supper this evening?"

"Oh, may we, Papa?" Polly asked.

"Please, Papa!"

Georgia held her breath waiting for his answer.

He didn't eat meals with his girls and she wasn't sure he'd agree.

"Thank you so much for your invitation, Mrs. Heaton, but another time perhaps?"

"Of course. I do apologize for the lateness of my invitation." She looked down at his girls and back at him. "And for any problems I might have caused with it."

"Please don't. Spontaneity is quite refreshing and I'm sorry I can't accept for us at this time."

He looked at Georgia. "We'll see you in the morning, Miss Marshall. Have a good afternoon and evening."

"Yes, you, too."

But something in his expression and the disappointment in his daughters' eyes told Georgia that the rest of the day might not be all that good for him.

She fell into step with her landlady on the walk home. "I'm sorry Sir Tyler didn't accept your invitation, Mrs. Heaton."

"Oh, don't be, dear. I wasn't sure if I should issue it anyway, but I do feel sorry for him in that big house, trying to raise his daughters without his wife. I'm sure the weekends are a little difficult for him with you not there."

"Do you think I should be staying overnight?"

"Oh, no, dear! You must have some time to yourself. You aren't in service and I certainly don't want you to feel as if you are."

"Perhaps I should broach the subject of working on Saturday and taking another day off during the week. It might make things easier on him and the girls."

"That would be your decision entirely, Georgia,

but I don't want you doing it because of anything I said. It could be that our way of doing things is a bit too spontaneous for Sir Tyler."

"More likely it's that he's not sure how his girls might act. He doesn't have his meals with them."

Mrs. Heaton stopped in her tracks. "Never?"

"Not since I've been there. He looks in on them after his breakfast while they have theirs, and again at lunchtime, if he's home. He did mention that the other nanny had brought them in for tea back in England, but we haven't done that since I've been there. He hasn't asked me to and Mr. Tate hasn't said anything about it, so we have it together in the morning room."

"What about dinner?"

Georgia shook her head. "He has his later than they do and, well, he does come up to hear their prayers and tuck them in at night, but I think that's mostly since I've been there."

"Oh, Georgia. He does need you—or at least his daughters do."

"He does love them, Mrs. Heaton," Georgia said, as she found herself defending him. "I think he just doesn't know quite what to do with them."

"Then perhaps it's up to you to show him."

"I don't want to overstep my bounds."

"I don't think you will. You can be very tactful, but perhaps it's time you use your experience as a teacher to help him along."

"Perhaps…" Did she dare? Or would she be a coward if she didn't? He might put her in her place, but she didn't think he'd fire her. At least she hoped he wouldn't. *Oh, dear Lord, please help me to know what to do.*

* * *

The next morning, Georgia followed Mr. Tate to Sir Tyler's study, where he was waiting for her.

"Good morning, Miss Marshall. Please have a cup of tea with me."

It sounded more like an order than a request, and Georgia couldn't help but wonder why he sounded so gruff this morning. He looked a bit out of sorts, but she couldn't imagine what she'd done to make him feel that way toward her. She sat down in the chair he indicated and then took the cup Mr. Tate handed her.

The butler left and Georgia took a sip of tea, waiting for Sir Tyler to give her an indication of what was troubling him.

Instead he smiled and said, "Now, tell me about this surprise you have for the girls. What is it you've planned for them?"

Evidently he had no intention of letting her know what was bothering him. Maybe her instincts had been wrong—which was in keeping with how they usually worked with her. It appeared they hadn't got any better.

"If it's all right with you, Betsy, the seamstress I told you about, is coming over after breakfast. We're going to look at their wardrobe and decide what still can be used and what we need to have made or purchase for them. Then we're going to take them to look at clothing so we can get an idea of what they like that is in style."

"That sounds like a very good plan," Sir Tyler said.

"We might have lunch out with them, if you agree," Georgia continued, "and then we'll come back here and look at the fashion plates Betsy has and the *Delineator* magazines that Elizabeth Talbot has loaned me. By the end of the day, I think we might have an idea of what is needed and I can report back to you."

Sir Tyler leaned back in his chair. "I'm impressed, Miss Marshall. And Polly and Lilly will be delighted at the outing. It's just what they need after last night."

Georgia sat up straighter. "Last night? Are they all right?"

"I believe so. But they both had a breakdown of sorts after I tucked them in and heard their prayers. Actually, it began on Saturday night. Evidently seeing Jenny with her mother and father made them miss their mother even more than usual, but they didn't want me to be sad, too, so they didn't mention it that night."

Sir Tyler got up and began to pace. "I thought things were fine and that they'd had a wonderful time at the housewarming. But Polly came to get me in the middle of the night because Lilly was sobbing again and she couldn't get her to stop, and then it all came out. It took a while but I got them settled back down. I thought everything was all right when we went to church yesterday morning and they were so pleased to see you."

"They seemed fine yesterday," Georgia said.

"They did. Until I turned down Mrs. Heaton's invitation to Sunday supper. Evidently that upset them and for the rest of the day they were quite difficult. I was tempted to tell you to put off your surprise because of it. However, I'm not certain that would be best." He sat back down and sighed. "To tell you the truth, Georgia, I... Pardon me—Miss Marshall... Most times I'm not sure what to do when it pertains to my daughters."

Georgia's heart had begun to hammer against her ribs when he'd called her by her given name. Now it overflowed with compassion for this man. "Sir Tyler, it isn't easy to raise children when both parents are involved, but to try to do so alone, during a time of grief, must be…" She was at a loss for words.

"It's the most difficult thing I've ever done. I wish I'd paid more attention to the things Ivy did for them apart from what the nanny did. And I wish—" He shook his head and stood. "I must let you get to the girls. They'll be afraid you aren't coming. I think your idea is a very good one, but I'll visit at breakfast and make sure they're in a better mood. If not, I'll make them stay home while you go out."

Georgia didn't say how that would be defeating her purpose. She needed to know what the girls liked. There'd be no point in them having new outfits if they hated them. Even little girls had likes and dislikes. "I'll go get them ready for breakfast now, Sir Tyler."

She wanted to say so much more to this man. Wanted to help in any way she could. And yet she must get her emotions where he was concerned under control. He was still grieving, just as his daughters were, and while her heart might flood with compassion for his situation, that was all she could let it feel. Nothing more.

She hurried upstairs to find the girls just opening their eyes. Poor dears. Her heart went out to them just as much as it did their papa.

"Miss Georgia! I'm so glad it's Monday and you're here. Two days is much too long, don't you think?" Polly said.

"But you saw me both of those days." She smiled

at the two of them. "I don't want you to get sick of me, you know."

"We saw you for only a little bit of the day," Lilly said as Georgia went to pick out their outfits to go shopping. "It's not enough. And Papa didn't let us go to Mrs. Heaton's for Sunday dinner!"

"We were angry with him," Polly said.

Georgia turned from what she was doing. "Girls, I am very sure your papa didn't refuse in order to upset you. He loves you both very much. Maybe it was because he wasn't sure how you'd act at a table full of grown-ups."

"How should we act?" Lilly's question showed Georgia that Sir Tyler might have been right.

"With your very best manners, of course. And at a dinner with adults, there are more utensils to use and you should know what they are for."

"Can't you teach us?"

"Why, yes, I can. I'll speak to your papa about it. But why don't you try to think of his turning the invitation down as trying to protect you from being embarrassed because you don't know what to do yet."

Polly dropped her head. "I didn't think of that."

"I didn't, either," Lilly said. "We weren't very nice to him after that."

"Do you think maybe you should apologize for your bad behavior?"

When both girls nodded, Georgia smiled. They loved their papa as much as he loved them, only none of them seemed to know how to relate to each other. "Good. Now go wash up and we'll get you dressed. I'll tell you about the surprise I have for you at breakfast."

"The surprise!" Lilly slapped her forehead. "I almost forgot about it."

"How could you?" Polly said. "Even I remembered, but when Miss Georgia didn't mention it, I thought maybe Papa said we couldn't have it after the way we acted yesterday."

At least the girls had the sensibility to know they'd acted badly. Georgia couldn't help but wonder what they'd put their father through the day before. She felt it must have been bad for him to even bring it up to her.

"Well, I think he will, but I expect you to be on your very best behavior or I will let him know. And a friend of mine is going with us. You'll like her a lot."

"We're going somewhere? Oh, I can't wait to hear about it!"

"Then you both had better get a move on!"

The two girls rushed into the bathroom to freshen up and Georgia laid their clothes out for them. These three needed her help. But in order to provide it, she had to find a way to guard her heart. And as quickly as possible.

Tyler had avoided thinking about this morning's conversation with Miss Marshall until Tate served his breakfast. But he could no longer keep the thoughts at bay. What had he been thinking to confide in her in such a way?

Not to mention that he'd called her by her given name! He'd totally overstepped the bounds of an employer-employee relationship. At least Tate hadn't overheard him—otherwise he'd have been sure to show his disapproval.

It was a wonder Georgia Marshall hadn't admonished him about it. But she'd looked so sympathetic to his plight with his girls, he couldn't seem to keep from talking to her about it. Or admitting that he was out of his depth when it came to knowing how to raise his daughters.

And wrong or not, he felt better for having talked to her. She was their nanny, after all, a teacher and a very lovely female who could relate to his daughters in ways he couldn't. And it'd become more than obvious to him that he needed her help with them.

But he must not let his attraction to her grow. He couldn't deny it was there, but nothing—nothing at all—must come from it. He'd suffered the kind of heartbreak he never wanted to go through a second time, and he wasn't going to take a chance on it ever happening again.

Nor was he going to think about it now—not with his girls giggling in the next room. Hearing that sweet sound cheered him up and he quickly finished his meal so he could look in on them.

"I can't believe we're getting new clothes, Miss Georgia!" Polly was saying as he entered the breakfast room.

"Only if you behave yourself while you're out today," Tyler said from the doorway.

"Papa! We are so sorry we weren't nice to you yesterday!" Polly exclaimed.

"Yes, we are, Papa. Will you forgive us?" Lilly asked.

The little scamps. He had a feeling this was just the beginning of them being able to twist him around their little fingers. "Of course I forgive you. How could I not? But I do expect you to be on your very best behavior on your outing today, or there will be *no* picnic on Friday."

"Yes, sir," the girls said in unison.

"Good, because I'd hate to miss it. I'm off to check out the work on my new office, but I look forward to hearing about your trip to the Ladies' Mile." He handed Georgia cash. "This is in case you purchase anything today. Then you can tell me where you'll be shopping and I'll open a line of credit for you at those stores."

Georgia hesitantly took the bills from him. "I'm not sure we'll actually purchase anything today, but thank you," Georgia said.

"At the very least, you're going to lunch with your friend and the girls and it's my treat today. Have a good time."

The huge grins his daughters flashed him warmed Tyler's heart, but the smile Georgia Marshall gave him shot straight into it and had him backing out of the room as fast as he could. Something about this woman drew him in a way he'd never experienced before and he had to find a way to ignore the pull. But how could he do that when his girls needed her so much? Maybe the best way was to get to the office, finish setting it up and stay there most of the day.

Chapter Eight

The morning sped by as Georgia, Betsy and the girls went through their wardrobes to see what was needed. They had Polly and Lilly try on everything to see if they could get more use out of it, but when Georgia had them put on the outfits they'd had on that first Sunday, she realized that both of them had grown even more in just that short amount of time.

"A few of their underclothes would work for a bit, but nearly everything else needs to be given away or refashioned in some way," Betsy said.

"I love this dress," Polly said. "I don't want to part with it."

"What do you think, Betsy? Can the hem be let down enough?" Georgia asked.

Betsy looked at the skirt closely. "I think we can get a little more wear out of it. But most of their things have already been let down as much as possible and all that we could do to them would be to add material or lace of some kind. It might work for a few things, but not all."

"Well, we'll add to the one Polly has on. Lilly, what about you? Do you want your dress to be let down like Polly's?"

"Yes, please, but I'm a little tired of the others."

"Yes, so am I," Polly said.

"Well, then, let's get started. We're going to lunch first and then we'll go looking for the style you like and the colors you love best."

"Will we buy anything today?" Lilly asked, her eyes shining with excitement.

"I don't believe so, but you never know. We might pick out some material so that Miss Betsy can get started on a few new outfits. It depends on how good you are and how much time we have."

"Oh, we'll be very good, Miss Georgia," Polly assured her.

And they were. Georgia was quite proud of them as she and Betsy took them to lunch at a small café down the street from Macy's and they behaved very well. It wouldn't take much to have them ready for a real dinner. Perhaps she should speak to their papa about it soon.

After lunch they went to several shops featuring children's clothing. At one, the proprietor clapped her hands when she saw Polly and Lilly. "Oh, what pretty daughters you have," she said to Georgia.

Georgia couldn't miss the look the two girls gave each other and she hoped the clerk's words didn't upset them, like seeing Jenny with her mother and stepfather had.

"Oh, yes, they are quite beautiful, aren't they? But I'm only their nanny."

"Oh! I'm sorry. They have your coloring and I—"

"It's all right. You couldn't have known."

Georgia decided not to tarry there long, however. She wanted to get the girls' minds off the woman's comment as soon as possible.

After visiting several other shops, they went to Macy's, where Emily worked, and the newer Siegel-Cooper store, where Stephen was employed.

By the time they were through, Georgia and Betsy knew what the girls liked and were happy with what they'd pointed out. They did purchase some trim and yard goods so that Betsy could lengthen the two dresses and get started on new Sunday outfits for them. They also bought new petticoats for both girls.

"The cost to buy them isn't that much more than making them and that will leave me free to concentrate on the more detailed sewing," Betsy said.

The girls were thrilled they'd soon have new clothing and Georgia was relieved that they didn't seem upset about the shop owner's remarks about them being her daughters. Perhaps it was she who was most affected by it, for a longing deep inside seemed to have risen up at the woman's words and Georgia realized how very attached she was to her charges. And how very proud she'd be if they *were* her daughters.

She'd barely got the girls down for their naps and joined Betsy in the morning room for tea when Sir Tyler surprised them by showing up.

"Good afternoon, ladies. Might there be enough tea for me, or should I ring for more?"

Georgia's pulse sped through her veins to jolt her heart at his sudden appearance. "I believe there is enough here. But we can ask for more."

Only it wasn't necessary because Mr. Tate must

have let Mrs. Biddle know Sir Tyler was home. For at that moment, Amelia brought in another cup and a fresh pot of tea and left as quietly as she came.

Georgia poured her employer a cup and introduced him to Betsy.

"Yes, I believe we met at the housewarming last weekend," Sir Tyler said, taking a seat on the chair nearest Georgia. "How did the shopping trip go? Did the girls behave themselves?"

"It went very well and they were very good. And we found they have wonderful taste in color and style for themselves," Georgia said.

"Much better than most girls their age," Betsy added. "It's going to be a pleasure to sew for them."

"Will you want to set up your machine here?"

Betsy shook her head. "I'll sew at Heaton House, if you don't mind. I have everything set up in my room at present and it will be less distracting to your household. I can bring things over here for fittings, or Georgia can bring the girls over there. Being just next door, either way will be easy for us."

Sir Tyler gave a nod. "I'll leave it to you two to figure all that out, then. Whatever you decide is fine with me. I'm sure that you'll make certain my daughters do me proud."

"Oh, yes, you may be assured of that," Georgia said. She wanted them to look as good as their mother would have had them do, or their grandmothers, for that matter. She certainly didn't want people talking behind Sir Tyler's back and wondering why his nanny hadn't brought the girls' wardrobes to his attention.

Sir Tyler drained his cup and stood. "I must send Mrs. Heaton some flowers. She somehow persuaded

Miss Marshall to agree to help me out and now another of her boarders is coming to our aid. The Lord definitely led me to the right house in the neighborhood. I'll leave you ladies to your planning. I'm going back to the office now. I just wanted to stop in and see how things had gone."

Georgia's heart softened as she watched him leave the room. He seemed to be taking more of an interest in his daughters now, and she prayed that he continued to do so.

She turned back to Betsy only to find her waving her hand in front of her face. "Oh, my, Georgia. He is even more handsome up close. You're going to have to be on guard of your heart—if you haven't lost it already!"

"Betsy! Shh!" Georgia turned to make sure Sir Tyler was out of hearing distance.

"He didn't hear me." Betsy chuckled.

Georgia hoped so, because truer words had never been spoken.

The next few days passed fairly smoothly, with the girls excited about the new outfits. There'd been no more frightening pranks, but they'd been whispering all day and she had a feeling something was about to happen.

She'd told them earlier in the day that she'd be leaving early the next day after the picnic and they hadn't been very happy about it.

"Leave early?" Lilly had asked. "Why would you want to do that, Miss Georgia?"

"Well, it's Mrs. Heaton's son's birthday and she's planned a surprise dinner for him."

"Oh," Polly said.

"But why do you have to go?"

"I don't have to. But I've been friends with Mrs. Heaton and her family a long time and I want to celebrate with them."

"Oh." Lilly sighed. "We like Mrs. Heaton, too. But we wish you didn't have to leave early."

"It's only for one night."

"But after the picnic we won't see you again until Monday." Lilly began to pout.

Georgia bent down and gave her a hug. "Now, Lilly, I'm sure I'll see you on Sunday."

"Maybe," the child said.

"We do like Mrs. Heaton and all, but did Papa say it was all right for you to go?" Polly asked.

"He did. It is for something special."

"Uh-huh."

"It's only a few hours early."

"Oh, okay," Lilly said, giving in.

"I'll tell your papa and maybe he will take you to the ice-cream parlor tomorrow evening."

"Really? Do you think so?"

"I'll see what I can do. Your papa will be coming up soon. Better jump into bed." The girls did as she asked and she went to get her reticule. But it wasn't where she usually kept it in the secretary in the corner of their room. Georgia bent down to see if it was in one of the cubbyholes, but it wasn't there, either.

"Girls, have you seen my handbag?"

"Is it gone?"

"It's not where I usually keep it."

"We'll help!"

They both jumped out of bed and began to look under their beds.

"Now, girls, you know I wouldn't put my purse there."

"But you could have dropped it and accidentally kicked it under," Lilly said.

"Possibly," Georgia said, bending to look under the secretary. But it wasn't there. Georgia turned to see them whispering again. She was almost certain they had something to do with this.

"Did you find it?"

"It's not under the beds."

"It's not under the secretary, either."

If she was wrong about the girls doing it, what could she have done with it? She always kept it in the same place—or tried to. But a time or two when she was about to leave, it seemed she'd misplaced it and the girls helped then, too. Once it was in one of the drawers in their wardrobe. She assumed she'd hurried to get their clothing out and just laid it down in there and forgotten it.

The next time it had been in one of the drawers that she never used. It was then that she began to suspect the sisters were pulling pranks again. And she was even more convinced they'd hid it from her this time.

The girls were giggling and running from one corner of the room to the other, looking behind chairs, the window curtains, anything and everything.

Then Lilly sat down on the settee and pulled something out from between the cushion and arm. "Here it is, Miss Georgia!"

"Now, what was it doing there, do you suppose?" She was certain she hadn't left it there—she hadn't sat down on that settee in days. "I think perhaps some-one hid it there. Lilly, did you?"

"Not me!" Lilly said, eyeing her big sister.

"No, but it was *your* idea," Polly said.

"Girls, did you or not hide it?" Georgia asked. They'd practically admitted it, but she couldn't let them get away with it any longer.

"We thought it would be fun to help you find it again," Polly said.

"And were you responsible for those other times, too?"

"We might have been," Lilly admitted, hurrying back to her bed.

"You're not mad, are you, Miss Georgia?" Polly asked as she slipped back into her bed.

"No, I'm not mad. But I think you two have pulled quite enough tricks lately," Georgia said as she covered them up.

"I'm sorry," Lilly said. "Tonight *was* my idea. We just wanted—"

"We didn't want—"

"And what is it you either did or didn't want?" Sir Tyler asked from the doorway. "I was wondering what was taking so long for Miss Georgia to let me know you were ready to say your prayers. Have you been hiding from her again?"

"No, Papa. We haven't."

"Then what have you done?"

Tears welled up in Lilly's eyes. "We just hid her reticule from her a few times."

"A few times? Today?"

"Not all today!" Polly said hurriedly.

"Oh, I see. So you've been pulling a few pranks on Miss Georgia again?"

Both girls nodded and Georgia hoped their truthfulness would keep them from getting into too much trouble.

At the glance Sir Tyler shot her, she wasn't sure he was too happy with her for not telling him, either. But the latest tricks hadn't been the same as hiding themselves from her.

"And what was your reasoning? Girls, Miss Georgia is here very long days to help us out and I'm sure that she's ready to go home at the end of them."

"We just wanted her to stay a little longer, Papa," Polly explained. "And we had fun helping her find it."

Georgia's heart melted right then and there. But was that all the pranks were? They didn't seem too upset that their papa was admonishing them. Was it to get his attention? He'd been out of the house a lot this week. Maybe it bothered them more than she'd thought it would to have him away.

"Girls, you must stop pulling these kinds of pranks on Miss Marshall. I know you might not totally understand, but what is sometimes funny to you is not always funny to her or to me. You don't want to run her away, do you?"

"Oh, no!" they said together as they turned to Georgia.

"We don't want you to leave, Miss Georgia," Lilly cried.

"Please don't quit," Polly added. "We're sorry!"

"Girls, I have no intention of quitting." At least not right now. They would only blame themselves and she couldn't have that. Then she'd blame herself and—

No, she wouldn't be quitting over childish pranks. They needed her and she needed a paycheck.

"Oh, thank you, Miss Georgia! We promise to be better, don't we, Lilly?"

"Yes, we do!"

"All right now. You've kept Miss Georgia extra time tonight—most of the week, actually—and I need to speak to her," Sir Tyler said. "I'll be back up to tuck you in and hear your prayers after I do."

"Do we still get to go on the picnic tomorrow?" Lilly asked, running to her father and blinking her big eyes rapidly.

Georgia watched as fat tears gathered in the corners of the girl's eyes. One more blink and they flew out of her eyes to roll down her cheeks. She'd just recently realized the child could produce flying tears at will. Literally. Did Sir Tyler know? Georgia watched as he picked her up and brushed the tears away. Evidently not.

"Now, don't cry. I will think it over and let you know. We'll talk about it when I come back up." He put her back on her bed and ruffled Polly's hair, as she was already in her bed.

"Good night, girls. Sleep tight and I'll see you in the morning." Georgia blew them kisses and headed for the door.

Sir Tyler joined her in the hall. "I'm not sure if I should let them get away with all of this so easily."

"Oh, I don't think it's easy for them," Georgia said quietly as they started down the stairs. "They're probably thinking you're going to cancel the outing tomorrow."

"Don't you think I should? They need to learn that their actions do have consequences."

"True, but so far they haven't been all that bad, have they?"

"We don't want them thinking they can get away with pulling pranks on a regular basis, do we?"

Georgia's heart seemed to turn a somersault at his question and the knowledge that he valued her opinion. "No, of course not. Is this something they do normally?"

"Not to my knowledge. At least not that I was aware of. It's possible they did, but their nannies never told me. But I did ask you to and you agreed—"

"Sir Tyler, I don't consider hiding my purse the same as the girls hiding from me. And at first, I thought I might have misplaced it."

"Why did they do it?"

"They said they wanted me to stay a little longer. How could I get angry about that?"

"I wonder if they're testing you in some way?"

"Testing me? Why would they do that?"

"Well, I do know that they hate to see you leave. In fact, they'd be more than happy if you lived here all the time."

"I can't, but—"

"I know. And I understand. And I've tried to explain all that to them. But they did tell me that with the last nanny, that if she didn't want to be their nanny, they didn't want her to be."

"But they know I like being their nanny. Still, I won't be here forever and they do know that, too. Besides, I wonder if it is *you* they are trying to get the attention of?"

They'd reached the front door and Sir Tyler looked totally confused. "Me? But I've been giving them more time than usual."

Georgia let out a sigh. She hated to bring up memories, but she knew she needed to bring this to him, for the sake of his girls. "I think perhaps they are acting out because of missing their mother so much. Sometimes, when memories begin to fade, people—children especially—sometimes feel guilty and they don't know how to deal with it."

"Oh."

She hated that she'd brought up his loss. He didn't seem to know what to say.

"I'm sorry. But I do believe that might be part of the problem."

"No, don't be sorry. I'm glad you've brought this to my attention. I would like to speak to you more about it, but the girls are waiting for me and I'm sure you'd like to get home. Perhaps we can discuss this more tomorrow?"

"Of course. What are you going to do about the picnic?"

"It's been planned since last week, and if what you think is going on with them is true, I don't want to make things worse by canceling it."

"Good. I'm glad."

Sir Tyler nodded as he opened the door for her. "I'll see you tomorrow. You've given me much to think about, Miss Marshall."

Georgia wished she hadn't had to, but something was going on with his daughters and the sooner they discovered what it was, the faster they could address it. Still, the look in Sir Tyler's eyes when she'd mentioned his loss… Well, she wouldn't be getting it out of her mind for a very long time.

Dear Lord, please show me what to do or say to help him and his daughters deal with their sorrow, if that is what You would have me do. Please comfort them tonight.

Tyler went back to his daughters' room to find them at the window. Probably watching Georgia going back to Heaton House. He cleared his throat and they quickly hurried back to their beds.

Hopefully they hadn't been at the top of the stairs listening to the conversation. "All right, girls. We will be going on the picnic tomorrow. But *only* if you promise me that you'll not be pulling any more tricks on Miss Georgia. If you are trying to test her like you did the last nanny, it is to stop now. Miss Georgia has no intention of leaving us yet, although she will eventually, and if you keep this up, probably sooner than later."

"We don't want that!" Polly said.

The very thought that she would be leaving at any time didn't sit any better with him than it did with his daughters. "But you must remember that she lives just next door and you will be seeing her even after we get a new nanny."

"Do you think so, Papa?" Polly asked.

"Really? We could still see her?" Lilly's eyes were full of hope.

"Of course you could." Tyler sat down on the side of her bed. He wasn't going to mention that it wouldn't be the same for any of them—they'd realize that on their own when it came about. But they'd had enough to deal with and for now his assurance seemed enough to calm them.

"But you won't hurry to get another nanny just yet, will you, Papa? Please don't," Polly pleaded.

"No, I won't. With setting up the new office, I don't have the time and I don't want to disrupt the household again so quickly." Still, he felt the need to give one more reminder, for it was something they would have to accept. "I know you've become quite fond of Miss Marshall, but you will need to remember that she won't be here forever. However, I think she'll be your friend as long as you want her to be."

"Do you really think so, Papa?" Polly asked.

"I do."

"And it's okay if we are fond of her?"

"Why, yes, of course it is."

"Sometimes…I forget what Mama looked like," Polly said out of the blue. "And I have to sneak into your room to look at her picture by your bedside to remember."

"Me, too." Lilly, who'd been almost too young to remember Ivy at all when she passed away, added with a small sob as she crawled out from under her covers.

Polly jumped out of bed and ran to him and he drew them both into his arms. "I know, but it's a natural thing and it happens to everyone who has lost someone they love."

"Does it?" Polly asked.

"It does." It broke his heart to know they sneaked into his room to see their mother's photograph. "And you can go into my room anytime. I'll write to your grandmother and ask her if she has any photos of your mama when she was growing up that she can give you two."

"Will you, Papa? That would be wonderful!" Polly exclaimed.

"I will. Now, no more pranks pulled on Miss Georgia, right?"

"Yes, Papa!"

"Let's hear your prayers, then. You need to get to sleep or you won't have a good time at the park tomorrow."

Tyler listened to first one and then the other's prayers, noticing that they each asked His forgiveness for pulling pranks and asked Him to let Miss Georgia stay for a long time as their nanny.

He pulled up their covers and kissed their brows before heading out the door, but he had a feeling they were asleep before he even left the room. Tyler made his way down to his study and dropped down into his favorite chair.

The new nighttime ritual went much smoother than he'd thought it might after hearing about their antics, and for that he had only one person to thank. *Georgia Marshall.* And if she was right about his daughters feeling bad because the memory of their mother was fading, and it seemed she might be, then he completely understood. For he had the same problem, only possibly worse.

Tyler dropped his head into his hands and sighed. Not only was the memory of his lovely wife's face fading, but it was also being replaced by the very woman who was striving to help his daughters get through their grief.

Dear Lord, what am I to do? I need to distance my-

self from Georgia Marshall, but because of my girls, I don't see how I can. I feel it would set them back to let her go, and yet with each day that passes, I find myself more drawn to her.

You know why I can't let her into my heart. I can't chance that kind of heartbreak again. Please help me to guard my heart and to accept what I must.

And please, dear God, help me to become the kind of father You would have me be to Polly and Lilly. And thank You for sending Miss Marshall to help me. In Jesus's name, amen.

Tyler raised his head just as he heard Tate clear his throat outside the door. His butler entered. "Your dinner is ready to be served, Sir Tyler."

"Thank you, Tate. I think I'll have it in here this evening."

"Very well, sir." Tate left and Tyler moved to the small table he'd had brought in for those nights when the thought of eating alone in the dining room seemed more than he could handle.

In only moments, Tate was back with his place setting and then quietly left the room. Mrs. Biddle had cooked his favorite roast beef and it was done to perfection. Much better than his appetite deserved. Still, Tyler made himself eat it all, not wanting to offend his cook by leaving any of his favorite meal on the plate.

When Tate came back in, Tyler told him not to bring dessert until a bit later with coffee. "Please tell Mrs. Biddle I appreciate her thoughtfulness in making my favorite meal. It was delicious and quite filling."

"She'll be glad to hear it, Sir Tyler."

"I hope so. She seems to be more content now. Do you think she's going to stay?"

"I believe so. She's gotten to know Mrs. Heaton's help better and I think they share teatime together once in a while."

"Very good news to hear."

The only thing better would be if Miss Marshall decided she didn't want to go back to teaching and would stay here. No. That wouldn't be a good thing. He was much too attracted to her to try to talk her into staying—no matter how much he might long to.

Chapter Nine

The girls were on their best behavior the next morning, and Georgia had no doubt they would be very good if they ever wanted their papa to take time off again.

He seemed in good spirits, too, as they took off. He'd ordered a hack to take them to the park, and once he helped his daughters into the cab, he turned to her.

She was holding the basket Mrs. Biddle had prepared for them, and he placed it between Polly and Lilly before helping her into the cab.

"Thank you," Georgia said as she tried to ignore her racing pulse. Being so close to the father of her charges seemed to have her all aflutter this morning.

"You're welcome," Sir Tyler said as he sat down beside her.

The driver took off and the girls' excitement showed in their eyes.

"Where are we going first?" Sir Tyler asked.

"We'd like to go to the carousel, but maybe we should save that for last, as it's our favorite. Perhaps the zoo?" Polly asked.

"The zoo it is."

They drove up Fifth Avenue with the girls getting more excited by the minute.

"Let's have our lunch and then we won't have to worry about some wild animal coming after it," Polly said.

Lilly gasped. "Do you think one would?"

Sir Tyler's husky chuckle warmed Georgia's heart.

"I don't think they'd be able to get to it. After all, they are caged up," he said.

Lilly let out a huge sigh and grinned. "Oh, that is good!"

"Yes, it is," Georgia said.

"Well, then, we can go look at them and have our lunch afterward," Polly said.

"I think that's a wonderful idea." Georgia smiled at the girls. It was obvious they were happy to have their papa along.

The hack stopped right in front of the zoo entrance, which was near the city arsenal. Sir Tyler helped her down, and she took charge of the picnic basket again while he helped his daughters down. He paid the driver and they made their way in. He paid the fee and then took charge of the basket as they began weaving their way around, looking at the animals.

The tigers were sunning themselves, while the monkeys scampered up and down trees making all kinds of noises. Polly and Lilly laughed at their antics, as did Sir Tyler and Georgia.

But the sea-lion pool proved to be a favorite of them all as they watched them dive and swim and then sun themselves before diving in the pool again. The girls almost hated to leave, but they were getting hungry and didn't put up a fuss when they left to find a place to picnic.

They strolled to a shady area not too far from the carousel, and Sir Tyler and his daughters spread out the picnic blanket Mrs. Biddle had put in the basket. Then Georgia laid out the scrumptious spread the cook had prepared. There were roast-beef sandwiches and still-warm escalloped potatoes, along with chocolate cake and a large jar of iced lemonade.

Georgia handed plates to the girls while their father poured the lemonade. Then he handed a glass to Georgia. Their fingers brushed together and her heart seemed to do some kind of twisting flip-flop. She quickly took a drink, trying to hide her reaction to the brief touch.

"Mmm, this is so good," Polly said.

"Why is it more fun to eat outside than it is to eat inside?" Lilly asked.

"I don't know—perhaps it's the fresh air, or maybe it's the company." Sir Tyler smiled at Georgia and sent her pulse to racing. What was it about this man that affected her so?

"I wish we did it more often!" Polly said.

"So do I!" Lilly added.

"Well, if you're very good, perhaps we could lunch outside once in a while this summer," Georgia suggested.

"Oh, could we?"

"I don't see why not," Georgia said.

"And I might join you once in a while," their papa said.

"Then we must do it!" Polly grinned at her father.

His comment reminded Georgia of what she'd

wanted to speak to him about, but she didn't want to bring it up in front of the girls. Perhaps she'd be able to talk to him about it on Monday.

But after they finished eating, cleaned up and re-packed their basket, Sir Tyler turned to her as the girls hurried out ahead of them to the carousel. "I'd like to speak to you before you leave today, if we have time."

"I am leaving a bit early to get dressed for Michael Heaton's surprise birthday party, remember?"

"I do. But it won't take long and I'll make sure we get home in plenty of time."

"In that case, there is something I'd like to talk to you about also."

"All right." Sir Tyler pulled out his watch. "We'll give them an hour or so more and then we'll head back."

He helped his girls on the horses they'd chosen. Polly picked a shining black one and Lilly went straight for a white one with a long mane. "Do you think we should stand beside them?"

"I do think we should, at least for the first time." Georgia took a place beside Lilly while Sir Tyler stood beside Polly. They all chuckled as music started playing and the carousel lurched forward. They'd been told that real horses below the ride went around in circles to put the carousel into motion and that they'd been trained to stop and start when the attendant hit his cane on the floor of the ride. But no one could see what was beneath the ride to make sure. All the riders knew was how much fun it was.

The girls did very well and Sir Tyler surprised Georgia by helping her onto an empty horse beside Lilly, causing her to catch her breath while her pulse took off in a gallop. He then got on the horse next to Polly. Before long they were grinning along with the girls, who seemed delighted that the adults in their life were having fun, too.

By the time Sir Tyler said it was time to leave, his daughters seemed a bit tired and gave no argument. Georgia thought they might actually sleep at nap time, instead of just resting, as they did most days now.

Once they reached the Walker home, she said, "I'll put the girls down for their rest and be back down."

"I'll take the basket to Mrs. Biddle and ask her to make us some tea."

"I can do that, sir," Mr. Tate said, taking the basket from him.

"Very well, Tate." Sir Tyler turned to his daughters. "I'll see you after your naps. Did you have a good time?"

"Oh, yes, Papa. The best ever time!" Polly said.

"We will be able to do it again, won't we?" Lilly asked.

"I believe so—if you continue to be on good behavior."

"Oh, we will try, Papa!" his youngest said before running up the stairs behind her sister.

The girls needed no urging to rest—the fresh air and fun, mixed with lunch outdoors, seemed to have worn them out, and their eyes were shut tight when Georgia left the room.

Mr. Tate was pouring the tea when Georgia entered Sir Tyler's study a few minutes later. He soon left with a slight nod in her direction.

"Please take a seat, Miss Marshall," Sir Tyler said

from a chair by a small table near the window. She took the one across from him.

"I wanted to speak to you about last night when the girls hid your reticule."

"Oh? Did they say something about it?"

"They did." He went on to repeat their conversation about how they wanted her to stay longer and had fun trying to help her find it. Then he cleared his throat. "And I wanted to tell you that I think you may be right about them feeling guilty about memories fading. In fact, I found out that they sometimes sneak into my room to look at the photo of their mother. I'm going to give it to them tonight to put on the table between their beds. I should have realized they needed pictures of her around."

Georgia had to blink to hold back the sudden tears that formed behind her eyes. "I'm sure that will make them feel better."

"I hope so." He took a sip of tea and sat back in his chair. "Now, what was it you wanted to speak to me about?"

Georgia stirred her cup, trying to get her emotions under control. "A couple of things, actually. When the girls seemed upset about my leaving early today, I mentioned that you might take them for ice cream this evening."

"Oh, you did, did you?" His eyebrow rose and she was sure she'd overstepped her bounds as a nanny. But then he chuckled. "Actually, that's a very good idea."

Georgia released a small sigh of relief but held her breath for a moment before she brought up the subject she most wanted to discuss. "And…I've been meaning to speak to you about preparing your daughters for the time when they might be included in a dinner along with adults."

Sir Tyler sat up a little straighter in his chair. "They're a little young for that, aren't they?"

"Not necessarily. Not here in America."

"Really?"

"In some circles, perhaps. And if that is what you wish, just tell me. But truthfully, they'll need to learn proper table manners at some point, and as a teacher, I feel the earlier they are taught, the easier it will be for them."

"And you will take this on?"

"Of course I will. But…"

"Yes?"

"Would you be willing to let them stay up just a little longer a few nights a week so that they could have dinner with you?"

"With me? Already?" He seemed a bit testy and she tried not to show her dismay at his reaction. She wanted to ask why not. But she didn't dare upset him further.

"Not every night, but it might be good for them to spend a little extra time with you a couple of nights a week. And then you'd be able to see how they're progressing so that if you were invited to something that included them for a dinner, you'd know if they were ready."

"Shouldn't you be able to tell me when they are ready?"

"I could, yes, of course. But teaching them in a setting at their dinnertime is not the same as a real dinner table setting, where they might dress up and get the feel of—"

"I'm not sure. This is not the way it is done in England. Not at all." Sir Tyler got up and began to pace.

"I realize that, Sir Tyler. And in some circles, possibly the ones you might be part of, I'm sure it is done the way you were raised. Still, children must have that time where they learn by watching others and doing, and I thought it would be better if they did it in the comfort of familiar settings, rather than out at someone else's home. I'd think you might feel more comfortable about that, too."

The man let out what could only be described as a frustrated sigh. But perhaps she was reading him all wrong.

But she wasn't ready to give up. "I don't see how it could hurt Polly and Lilly to know how to act in any circumstance they might be in. They could be invited to any number of places—whether to tea with other children of your social set or to a Sunday dinner again at Mrs. Heaton's. I—"

Sir Tyler held up a hand, stopping her in midsentence, then dropped down in his chair once more. "I'll think about all this over the weekend and let you know what I decide on Monday, Miss Marshall."

Evidently he'd heard all he wanted to hear from her for now. But at least he said he'd think about it. She took one last sip of tea and stood. "Yes, sir. I'll go see to the girls now."

"Thank you for caring about their welfare, Miss Marshall. I know you have what's best for them at heart. I do appreciate that. And I enjoyed the outing today."

"So did your daughters."

"And you?"

Something in his expression had her heart skipping a beat and then two. "I enjoyed it very much."

He smiled and nodded. "I'm glad. Have a good weekend and please tell Michael Heaton happy birthday for us."

"I will." With that, she dashed out of the room as fast as she could. Would she ever stop reacting so to that man's smile?

Tyler hurried up to check on his daughters after Amelia told him they were ready for him to come listen to their prayers. But he stopped in his room first, going over to his nightstand and picking up the photo of Ivy.

She'd been a very pretty woman, with a beautiful smile, which he got glimpses of in his daughters'. And he missed her still. But even he had a hard time remembering what she'd looked like without gazing at her photo now. And if he was honest, he hadn't been looking at it quite as often lately.

He was in his daughters' room each evening and he could see it there. They shouldn't have to feel like they had to sneak into his room to remember what their mother looked like.

He'd write to Ivy's mother when he got back downstairs and ask about any photographs she could send the girls. He hid the frame behind his back, crossed the hall and entered the girls' room.

"Papa, we thought you weren't coming!"

"Now, Lilly, you know better. But I did take a few

extra minutes to bring you two something I should have given you before now."

"What is it, Papa?" Polly asked as he sat down on the side of her bed.

"Yes, Papa, what do you have for us?" Lilly jumped out of her bed and over onto her sister's to join them.

He pulled the photograph out from behind him. "I want you two to have this photograph of your mother—at least until we can find more."

"Oh, Papa, thank you!" Polly said, taking the photo and gazing into it.

Lilly scrambled to her side and smiled. "She was so pretty."

"And you both remind me of her."

"We do?" Polly asked.

"You do."

"Thank you, Papa," Polly said. "Now we won't have to sneak into your room to see it."

"No, you won't have to do that. Let's put it here, on the table between your beds." Tyler took the photo and set it down in the middle of the table, feeling a sense of peace that he'd done the right thing.

"Now back to bed with you. Lilly, it's time to hear your prayers." She gave him an extra hard hug as he picked her up and took her back to her bed.

He took turns with who was first to say their prayers each night, and tonight he listened first to her prayers and then to Polly's. He kissed them both good-night once they'd finished. "See you in the morning. Sleep well."

"You, too, Papa," they said, echoing each other.

Tyler looked back at the door to see them both gazing at the picture of their mother and his heart turned over. They'd lost her much too young. He hoped being able to see her photograph anytime they wanted to would help.

He hurried downstairs and back to his study. Law books lay open on his desk, a notepad beside them. He'd be taking his bar exam in the next week and prayed that he would pass it. He'd graduated from Oxford with honors and he'd been studying American law books at night for months now—even before they moved from England. He and Ivy had planned on moving to the United States and he'd wanted to be able to set up a practice when they did. Surely he was ready for this test.

After an hour or more of note taking, Tate brought in tea and Tyler was glad for the break. "Your timing is perfect, as usual, Tate. If I read any more tonight, I don't think I'll retain a bit of it."

"I was thinking it was time for you to take a break, sir." He poured the tea as Tyler moved from the desk to his easy chair.

"Well, you were right. I'll be glad to have this test behind me."

"I'm sure you'll do well, sir."

"Thank you, Tate. I appreciate your confidence in me."

"You always have it, sir. Will there be anything more?"

"Not now, Tate."

"Very well, Sir Tyler."

With that, the butler left the room and Tyler leaned his head back against his chair. He sighed and took a sip of his drink. His daughters were struggling with their memories and feeling bad about it. He hoped his talk with them helped, for it hadn't done a lot for him.

Not when Georgia Marshall came to mind off and on all day. He had to admit he'd been a bit put off when she'd suggested that his daughters eat dinner with him. In England children their age did not eat in the main dining room with the adults. They just didn't. He and his siblings certainly hadn't, although they had been allowed to have dessert with them occasionally. But it wasn't until they were in their teens— and then only if they knew their table manners, which the nanny taught them—that they'd been allowed to have an entire meal.

So, yes, she should be in charge of teaching them, but at the dinner table with him? It wasn't that he didn't enjoy being with his daughters, but dinner was sometimes a lengthy meal unless he had it in his study. Still, she had made him think about them needing more time with him. But dinner in the formal dining room? Surely they were too young for that.

Tyler took another sip of tea and rubbed the back of his neck. Just because it might be unusual didn't mean it was wrong for them to dine with him occasionally, did it? And she'd said the earlier they learned, the easier it would be for them.

It did get lonely to dine alone at that long table night after night. There'd been times when he'd been tempted to take his law books in with him, but Tate might have had a heart attack had he done so. Might have one if he found Miss Marshall wanted the girls to dine with him.

What am I to do? Lord, I seem to be so undecided about what to do with the girls—and now the woman I thought would help seems to be making things even more difficult. I don't know what Ivy would have said about it and I don't want to ask Mother or Ivy's mother their opinion. I'm afraid they'd try to take over and I know I don't want that and neither would Ivy. I want to do what is right for them, Father. Please help me to know what answer to give Miss Marshall on Monday.

He drained his cup and set it down before looking back at his desk. He was tired. But it'd been a good day. He'd enjoyed the outing at the park with his girls and Miss Marshall.

He was almost out of the room before he remembered he hadn't written the letter to his mother-in-law. Where was their next stop? He hoped the world trip they'd taken helped with their grief, but they'd still have to come back and take up their lives again. Distractions didn't do it. Only living life, regular day-to-day life, and trusting the Lord would get one through it.

Thank You, Lord, for my girls—and for bringing Miss Marshall to help during their time of grief... and mine.

Chapter Ten

Georgia woke on Monday morning, excited to find out what Sir Tyler had decided about the girls having dinner a few nights a week with him. From their conversation the Friday before, she was afraid he might refuse, but she hoped not.

She hurried to freshen up and get ready for work, thinking back over the weekend. It'd been very exciting for the Heaton House group. With Michael's birthday party starting it off, everyone was in high spirits when John Talbot telephoned early on Saturday to let them know that Elizabeth had given birth to their first child—a little boy they'd named John William.

Everyone raced downtown to buy gifts now that they knew what gender the baby was. The next afternoon, after Sunday dinner, there seemed to be a trail of boarders past and present going to see mother and newborn. Mrs. Heaton and Rebecca went right after lunch, and then Georgia, Julia, Emily and Betsy went.

The baby was beautiful and Elizabeth was glowing. John was grinning from ear to ear and Elizabeth's father and stepmother—her aunt Bea—couldn't take their eyes off of little John William. Georgia was glad she'd waited to get a gift, for she'd thought for sure Elizabeth would have a girl!

Now she took one last look in the mirror and hurried downstairs and over to Walker House. Since finding out Sir Tyler didn't have breakfast with his daughters, she'd made a point to always eat with them and have breakfast at Heaton House only on the weekends.

"Good morning, Mrs. Biddle," she greeted the cook as she entered the kitchen. "How are you today?"

"I'm fine. I hear you've had some excitement this past weekend."

Georgia was glad that Mrs. Biddle had become friends with Gretchen and Maida. "We did. The baby is precious. I'll go get the girls up and ready and we'll see you at breakfast."

"Very good, Miss Georgia. Tell them I'm making French toast today."

"Oh, one of their favorites, and mine, too, I might add."

"I'm glad."

Georgia hurried upstairs to find the girls looking at a photograph frame. Her heart warmed as she realized that Sir Tyler had given them their mother's photograph as he'd said he intended to do.

"Good morning! What's that you're looking at?"

"Oh, Miss Georgia, it's a photograph of our mother. Wasn't she pretty?" Lilly held the picture frame out for her to take.

Ivy Walker was indeed a pretty woman with blond hair and blue eyes. Georgia was sure that she and Sir

Tyler had made a handsome couple. "She is. And you both look a lot like her, you know."

"That's what Papa told us," Polly said.

"And he's right. I'm glad you have this photograph of her." She set it down on the bedside table. "Now, let's hurry or Mrs. Biddle will wonder where we are. And Betsy will be over later for a fitting."

Excited about the prospect of seeing new outfits, the girls hurried to get dressed and stayed still while she did their hair.

They hurried down to the breakfast room and slid into their seats just as Mrs. Biddle brought in their breakfast.

"French toast with bacon!" Lilly exclaimed. "It's my favorite, Mrs. Biddle!"

"Mine, too," Polly added.

"I know. That's why I made it," Mrs. Biddle said. "And Miss Georgia loves it, too."

"I do."

Mrs. Biddle set down the girls' plates and then went back to get Georgia's. She quickly returned and set it in front of her, then poured her a cup of coffee.

"Thank you, Mrs. Biddle."

"Yes, thank you!" the girls said, bringing a smile to the cook's face.

"You're quite welcome." She left the room and Georgia said the prayer.

The French toast was delicious and it appeared the day was off to a good start. Maybe now was the time to bring up teaching them mealtime manners. They did fine for their ages and the meals they had now, but she wanted them to be ready when the time did come that they were expected to know which utensil to use. Of course, she might need Mr. Tate's permission to use a full service of silverware. Perhaps they could have pretend meals in the dining room. Oh… Georgia wasn't sure how he would take to all that. Maybe she should wait until Sir Tyler told her what his decision was.

"What are we going to do today, Miss Georgia?"

"We're going to start your American history lessons this morning after you do your writing and math lessons."

"All that in one morning?" Lilly asked, her brow furrowed.

Georgia couldn't help but chuckle. "I'll be sure not to make the lessons too long. You do want to learn about America, don't you?"

"Well, I do, even if Lilly doesn't," Polly answered.

"I want to, too," Lilly insisted. "I was hoping we wouldn't have to do our letters."

"I love doing letters!"

"Well, I like doing numbers better." Lilly frowned at her sister.

Oh, my. Perhaps the day wasn't going to go quite as smoothly as she'd first thought. "Girls, we'll get to both. I realize it's not all fun for you all the time, but these are subjects you must learn, along with reading—"

"Reading!" Lilly interrupted. "Oh, I want to learn to read!"

"So do I!" Polly exclaimed. "Nanny had said we were going to start, but we never did."

"Well, we're going to start very soon. But to do that, you must learn your letters and how to use them," Georgia said.

"We will, Miss Georgia!"

It always surprised her how often they said the same thing at the very same time.

"Good. Now finish your breakfast so we can get started. Remember, Betsy is coming this afternoon—if you're good."

"We'll be good!" Both girls clapped and went back to eating their breakfast.

"You'd better be," Sir Tyler said, coming in from behind Georgia and kissing each girl on the cheek.

She was going to have to change where she sat. He seemed to always be sneaking up behind her. Well, that really wasn't fair to him. This was his home, after all, and he did check on his daughters each morning.

"Yes, Papa!" the girls said.

Sir Tyler took the empty seat, and Mrs. Biddle must have been waiting to see if he stayed, for she burst in with a cup of coffee for him and refilled Georgia's cup.

"Excellent breakfast this morning, Mrs. Biddle," he said.

"Why, thank you, sir." The cook seemed a bit flustered as she smiled and hurried out of the room.

"I heard all you have planned for the girls today, Miss Marshall, and—"

"Do you think it's too much?"

Both girls sat up straight, all ears to see what their papa might say, and Georgia realized she should have waited to ask the question when they were not present.

"Not at all."

Georgia had to stifle the urge to chuckle at the look on his daughters' faces as they bent over their plates, their hopes that he would say yes dashed.

"In fact, perhaps we should add a new lesson or two, don't you think?"

She could see the teasing expression in his eyes, but when he winked at her, she caught her breath and all thought of how she should answer disappeared.

"Miss Marshall?"

"Yes?" What was it he'd asked?

"Don't you think you could add a new lesson or two to their day?"

"Papa! She did already. We're going to start reading lessons soon," Polly said.

"Hmm, I'm not sure that's enough."

Georgia loved seeing him tease his daughters like this, but she didn't like her reaction to his innocent wink at all. She was sure he had no idea how it affected her and she wasn't sure at all why it had. Except that he was even handsomer than unusual when he was in a playful mood like now.

"Oh, Papa, you're teasing. Isn't he, Miss Georgia?" Lilly asked.

"Oh, I don't know..." She played along with Sir Tyler.

"Miss Georgia!"

"In fact, now that you girls are through with your breakfast, I need to talk to Miss Geo— Miss Marshall about your lessons. So if it's all right with her, perhaps you could go out into the garden while we have our talk."

The girls' woebegone expressions changed immediately and they were all smiles.

"Oh, may we, Miss Georgia?" Polly asked.

Georgia certainly wasn't going to argue with her employer, but not knowing what it was he was going to say, she decided it would be best if they weren't in the same room. "That's fine. I'll come get you shortly."

The girls slipped out of their chairs and hurried out of the room. In only a moment or so, she and Sir Tyler could see them run to the rope swings he'd put up for them. Georgia was glad they didn't have their new clothes yet, for she hadn't planned on them playing outside in what they had on. But she couldn't help but smile as Polly helped get Lilly started before taking her swing and pumping herself up to speed.

Georgia turned away to find Sir Tyler watching her, and something in his expression sent her pulse on a collision course with her heart.

Tyler observed Georgia watching his daughters and smiled. She was so good with them, no wonder they hated weekends without her.

And even though this one had gone much better than the past few, they'd talked about her all weekend. It was Miss Georgia this and Miss Georgia that, and what would Miss Georgia think about that from morning till night.

And no matter how hard he tried to put their nanny out of his mind, it was near impossible when they brought up her name so often. But were they really to blame for his thoughts of her? Hardly. Most times he'd had her on his mind when the girls brought her up.

"Looks like they'll be fine for a while."

Tyler's heart slammed against his ribs as Georgia Marshall turned back to him and smiled. She was more than just lovely. She was a caring, compassionate woman who wanted to help his girls get through this trying time for them. And in the process she was helping him to recognize how he could help them, too.

"Would you like more coffee? I can ring for Mrs. Biddle."

"No, thank you, I'm fine. What other subjects were you thinking I should add to their studies?"

"Only the one you suggested to me. And yes, they may have dinner with me two times a week once you believe they are ready to."

"Oh, Sir Tyler, thank you."

"And only if you take dinner with us."

"But if they are ready—"

"Only if you stay for dinner, Miss Marshall," Tyler said as firmly as he could.

"All right. I'll stay."

Tyler wished she sounded a little more enthused— this was all her idea, after all. Well, maybe not to have dinner with them, but still…

"And thank you for agreeing to my idea," Georgia said, soothing his ego a bit. "I think you'll be very happy with the outcome."

Tyler hoped so. One thing he knew was that the prospect of having Georgia Marshall at his dinner table was something he looked forward to.

"What evenings would you want to choose?"

"Whatever works best for you. I will begin to accept a few dinner invitations before long so that I can make contacts for my law practice, but I won't be going to all of them. Maybe one or two a week—no more than that."

"How about an evening midweek and then perhaps a Saturday when you don't have an invitation?"

"But that would interfere with your weekend. Are you sure?"

"I've been thinking that might be a way to break up the girls' weekend and give them something to look forward to. It's only for a few hours, and if you have a dinner engagement we can move it to Friday evening. We don't have to have a set schedule."

Tyler couldn't believe she was willing to give up part of her time off for his family. She must care a great deal for his daughters, and if teaching them meal-time manners was that important to her, he surmised that it should be that important to him, too. "Thank you. I believe that plan will work quite well and I know the girls will love it."

"We won't start the dinners with you until I'm sure they're ready. That won't mean that they won't pick up the wrong utensil or slouch once in a while, but that is why believing this is something special will help them when they do eventually dine with other grown-ups."

"You're a very intelligent woman, Miss Marshall. I suppose we should let Mr. Tate and Mrs. Biddle know our plans." He got up and pulled the cord that would summon the two servants. In only a few moments they both entered the breakfast room from different directions.

"Tate, Mrs. Biddle, Miss Marshall and I have decided that the girls need to learn table manners as one of their lessons. And I want them prepared to have dinner with me and others for when the time comes that they need to be."

"But aren't they a bit young for that now, Sir Tyler?" Mr. Tate asked.

"We believe that the earlier they learn, the easier

it will be on them—and me. We were recently asked to dinner and I turned it down because I wasn't sure they'd be ready."

"Really? Children are allowed to eat with adults here?" Mrs. Biddle looked at Georgia for confirmation.

Tyler was relieved when she immediately explained, "Not everywhere and not in every social gathering. But Sir Tyler wants his daughters to be comfortable in any circumstance they find themselves."

"I don't want them or me embarrassed by not knowing something Miss Marshall is willing to teach them."

Mr. Tate gave a slight nod. "That does make sense, I suppose. Especially in new surroundings, in a new country."

"I think so, too," Tyler said. "But we will need your help. Miss Marshall will need to have access to the table settings for the lessons and for their meals."

Mr. Tate and Mrs. Biddle looked to Georgia for more explanation of what she might need. "I'd like to have the table in here set as if they were eating in the formal dining room with their father, so that they can get used to choosing the proper utensils. At lunchtime and their supper time, I'd like to have the table set about a half hour before the meal, so that we can practice."

"But what about the different courses?" Mr. Tate asked.

"If you will put the different plates and all that would be needed for either meal—as if they were having what Sir Tyler has—on the sideboard, I can serve them. I'll tell them what is supposed to be on each one so they can pick the right eating utensil to use. We'll pretend that they're eating what their father is having later that evening—that is, until it's time to actually eat whatever Mrs. Biddle has prepared for them. I'm hoping to make it fun for them."

"Like a game of some kind?" Sir Tyler asked. "It does sound fun."

"I won't mind doing the serving, if you'd like, Miss Marshall," Tate said.

"But where do I come in?" Mrs. Biddle asked.

"If it's not too much trouble, I'd like their meals to be served in courses, when possible. Just like you'd do for their papa."

Mrs. Biddle gave a little bobble with her head and smiled. "It sounds like fun for all of us."

"Oh, thank you. I think it will be. And then when I think they're ready—"

"They'll graduate to having dinner with me in the dining room a couple of evenings a week. By the time they have to know those manners, they'll make us all proud," Tyler said.

"Yes, they will," Tate said with a nod. "We'll see to it, sir."

"Will dinner with Sir Tyler be at his time, or—"

"Oh, I'm glad you brought that up, Mrs. Biddle. We hadn't actually discussed that. What do you think, Miss Marshall? I do eat several hours later than they do. Perhaps we should eat in between the two times? Would six o'clock work for all of you? It won't hurt me to eat a little earlier a few times a week."

"I think that's a wonderful idea," Georgia said. "If it works for Mrs. Biddle and Mr. Tate, of course."

"That should work just fine for us, don't you think, Mr. Tate?" Mrs. Biddle asked.

"Yes, I believe it will."

"Then six o'clock it is. Thank you both. I knew I could count on you to help Miss Marshall with this project," Tyler said.

"Thank you for asking for our help, Miss Georgia," Mrs. Biddle said. "When would you like to start?"

"How about tomorrow? That will give you time to plan a menu and for Mr. Tate to figure out what settings to use. I don't think we need the best china, but if you have something that will make it feel special for them, that would be nice."

"I'll take care of it."

"I believe that's all, then. Thank you both for your support," Tyler said.

They quickly left the room and he turned to Georgia. "That went much easier than I thought it would. They both seem quite excited about it."

"They do and it will make it much more special to the girls. And I promise you, Sir Tyler—by the time they have their first dinner with you, you'll be quite pleased."

Somehow he had a feeling he would be. "I'm almost looking forward to it."

Chapter Eleven

The next morning, Georgia hurried to dress and get over to Walker House. She couldn't wait to start the table-manners lessons and was delighted that Sir Tyler had agreed to her plan. And that Mr. Tate and Mrs. Biddle were willing to help.

When she'd first seen the furrow on Mr. Tate's brow that the girls learn adult table manners, and then when he suggested they were too young, she thought her plan might be doomed. He was the butler of this house, after all.

And when Sir Tyler had told him his daughters would be dining with him several nights a week, why, Mr. Tate's eyebrows seemed to almost disappear into his hairline. But in the end, it was obvious that he didn't want his two favorite little girls, or their papa, to be humiliated in any way.

The girls had been thrilled about the new lessons, thinking of them as a game as she'd hoped they would. As a teacher, she'd learned earlier on that her students found it much easier to remember lessons if they enjoyed them.

Now as she helped them get ready for breakfast, they were more than a little excited.

"We're really going to learn how to behave for eating dinner with grown-ups?" Polly asked.

"You are. And once I believe you're ready, we'll begin having dinner with your papa a couple of nights a week."

"We? Does that mean you'll eat with us?" sharp-as-a-tack Lilly asked.

"It does. I'll be there so that if you forget which fork or spoon to use, you can watch what I do."

Sir Tyler's youngest child let out a huge breath that must have come from her toes. "Oh, that is a relief!"

"Oh, Lilly, you are so dramatic!" Polly said. "You should know that Miss Georgia wouldn't leave us on our own—not at first, anyway. We'd be too nervous without her, wanting to impress Papa."

Well, she might have if their papa hadn't insisted she be there, but after seeing their response, she was glad he had. She certainly didn't want the girls to think she'd deserted them.

They hurried downstairs to see that the table had been set differently and had more forks than they usually used.

"Oh, the table looks so nice!"

"Thank you, Miss Polly," Mr. Tate said from behind her. "I'm going to be helping Miss Marshall with your lessons."

"You are?" Lilly asked as she jumped into her chair.

"I certainly am."

"And so am I," Mrs. Biddle said as she came into the room with small fruit cups, filled only halfway with fresh berries. She set the cups in the middle of the plates in front of them.

"Oh, how pretty," Polly said, grabbing a fork from beside her plate.

"No, Polly. That isn't the right fork," Georgia said.

"It isn't?"

"No, there are forks and spoons and knives for different dishes, and one of the first things you'll learn is which one to use."

"Well, which one *do* we use?" Lilly asked.

"The general rule is to work from the outside in, so you would pick up the small fork that comes first. But first, girls, we'll say a prayer."

"Yes, ma'am," they said in unison.

"Dear Lord, thank You for this day, thank You for Mr. Tate and Mrs. Biddle, who are helping with these lessons, and thank You for the food we are about to eat. In Jesus's name, amen." Georgia raised her head and the girls looked to her for guidance. She picked up the fruit fork and said, "You may begin."

The girls followed her example and picked up the right utensil, then began to eat the first course of their breakfast. Just as they finished that, Mr. Tate came back in to remove that dish and Mrs. Biddle brought in the next course. It was served on a child-sized plate and was one piece of bacon and a scrambled egg.

"Now what fork, Miss Georgia?" Lilly asked.

"The one that is left, silly," Polly said.

There was only one fork left next to the plate. Both girls giggled as they picked up the remaining fork and began to eat. They were having fun and Georgia was pleased.

They were just finishing up when Sir Tyler entered the room. "From what I've been hearing in the dining room, your table-manner lessons are going quite well."

"Oh, Papa, they are. We know what fork to use for fruit and for eggs!" Lilly said.

"And we know to start at the outside and work in," Polly said.

"And we have a water glass and a milk glass!" Lilly added.

Sir Tyler grinned at their enthusiasm. "I'm glad you're enjoying your lessons."

"I'm looking forward to the noon meal. I wonder what Mrs. Biddle is making and how many forks and spoons and knives we'll learn to use then," Polly said.

"I don't know, but I'm sure Miss Marshall will guide you through it."

"I think it's time we got some other lessons done now," Georgia said. "You have another fitting this afternoon, remember?"

"Oh, I can't wait!" Polly said as she and her sister each received a kiss from their papa and then hurried upstairs.

"I'll be right up, so get out your tablets."

"Yes, ma'am!"

Sir Tyler chuckled. "They seem quite excited about all this. I believe you're right about them starting early. Making a kind of game out of it has got to be more fun than making it tedious for them."

"I'm glad you approve. I think they're going to catch on very fast." She smiled. "I'd best get them started on their numbers. We took a bit of extra time with breakfast this morning."

"I'm sure it will be worth your effort by the time they dine with me."

"I think so." And Sir Tyler would be dining with his daughters much sooner than he expected.

Tyler watched Miss Marshall hurry out of the room and then he headed toward his study. His office would soon be ready for him to work out of and all he needed was to pass the bar exam he was taking that morning.

He entered the study and sat down at his desk. He had notes he wanted to go over before leaving, and as if Tate could read his mind, he brought in a pot of coffee and poured him a cup.

"Thought you might need this, sir."

"Thank you, Tate. I do."

"You'll do fine. I have no doubt of it."

"I hope you're right. I'll know soon."

"I'll be praying all goes well."

"That will help most of all. How did Miss Marshall's first lesson go? From what I could hear, it was a great success with the girls."

"It was, sir. They did very well, I must say, and they had fun. It was good to hear their laughter."

"Yes, it always is. And they do seem to be doing more of it lately, don't they?"

"I believe they are."

"It's not too much extra work for you or Mrs. Biddle, is it?"

"Not really, and we're glad to help Miss Marshall. I believe we both enjoyed it."

"Good. Thank you, Tate. That will be all."

His butler gave a nod and left the room. Tyler was thankful that Mr. Tate had agreed to come to America with him. He surely didn't know what he'd do without him.

He drank his coffee, looked over his notes and whispered a prayer. "Father, thank You for my many blessings and for sending Miss Marshall to us. She's been such a wonderful help to my daughters and I believe to my whole household. Everyone seems more settled since she's been with us. I ask that You help me pass this exam, knowing how important it is that I'm able to practice law here. In Jesus's name, amen."

Tyler glanced at the clock and took one last swig of coffee before heading out. Tate was at the door to help him on with his jacket and then he handed him his hat.

"I'm not sure how long this is going to take. Tell Mrs. Biddle I won't be home for luncheon."

"Yes, sir."

Tyler headed out the door and took the hack Tate had called for him. It didn't take long for him to get to the building where the New York Bar Association was housed, and he hurried in and up the elevator to the office.

He was welcomed in and the test was administered right away. It took most of the morning and Tyler was thankful that the Lord had given him ready recollection as he made his way through it.

The examiners had already checked into his background and knew that he'd passed all tests in England, so that was one hurdle he didn't have to worry about. After the last question, he went back over the test to make certain he'd answered them all and then turned it in.

"We'll let you know within the next week, Sir Tyler," one of the examiners said. "We hope to welcome you to the New York State bar very soon."

"Thank you, sir. I look forward to hearing from you." Tyler nodded to each of the other men and left the room. He released a huge breath and took the elevator down to the lobby. That was done. He felt confident he'd passed; still, he wouldn't totally relax until he got official word that he had. In the meantime, he'd turn it all over to the Lord.

Tyler pulled out his pocket watch and noted that it was well past lunchtime, but he really wasn't very hungry. Mrs. Biddle had made him a large breakfast, knowing he was going to take his test that morning. He decided to go to his office and make sure the telephone had been installed.

He made his way to the Heaton Building and took the elevator to the top floor, only to be met by Michael Heaton when the door opened.

"Sir Tyler! Good morning. It's good to see you. How did the test go?"

"I believe it went well. Should know before long."

"I was just going down to grab something to eat—want to join me?"

Tyler chuckled. "I wasn't hungry when I got through but I believe I will join you. My appetite seems to be coming back now that I have that exam behind me."

The two men entered the elevator. "I was just coming by to see if the telephones had been installed."

"They were put in this morning. I was going to telephone you to let you know."

They entered the café and were shown to a table, where they both ordered the day's special of roast-beef sandwiches.

When the waiter left, Tyler leaned back in his chair and asked, "How was your birthday party? Did they manage to surprise you?"

Michael grinned. "They did. It was very nice. Thank you for letting Georgia off early so she could make it."

"That was the least I could do after all she's done for me. My girls love her."

"She's a good woman."

"I believe so." And he did. His esteem for Georgia Marshall seemed to grow with each passing day. He didn't even want to think about the day she'd leave them. But she'd made it clear in the beginning that she wouldn't stay and he'd hired her on those terms. Still, he wished there was a way to keep her on. Yes, he surely did.

The girls were down for their rest when Sir Tyler returned from taking his bar exam. Mrs. Biddle had told Georgia that he'd gone to take it and she'd been praying for him off and on all day.

Lunch had gone wonderfully well. Mrs. Biddle had again given them child-sized portions of what she'd made for Georgia and with enough courses that the girls had to try out using different utensils.

After they'd lain down for their rest, Georgia had come downstairs to speak to the cook and thank her and Mr. Tate for their help.

"Oh, I'm having such fun trying to decide what to make," Mrs. Biddle said. "And actually, it's making things a bit easier on me to serve them the same thing I serve you and Sir Tyler—well, his is a bit more elaborate the way it's served, but I thought it'd be best to start them out a little more simply. Is that all right with you?"

"Of course it is. No need in doing anything complicated. If we ease them into it, it will be easier on them. I'll leave the menu planning to you, as you know best what the family likes."

"Thank you, dear. I appreciate that. Would you like some tea now?"

"I'd love some. I'll be in the morning room." She'd gone to Mr. Tate next and he was as gracious as Mrs. Biddle had been.

She'd just entered the morning room when she heard voices in the foyer and her heart flipped as she recognized Sir Tyler speaking to Mr. Tate and then footsteps heading her way.

"Miss Marshall, Tate told me I might find you here." He sat down across from her at the small table by the window.

Amelia entered the room just then with a tea tray.

"You wouldn't happen to have an extra cup there, would you, Amelia?" Sir Tyler asked.

"I would. Mrs. Biddle sent one for you just in case, Sir Tyler." The maid poured them both a cup and left the tray that also held some of the tea cakes the cook knew they were both fond of. She quietly left the room.

Sir Tyler needed no prodding as he reached for one of the sweets and popped the whole thing into his mouth. Georgia took one for herself, only she set it on a small plate after taking a bite.

"I wanted to see how the girls did on the table-manner lessons at lunchtime."

"Very well. And Mrs. Biddle and Mr. Tate have helped tremendously. Thank you for getting them to support my plan."

"You're welcome."

"Mrs. Biddle told me about you taking your bar exam today. I hope it went well."

Sir Tyler's smile turned her heart to mush. "Thank you, Miss Marshall. I believe it did, but I won't know until I get notice from the association."

"I'm sure you passed with flying colors."

He laughed and shook his head. "I'm not sure I did that well, but I do think I passed."

"I'm praying that you did."

Something in his expression changed and Georgia held her breath. He looked touched and a little surprised at her words. Perhaps she'd been too open with her thoughts.

Sir Tyler cleared his throat. "Thank you, Miss Marshall. It means a lot to know that you are. Once I have that notice, I'll be ready to start working at the office most days. I checked it out before I came home and it's ready. I'll be over there for part of the days this week—putting up my law books on the shelves and setting up my desk. Polly and Lilly's grandparents—my in-laws—will be coming home from their voyage before too long and they'll want to see it. I think that will prove to them that I mean to stay here."

"Do they fear you might go back to England?"

"I think they might. But this is our home now and I'm not going back except for a visit once in a while.

I'm hoping my own parents will come over before long."

"They must be missing their granddaughters," Georgia said. "They are quite easy to get attached to and I'm sure it was hard on them to see you leave."

"Perhaps not quite as much as you might think," Sir Tyler said.

Her heart broke a little for him. Was he not close to his family? She didn't dare ask.

"I'm sorry—that didn't quite come out right," Sir Tyler said. "I know my parents love me and my daughters, but my brother is there, married with five children, and he is the one who will inherit the bulk of their estate. In some ways I feel sorry for him, for much is expected of him. I've had more freedom to make my own decisions than he has and I'm glad."

"I really don't understand English ways, I must admit."

He laughed. "I wouldn't worry about it, if I were you. I don't understand these new American ways very well, either, but I do find them very interesting."

The clock in the foyer chimed and Georgia jumped. "Oh, I must go see about the girls. They're probably up there wondering where I got off to."

"I'm sure they're fine. Finish your tea, then go up."

Georgia took one last sip of tea. "I'm through."

"I've enjoyed your company, Miss Marshall." He drained his cup and stood. "Tate said I had mail to go through, so I'll leave you to see to my daughters. Thank you for listening to my rambling."

He walked out of the door and Georgia blinked

back the tears that wanted to form. Her heart twisted at the thought that he had no one but his servants to "ramble" to. How lonesome he must get at times.

Chapter Twelve

When Georgia got back to Heaton House that evening, she was more than thankful she lived there. Sir Tyler's words had haunted her all afternoon. At the boardinghouse there was always someone to listen to anyone who needed to talk, but he really had no one close to him now.

Oh, she was sure that Mr. Tate had become his sounding board over the years, but that wasn't the same as talking things over with a wife. How he must miss her! Georgia could only imagine, for she'd had no husband, but she did know how her parents seemed to always seek each other out to talk over all manner of things.

And her boardinghouse family wasn't the same, either, but they were there and she felt a sense of homecoming every time she walked in the door.

"Georgia," Julia called from the parlor, "come tell us how your table-manner lessons went today!"

She'd told them all about it the night before and they'd been very supportive. She hurried into the room and took a seat. "It went even better than I expected. And the girls are having such fun and catching on very fast!"

"Should I start on an outfit or two for those dinners with their papa?" Betsy asked.

"Oh, I'd say yes. Sir Tyler mentioned that his in-laws will be returning to the country soon, and should they allow them to have dinner with them, they'll look their best."

"Do you think they would refuse to eat dinner with their granddaughters?" Mrs. Heaton asked.

Georgia knew that Mrs. Heaton would be appalled if they did. "I have no idea. I would hope not! And these are the American ones, so—"

"One never knows these days," Mrs. Heaton said. "But these are their granddaughters and it would most likely be a family dinner, so surely they would be happy for any time they might have with them."

"I certainly hope so. And I want to have them ready for when they do get here," Georgia said. "Maybe we can choose some fabric on Saturday?"

"That sounds great. We know the styles the girls like and the colors, so I believe we can pick something out they'll love."

"Thanks, Betsy. They'll love it."

The boarders decided to make a quick trip to the ice-cream shop and Georgia was happy to join them. But as they passed Walker House, she wondered what Sir Tyler was doing. He'd taken his test, so he wouldn't be studying as he had ever since she'd been working there.

For a moment she was tempted to stop and ask if he wanted to join them. But her good sense stopped her.

He was her employer, after all! Not just a neighbor. Not even a friend, although she thought of him that way sometimes. Wished he was. Well, she'd best get that kind of thinking out of her mind. His social set didn't make friends with working people. Not really.

"What are you woolgathering about now?" Julia asked after they'd passed the house and headed on to the ice-cream shop.

Georgia shook her head. "Nothing much. I just hope I can get the girls ready before their grandparents arrive. I'd like them to have some practice time with their papa before then. I think he'd be more apt to want them at the table while they're here if he sees how well they'll do."

"And you're sure of that?"

"Not that he'll have them at the table for visitors, but that they'll be ready before the practice, yes, I'm sure of it."

"Maybe you should open your own etiquette school, Georgia. You seem to be very excited about all of this."

"I am. I think manners—not just table manners, but all manners—help keep things civil."

"You won't get any argument from me on that count," Stephen said. "Manners were drilled into me early on, but I've run across many who were never taught them."

"Perhaps their parents weren't taught," Emily said.

"I'm sure that's the case," Georgia said. "But it's not that hard. You teach by doing. Saying 'please' and 'thank you' to a child teaches them how, and under what kinds of circumstances, they should do the same. From there, it's 'excuse me' or 'pardon me.' I'd think table manners—most any kind—can be taught by showing and doing. Like the most important ones, being kind to one another and loving our neighbors—"

"And is there a neighbor you particularly love?" Julia teased.

But Georgia's heart banged against her chest as she realized what she'd just said. "Julia! The Bible teaches us to love our neighbors!"

"It does. I was just asking," Julia said.

It was time to change the subject. "Have you given any more thought to going out West?"

"Not lately. Mama hasn't been feeling well and I don't see how I can just up and leave now."

She sounded a bit down and Georgia wished she hadn't asked. She looped her arm through her friend's. "Maybe one day."

"Perhaps. But I won't hold my breath. My dream seems to be dying with each passing month."

"Oh, Julia, I am sorry I brought it up. I didn't mean to make you feel bad."

"I'm fine. Don't give it a worry."

But Georgia felt bad and sent up a silent prayer that Julia's dream would come true.

They arrived at the shop, ordered their ice-cream cones and started back to Heaton House under a big full moon and stars that glittered in the sky. As they passed Walker House once more, Georgia noticed a faint light through the window coverings in the darkened parlor…probably from back in Sir Tyler's study. What was he doing?

Sadness for him rushed over her at the thought of how lonely he must be once his daughters went to sleep. She wished she'd been brave enough to ask him to come with them. He needed a social life. Needed to get out and about. But the thought of him doing so didn't sit right with her. On one hand, she wanted him home with his children, and on the other…well, she dreaded the day he found someone he might consider marrying.

Tyler was restless. He'd heard the Heaton House group walk by his home around an hour or so ago, talking and laughing. He had wondered where they were off to. Probably to the ice-cream shop. He wished he could have just walked out and joined them. But they probably wouldn't welcome him into their circle.

Oh, they were all very nice, but for the most part they seemed a bit guarded around him, as if they didn't quite know how to act around someone in the gentry— no matter how low on the ladder he was.

He pulled the day's mail toward him and noticed a couple of posts that appeared to be invitations of some kind. Much as he knew he needed to make more contacts in the city because of his business, he didn't look forward to entering the social scene. But there seemed no way around it if he wanted to attain clients for his law practice.

Still, he was determined to control the number of invitations he accepted. He wasn't going to let any social life he might have control him or his time. His daughters' well-being was his top priority. Raising them to love the Lord, to know they were loved and to be kind and caring to others. He wanted them to be like…Miss Georgia. She was a wonderful example for them to follow—he could think of no one better, except their mother. But they no longer had her and he grew more thankful each day that Georgia Marshall was in their lives.

Tyler took a letter opener and slit open both envelopes before pulling out the contents. Oh, yes, they were invitations. One was from Mr. and Mrs. Adam Fletcher to dine the Thursday of this week at the Waldorf-Astoria, and the other was from Mr. and Mrs. Reginald Wellington for dinner at their home on Friday of next week. The hour would be after his girls were sound asleep and he had no real excuse not to accept.

Dread seeped into Tyler's every pore. These were friends of his in-laws, so he couldn't very well refuse. But they also knew he was widowed and they both had daughters, if he remembered right. Oh, please, dear Lord, don't let these invitations be schemes to get him married off.

He wasn't in the market for a wife. Not yet, anyway. Suddenly Tyler realized what his thought meant—that he might be in the future. But that wasn't true. He wasn't in the market for a wife ever again.

Tyler wrote acceptance notes and got them ready for Tate to put in the mail the next day. Perhaps he could handle one engagement of this sort a week. He did need the contacts. If not, those notes would have respectfully declined the invitations.

Tate brought in tea and he handed the notes to him. "I've accepted dinner invitations for this Thursday and Friday of next week, Tate."

"Very good, Sir Tyler. I'll get them in the mail first thing tomorrow. I'm glad to see you'll be getting out from time to time."

"Only because I must, Tate. But I do have a business to build and that requires a certain amount of socializing, I suppose."

"I believe it does, Sir Tyler. Will that be all?"

"Yes, thank you, Tate. I'm going to take a walk around the park."

"It's a nice night for it."

Tyler drank his tea, and then, after grabbing a key to Gramercy Park, he went out onto his porch, down the steps and across the street. The night was still and bright. It'd be a nice evening to share a walk with someone. And lately, he'd wished— No. He wasn't even going to finish that thought.

He let himself into Gramercy Park. He loved that it was a private park, available to only the residents around it. He sat down on one of the benches and looked straight up at the open sky. He caught the scent of some sweet bloom nearby but he hadn't a clue what it was. Lights shone down from the homes around the park and he could hear the muffled sound of traffic over on Fifth Avenue. But for the most part it was still and he let the peacefulness of the night wrap around him.

But that only lasted but for a few minutes as he began to hear laughter coming from down the street. Must be the group from Heaton House on their way back from the ice-cream parlor.

He wondered if Miss Marshall was with them. Surely she was. The group seemed quite close and did a lot together. Should he stay where he was or make his presence known?

Tyler settled back on the park bench. No. Miss Marshall gave his family enough of her time. She deserved to have a life outside of his home. But he listened for the sound of her voice as the group passed by.

But all he heard was a man's voice saying "It won't be long until we have to stay there to eat our cones—they'll melt before we can get halfway down the street."

Everyone chuckled or agreed with him and it was a musical laugh that told Tyler Georgia was with them. He liked hearing her laughter almost as much as he liked hearing his girls' giggle. But the sound of it wound down as they hurried to Heaton House and disappeared behind its door.

Tyler sighed while the tranquillity he'd enjoyed only moments before turned to a longing he couldn't ignore. But he had to face, and then accept, that what he longed for would never come to pass.

Over the next few days, Polly and Lilly made very good progress in their table-manners class. It wouldn't be too much longer before they were prepared to have dinner with their papa. Georgia prayed he'd be ready when they were.

On Thursday she took them over to Heaton House for fittings and to have tea with Mrs. Heaton afterward. They'd been asking if they were ever going to get to go, and finally, Georgia had remembered to ask the night before.

They were to go after their midday rest, and once the girls had lain down, Georgia went to let Mrs. Biddle know they wouldn't be there for tea.

The cook was sitting with her feet propped up for a few moments, and when Georgia appeared at the kitchen door, she jumped up.

"Oh, please don't get up, Mrs. Biddle. Give your

feet a rest. I just wanted to let you know I'm taking the girls next door for tea—I meant to let you know at breakfast and then at lunch, but with the lessons and all, I forgot."

"That's fine. Would you like to share a cup with me now?"

"I'd love to." Georgia pulled a chair out on the other side of the small table.

"This is a rare day. No tea for the girls and no dinner for Sir Tyler."

"Oh?"

"He's been invited out for dinner—Mr. Tate says at the Waldorf-Astoria, no less."

"Oh…" Georgia didn't even know what to say. Dining at any dining room in that hotel was something so far out of her social standing that she didn't even dream about it happening.

"Yes. Mr. Tate says he's not looking forward to it and I believe him. Sir Tyler and his wife were not big socializers even back in England. But I suppose with starting his own business here, he feels he must."

"I'm sure you're right," Georgia said. But somehow the thought of Sir Tyler beginning a social life here in the city unsettled her. He was very handsome and very eligible. Would he look for a new wife? What would his daughters think if he did? And would it be someone who would love them? Her chest felt tight at the very thought of it.

"Here you go." Mrs. Biddle set a cup and saucer in front of her and poured her some tea.

Georgia stirred some sugar into the cup and let go of a shaky breath. It was none of her business what her employer did. But she was sure that he'd have more invitations as the days went by, once the parents of eligible daughters were introduced to him. He'd have a bevy of women to choose from and—

"I wonder if he'll ever remarry?"

For a moment Georgia thought the words had come out of her mouth until she realized the cook was asking the question.

"Why would he not, eventually?"

Mrs. Biddle shrugged. "He was so devastated when Lady Walker passed away and—"

"Mrs. Biddle," Mr. Tate called from the doorway. "Sir Tyler has just returned home and would like his tea."

"I'll prepare it now." The cook's face paled as she jumped up from the table and grabbed a warm teapot. In only a few minutes, she had a fresh pot on a tray, along with the toasted tea cakes Georgia had come to recognize were some of Sir Tyler's favorites. She handed the tray to Mr. Tate to take up.

She finished her tea quickly and turned to the cook. "You make wonderful tea, Mrs. Biddle. Thank you."

"You're welcome. You come down anytime."

Georgia had a feeling that Mr. Tate might scold Mrs. Biddle for talking to her about Sir Tyler and his deceased wife, once she wasn't there—if he'd heard any of their conversation. But perhaps he hadn't and Georgia sent up a prayer that was the case and that Mrs. Biddle wouldn't get into trouble.

She hurried back up to the ground floor and was about to go up the stairs to get the girls ready when she heard a cheer of joy come from Sir Tyler's study.

Then she heard Mr. Tate say, "That's wonderful news, Sir Tyler! Congratulations!"

Georgia grinned. Surely that must mean that he'd passed his bar exam! She certainly hoped so. She headed upstairs with a smile on her face. It was good to hear such elation in his voice.

Chapter Thirteen

Mr. Tate's congratulation was quite welcome, but Tyler wanted more. He wanted to tell the world that he was now able to practice law in New York State. And he wanted to celebrate in a big way. But his Ivy wasn't here and there was no one else he could do so with. Besides, he had that dinner tonight. And because he could begin practicing law now, it was more important than ever that he go.

Still, there were those he wanted to share the news with and they were right here in his home. He hurried out of his study and was about to rush upstairs when his daughters spotted him at the bottom and hurried down to meet him.

"Papa! Guess what?" Polly asked.

"We're going to Heaton House for fittings and to have tea with Mrs. Heaton!" Lilly said before Tyler had a chance to guess.

"You are? That sounds wonderful! I have some news I want to share with you."

"What is it, Papa?" Lilly asked.

Tyler took a seat on the second step and they sat down with him, one on each side.

Then Polly looked up and said, "Come join us, Miss Georgia! Papa has some news!"

Tyler looked up to where Miss Marshall stood at the top of the stairs, a smile on her face.

"Yes, please do come down." He waited until she'd reached them and then motioned for her to take the step above them. Once she sat down he grinned. "I just received the letter. I passed the bar exam!"

"Yay!" Lilly said, hugging his neck.

"That's wonderful news, Papa," Polly said, hugging his arm.

The smile on Miss Marshall's face warmed his heart as much as his daughters' hugs did, and he knew that it was her approval he most wanted at this moment.

"Congratulations, Sir Tyler. That is quite an accomplishment and I know it took a lot of extra work. I'm very happy for you."

"Thank you, Miss Marshall and girls. I can't think of anyone I'd rather share the news with."

His gaze caught Georgia Marshall's and he suddenly knew that the only other thing that could make this day perfect would have been to have supper with her instead of potential clients. But that wasn't to be and he'd have to settle for taking the memory of her smile with him instead.

After the girls left for their fittings, Tyler headed over to his office to tell Michael his good news. At the moment, he felt more relieved than anything, knowing that his in-laws had been telling all their friends about him, trying to get him clients before he even opened up for business—and how embarrassing it would have been had he failed.

"Sir Tyler!" Michael called from his office. "Good to see you today." He got up from his chair and joined Tyler in the reception area. "Come see your door. The workers just finished today."

Tyler followed him to his office, where on the frosted glass of the door window, in two lines, read: Sir Tyler Walker, Attorney at Law. It wasn't printed quite like it would have been in England, but this was America, and if it was done this way, it was fine with Tyler.

He turned to Michael Heaton and held out his hand. "Thank you, Michael. They finished just in time. I passed the exam."

Michael slapped him on the back. "Wonderful news! When do you open for business?"

"This coming Monday. I don't know how many clients I might have, but I'll be in business."

"Well, take it from me. Getting a new business up and running does take a while, but being your own boss is worth it."

"I certainly believe it will be." They entered the office and Tyler smiled. The painters were finished, his furniture fit perfectly and all that was needed were clients. "It looks great, Michael."

"I'm happy you like it and hope you'll be here for a long time to come."

"That's the plan."

"Are you celebrating tonight?"

"Not really. I have a dinner engagement, but it's certainly not a celebration. More a working dinner to drum up clients."

"I understand. I've been on plenty of them," Michael said.

"And it's with friends of my in-laws. They've given my name out and I'm grateful. But..."

"I think I understand," Michael said. "You're in a new city, a new country. That's adjustment enough. It'd be easier if you were back in England dining with friends of your family."

Tyler laughed. "You're right about the new adjustments. I'm not so sure that dining with friends of my family would be any easier, though. Even when you aren't the heir of the family, there is pressure—will you make it on your own? Will you be successful in your own right? I think it may be easier starting out on my own here."

"I hope so. And you know, you do have a friend in the city. Anytime you need to talk, I'm here."

"Thank you, Michael. I'm very glad I bought that house next to your mother."

They walked back to the elevator and Tyler headed home. His thoughts ran ahead of him to how sweet his daughters and Georgia Marshall had been over his passing the bar exam and he wished he could take them all out to dinner.

Were they back from their fittings and tea at Heaton House? They'd been so happy lately and he could only give the credit for that to their nanny. Only Georgia was becoming more than a nanny. She was very important to them, perhaps too much so—not only to them, but also to him.

When Sir Tyler came to hear his daughters' prayers and tuck them in that evening, Georgia's breath seemed to jump into her throat. Something did because she couldn't seem to catch her breath.

He was in evening dress—a black wool tailcoat over a white formal shirt with black waistcoat and straight-cut black wool trousers. Dress studs and cuff links were worn at his wrists. Never had he looked hand-somer. Georgia forced herself to breathe as he greeted her and his girls.

"Good evening, Miss Marshall. Polly and Lilly, I can't stay too long. Remember I told you I had to go out tonight for business and you promised to be very good for Amelia?"

"Yes, Papa, we remember," Polly said.

"And we'll be very good," Lilly assured him.

"I count on it."

He'd come in a bit earlier than usual, but that was understandable if he wanted more time with his daughters. "I'll take off now, but I'll see you in the morning," Georgia said on her way out the door. "I hope you enjoy your evening, Sir Tyler."

"Thank you, Miss Marshall. I'm not sure it will be enjoyable. I'm only hoping it will be worthwhile."

His smile made her heart skitter and she backed out of the room. "I hope it is. Night, girls."

"Good night, Miss Marshall," they chimed to-gether. "See you in the morning."

"See you then." Georgia hurried down the stairs to find Mr. Tate at the door.

"Good evening, Mr. Tate," she managed to say.

"And to you, too, Miss Marshall," the butler said, opening the door for her. He looked closely at her. "Are you all right? You seem a bit flushed."

"I'm fine, thank you."

He gave her his customary nod. "See you tomorrow."

"First thing." Georgia managed a smile and hurried down the steps. But instead of hurrying home, she turned in the opposite direction from Heaton House and crossed the street to walk along the park.

She needed a few minutes before she joined the others in the parlor. If she ran straight upstairs, the other women would be up there before she could even shut the door, wanting to know if anything was wrong with her.

And she wouldn't be able to lie. She wasn't all right and she didn't know why. That wasn't true. She did know why. Sir Tyler was resuming his social life, and whether it was for business reasons or not, after this evening, he'd be deluged with invitations. And many of them would be from the parents of marriageable daughters.

She tried to tell herself she was concerned for Polly and Lilly's future. Should their father marry again, she prayed it would be to someone who would love them as much as she did.

But deep down there was a little stab of jealousy that some young woman might catch Sir Tyler's eye and he might fall in love with her. She shouldn't care. Couldn't let herself care. She wasn't going to give her heart to anyone again—least of all one who would never consider her wife material.

She was attracted to him and there was no denying it any longer. And she had to get her runaway pulse under control so that it didn't race every time he smiled at her or came into a room. Or looked handsomer than any man ever should.

But more than all of that, she truly cared about Sir Tyler. Cared that he was still mourning the loss of his wife, cared that he was raising his daughters alone and cared that he might be lonely.

Georgia looked up at the evening sky, where stars were beginning to come out as she continued walking. "Dear Lord," she whispered, "please protect my heart from my growing feelings for Sir Tyler. I don't want it broken again. I probably should resign—but I do need this job and, well, I believe he and his daughters need me. I can't bring myself to turn my back on them, and yet I'm afraid that I'm beginning to care too much for the three of them. Please help me to keep in mind that he is my employer and they are my charges and that is all. In Jesus's name, I pray. Amen."

Georgia made it around the park as the evening sky darkened. The streetlights were just being lit and there were more lights shining from the windows of the houses surrounding the park. She rounded the corner at the same time a hack did and watched it come to a stop in front of Sir Tyler's home.

She crossed the street behind it, as Sir Tyler came out of his home. She hoped he didn't see her as she hurried up the steps to Heaton House, opened the door and quickly went inside. *Dear Lord, please let him have a nice evening—but maybe not too good.*

"Georgia, is that you?" Betsy called from the parlor. "Come on in. We need another player for charades."

"I'm coming!" Georgia took a deep breath and forced a smile as she crossed the foyer to the parlor.

* * *

Tyler glanced out the back window of the hack. Had that been Georgia he caught a glimpse of, entering Heaton House? What was she doing back out this evening?

Surely it wasn't her. Maybe she'd stopped to speak with Mrs. Biddle about the menu for the girls the next day before going home. And if she'd had an errand to run, it really wasn't any of his business. He was only her employer, after all. Still, his protective instincts where she was concerned seemed to grow with each passing day. If it had been Georgia, she was safe and sound now and he told himself to relax.

Except, much as he dreaded the evening out, that was impossible to do. *Lord, please help me get through this dinner and gain a client or two in the process.*

Tyler tried not to look out the windows as the hack driver dodged first one and then another vehicle while he raced up Fifth Avenue to Thirty-Fourth Street to pull into an entrance featuring a glass-enclosed promenade for pedestrians.

The driver stopped at the restaurant entrance and Tyler paid him upon getting out. Inside, he was shown the way to the Rose Room, where he was to meet his party. The hotel was magnificent, the decor something that would make even his mother catch her breath, and he hoped that one day he'd be able to bring his parents here.

At the entrance to the Rose Room, he told the maître d' whom he was to meet and was immediately shown to their table. Tyler had little time to take in the decor before his hosts, Mr. and Mrs. Fletcher, stood and welcomed him.

"Sir Tyler, we're so happy you could join us," Mr. Fletcher said. He introduced him to several other couples—Mr. and Mrs. Thornbrook, the Gregorys and the Middletons—and then to the woman Tyler surmised he'd be sitting next to, as it was the only empty seat at the table. "And this is our daughter, Felicia."

Tyler bowed over the woman's outstretched hand and smiled. "A pleasure to meet you, Miss Fletcher."

"I'm very pleased to meet you, too, Sir Tyler," the young woman said.

She had blond hair and pale blue eyes and was very attractive. And from the expression in her eyes, and in her mother's, it became clear to Tyler that, although he might leave here with the possibility of a client or two, the main reason he'd been invited was to meet Felicia Fletcher.

He took his seat next to her, and even though he was asked for his card from the other gentlemen at the table, the rest of the evening was spent listening to boring small talk about people he'd only heard of, but truly knew nothing about. Still, for business reasons, when someone was pointed out or a couple came up to their table, he made an effort to record their names to memory in case they might meet again.

The meal was superb and he did enjoy it, while trying to seem interested in what everyone was saying. But his thoughts drifted back to the start of the evening when he'd thought it was Georgia he'd seen going into Heaton House.

He wondered if she'd ever been here for dinner. If not, he'd love to bring her and—

"Sir Tyler, I wonder if you might be free two weeks

from this evening?" Mrs. Fletcher asked. "We're having a dinner party and we'd be honored if you would come."

"What a nice invitation, but I'll need to check my calendar before I can commit."

"I'll get an invitation out to you and hope to have an acceptance, then."

"What about lunch one day next week?" Mr. Thornbrook asked. "I'd like to talk some business over with you if you have the time."

"I'm free for lunch on Tuesday, if that works for you," Tyler said.

"Let's meet at the Astoria Gentlemen's Café, say one thirty?"

"I'll put it on my calendar when I get home."

"Odd how you know what you have open next week, but not the week after," Mrs. Fletcher said.

Tyler grinned. "That's a week later. And besides, I do have my children to consider."

"Don't you have a nanny for that?" Felicia Fletcher asked in a tone that seemed to totally dismiss his daughters.

"I do. But my wife and I liked—" Why was he explaining things to this woman? Especially with the attitude she had—as if dining with them should take preference over his daughters!

"Never mind. I'll check when I get home." And he'd make sure he had something planned for that evening. Tyler looked over at Mrs. Fletcher, who was watching them intently. Oh, yes, this dinner was planned with only one thing in mind. And that was to find her daughter a husband. Well, he wasn't going to be a candidate. Not even if it cost him a client or two.

He finished the meal as politely as he could and lingered over the dessert and coffee. But then he rose from his chair. "It's been a pleasure to meet you all. Thank you for the invitation, Mr. and Mrs. Fletcher."

"You're leaving already?" a pouty Felicia asked.

"I'm afraid I must."

"I'll see you on Tuesday," Mr. Thornbrook said. "The café is here in the hotel."

"I look forward to it," Tyler said. He nodded to those at the table, turned and strode back in the direction he'd come from. He had a feeling that he was the topic of conversation and that he'd come up woefully lacking as a prospective husband for Miss Fletcher. But hopefully the men at the table wouldn't take that into consideration in doing business with him. Only time would tell.

Chapter Fourteen

The next morning, the girls were in the middle of their table-manners lesson when Sir Tyler came into the breakfast room.

"Papa! Good morning. Did you have a good time last night?" Polly asked.

"I don't know that I'd call it a good time, but the restaurant was very pretty and the food was delicious. I wasn't impressed with some of the company, but I do think I may acquire a new client out of it."

"Then it was a good time," Lilly said matter-of-factly.

Tyler chuckled at his youngest. "Yes, I suppose you could say that, Lilly-bug."

Georgia's heart warmed at the way his daughter had got him to look on the bright side of it all and his use of a nickname for Lilly. Much as she hated to admit it, she felt better that he evidently hadn't enjoyed the evening as much as she'd feared he might.

"We're nearly ready to dine with you, Papa!" Polly said. "Miss Georgia says it won't be long now."

"Really?" Sir Tyler looked at Georgia for confirmation.

He looked so surprised Georgia couldn't help but smile. "Really. I believe next week, if you're agreeable to it."

Sir Tyler rubbed the bottom of his chin and looked at his daughters. "And do you two think you're ready?"

"Oh, yes, Papa!" Lilly said.

"We are!" Polly added.

How could he possibly ignore the pleas in their eyes? Georgia held her breath waiting for his answer.

Then he smiled. "All right. What evening? I do have an engagement on Friday, but any other night would work."

"Perhaps next Saturday?" Georgia suggested. "I'll come a bit early to get the girls dressed."

"Dressed?" Sir Tyler asked.

"Why, yes. They're having dinner with you. Won't the people at your dinner on Friday be dressed up?"

"Yes, of course. And the girls will want to look their best, too."

Thank You, Lord. Finally, Sir Tyler seemed to realize how important dining with him would be for them. And that the purpose of dressing for dinner would be so that they knew what was expected of them. They could hardly come to dinner in their nightclothes.

"Will you let Mrs. Biddle know? And plan the menu for that night?"

"If that's what you'd like me to do, of course I'll speak to her."

"Good. Then next Saturday evening it is. I'll put

it on my calendar." He looked at his girls, who were clapping their hands. "And I look forward to it."

Georgia hoped he did, for she was very sure he'd be quite pleased by the end of the night and that he truly would look forward to the next time.

"Well, I'm off to the office—to actually do some work. I hope you all have a good day."

"We hope you do, too, Papa!" Lilly said.

Sir Tyler gave them both a pat on the shoulder and turned to Georgia. "I'd like a few minutes of your time before you leave this evening, if you don't mind."

"Not at all." Georgia wondered what it was he wanted to speak to her about. Things had been going pretty smoothly lately and she couldn't imagine what it might be.

But he didn't seem upset about anything, so she wasn't going to let herself worry until she had something to be concerned about.

"See you all later."

Sir Tyler left and Georgia turned to his daughters. "Are you excited?"

"Oh, yes, Miss Georgia!" Lilly said.

"And he's going to be so surprised to see the outfits Miss Betsy made just for having dinner with him!" Polly said.

"He will. I'll have to tell Miss Betsy that they must be finished by next Saturday and we'll keep working to have you ready for the first dinner with your papa. For now, though, hurry upstairs and start on your letters. I have the work laid out for you. I'm going to speak to Mrs. Biddle about the menu and then I'll be up."

"Yes, Miss Georgia!" Lilly slipped out of her chair. "Come on, Polly."

"I'm right behind you."

The girls did hurry and she could hear their steps on the stairs before she turned to go down to speak to Mrs. Biddle.

The cook was having a cup of tea, probably just waiting until they finished up in the breakfast room to get on with her work.

"Sir Tyler will be having his first dinner with the girls and me next Saturday."

A broad smile split the cook's face. "Wonderful. What shall we have?"

"That's what I've come to speak to you about. I thought you might have some ideas."

"I have some for sure." The cook listed several options and Georgia thought any of them could work.

"You know the tastes of everyone better than I do, so I'll leave the menu to you, Mrs. Biddle. Just let me know what you finally decide. I'm sure whatever it is will be delicious."

"Thank you for your trust in me, Miss Georgia. I won't let you down."

"I know you won't. I'm sure Sir Tyler will be quite surprised and happy with the young ladies he'll be entertaining that night."

Mrs. Biddle chuckled. "Oh, yes, he will. It's been a pleasure to help with your lessons."

"And we'll need to continue them. There are some utensils they haven't had a chance to use yet, but as time goes on they'll need to know how."

"It gives Mr. Tate and me great joy to help and

see their progress. They're very special to us, as we can see they've become to you, too, Miss Georgia."

Georgia swallowed around a knot in her throat. The cook was very perceptive. She did care about Polly and Lilly—more each day. "It'd be impossible not to care about them."

"They are quite a team."

Georgia chuckled. "Yes, they are. And I must get up there and see to it that their lessons get done. We'll see you at lunch."

She hurried back up to the ground floor and then up the stairs to do her job. Only it didn't feel that much like work—not any longer. She loved being here, taking care of them, and if she wished for more, she tamped it down, telling herself again that there was no sense wishing for the impossible.

Tyler was quite pleased with his day. He'd had a telephone call from Mr. Gregory, whom he'd met the evening before, and he'd asked for an appointment for the next week also.

Then right before he'd left to go home, Michael Heaton had come over to introduce him to a friend of his, who also wanted to make an appointment to talk over some business decisions he was thinking of making. It appeared his law firm might get off to a faster start than he'd thought it would and there was a decided spring in his step as he walked home.

As always, Tate opened the door for him. "Good afternoon, Sir Tyler. I hope you had a good day."

"I did, thank you. How were things here? Did the girls do well with their lessons at lunch?"

That brought a smile to the butler's face. "They did. Miss Georgia tells us that they'll be having their first dinner with you next week."

"They will. She'll be joining us for those meals, too. Did she tell you?"

"She did."

"And you have no problem with that?"

"I might have at first, sir. But I think it's a good idea for her to take dinner with them and you. That way, she'll be able to remind them if they forget something or find out what they need to practice more of."

"I'm glad you aren't upset about it."

"Well, we are in America now, sir. I must accept that some things are done differently here."

"Yes, so must we all, I suppose. But I do think we'll adjust quite well, in time. Have the girls had their tea?"

"They have, sir. Would you like me to bring you some?"

"Yes, please. Has the mail come today?"

"It has. It's on your desk. There was a post from Mrs. Altman. I put it on top."

"Thank you, Tate." Tyler made his way back to his study, grabbed the mail off his desk and took a seat in his favorite chair. He opened the letter from his mother-in-law and began to read.

Dear Tyler,
I received your letter asking about photographs of our Ivy and will go through what I have as soon as we return home. I should have realized the girls would need some of them and I apologize for not thinking of it myself.

Our trip has been good for us and we now realize that it doesn't matter where we are, we will
always miss our daughter. But we can't wait
to see Polly and Lilly and you, too, of course.
You all are our family and we are thrilled to
be on our way back to New York and you all.
Peter will telegraph you the date and time our
ship will arrive. We've been telling all of our
acquaintances about your law practice and we
hope you'll have more clients than you know
what to do with soon.

Please give our granddaughters a hug from
us and tell them we can't wait to see them.
Sincerely,
Margaret

Tyler smiled and slipped the letter back in its envelope just as Tate brought in his tea.

Tate poured his tea and then said, "I trust that all
is well?"

"Yes. They'll be home before long. The girls will
be thrilled. Although…I'm not really sure about that,
either. It's not as if they know these grandparents
that well."

"I'm sure they will grow to love them, sir."

"Yes, of course they will." He only hoped their
grandparents didn't somehow undo all the good Miss
Marshall had accomplished since she'd been there.

"Will you be needing anything else, sir?"

"No. That's all for now, Tate."

Tyler leaned his head back on his chair as his butler left the room. It was good to be home.

He truly hoped his girls and their grandparents would grow close. Since he'd been widowed, his daughters had become more important than ever, and because of Georgia Marshall, he'd come to realize that more time together was what he and his girls needed. He still probably didn't spend enough time with them, but the comment from Felicia Fletcher last night had made him realize how valuable Georgia Marshall was to his family. Without her, he wouldn't be looking forward to hearing his daughters' prayers or tucking them in at night. That special time had come to mean a great deal to him.

And he knew that without her, he'd never be planning to have dinner with them to see how well their lessons were coming along. He had to admit that he looked forward to it, as he knew his daughters did. And Georgia would be here on a Saturday evening. It'd break up the weekend without her for all of them. Yes, he liked the idea a great deal.

Tyler sipped his tea and then went over to his desk to add the dinner to his calendar before writing his mother-in-law back to tell her they were looking forward to seeing them again.

Then he telephoned Michael Heaton at home to thank him for the introduction earlier that day. They made arrangements to meet for lunch the next week, and when the call ended, Tyler smiled. Not only had he gained a few clients this week, but he also realized Michael Heaton was going to be a true friend. The Lord was certainly looking over him when he led him to this home next to Mrs. Heaton—in all kinds of ways.

* * *

Georgia hurried down to let Sir Tyler know the girls were ready for him to tuck them in and to find out what it was he wanted to speak to her about.

Mr. Tate led her to the study. "Miss Marshall, Sir Tyler."

"Thank you, Tate. Come in, Miss Marshall." Tyler rose from his seat and motioned to the chair adjacent to his favorite one. "Please have a seat."

Georgia sat down, her pulse pounding in apprehension. What was it Sir Tyler wanted to speak to her about? She'd managed to put it out of her mind all afternoon, but now that she was here, she wanted to know. And she didn't wait for him to bring it up. "What was it you wanted to discuss with me, Sir Tyler? Is something wrong?"

"No! Not at all. I'm sorry if I gave you that impression."

"You didn't. Not really. I just—"

"Well, let me assure you that nothing is wrong. As a matter of fact, I wanted to let you know what a fine job you've been doing with my daughters and how much I appreciate you stepping in and helping us. And I'm hoping you'll change your mind about leaving at all. I'd like you to stay."

"Oh. I…" Georgia had no idea what to say. Deep down she knew it'd be best for her if she did leave and the sooner the better. But as for what she wanted to do? Her heart called out for her to stay. She cared so much about this family, her heart twisted at the very thought of leaving.

"I'm not asking you to decide right now, Miss Marshall. But I am asking you to consider staying. My daughters have been much happier in the last few weeks and I hope you'll think about making your position here permanent."

His words shot through her heart, warming it at the knowledge that he wanted her to stay, but shooting it with pain for reasons she couldn't even consider at the moment. "I'll think about it. But I don't know when I can give you an answer."

"As long as you don't intend to up and quit, that's fine. It's an open offer."

"Thank you, Sir Tyler. I appreciate it."

"And I'm giving you a raise. You've earned it."

"Why, thank you. I wasn't expecting a raise in pay." He certainly was making it more difficult to leave. "So this is what you wanted to speak to me about?"

"Yes. Somehow last evening, I was made to realize just how valuable you are to my household. Even Tate and Mrs. Biddle seem more content here since you've joined us. And I can go to work knowing that my daughters couldn't be in better hands when I am not here."

"Thank you. That means a great deal to me. Even more than the raise, in fact."

Sir Tyler chuckled. "You are truly one of a kind, Miss Marshall. I do hope you'll seriously consider staying on."

Something about the way he looked at her had her pulse skittering so fast she could feel it in her fingertips. But she couldn't take his wanting her to stay as anything personal. He wanted his girls to feel secure and he didn't want to have to worry about finding anyone else. That was all there was to it.

And she didn't want him to think that flattery

would have any effect on her—although, of course, it did. "I will consider it."

"Thank you. I'll let you go. I imagine the girls are wondering what's keeping me, and you would like to start enjoying your weekend."

"I'm sure they are waiting for you, Sir Tyler. And I warn you, they are already hoping they can talk you into taking them for ice cream this weekend."

"Yes, I thought they might. I'll take them, but I'm not going to let them know just yet. It's a good way to help them be on their best behavior."

Georgia chuckled. "Yes, it is. I'll see you all at church on Sunday. Good night."

"Good night."

She turned and hurried out of the room. She hadn't even thought about when she might leave—hadn't inquired as to what openings there might be come fall. But now she didn't know what to do. She'd think on it later and pray. She feared she was in danger of losing her heart to Sir Tyler—that he might already own a small part of it. And the only thing she knew for certain was that she needed guidance in this situation and she needed it as soon as possible.

Chapter Fifteen

The weekend seemed longer than usual even though Georgia had stayed busy. Once she'd told Betsy that the girls would be having their first dinner with Sir Tyler the following Saturday, the seamstress insisted they choose new trim for the girls' dresses she was almost finished with. So after breakfast the next morning, they, along with Julia, took off for the Ladies' Mile with swatches of the material each girl's outfit was made of.

"But what about you, Georgia? What are you going to wear?"

"Something I already have. They've never seen any of them and whichever I choose will be fine."

"Well, if you want my advice," Julia said, "I think you should wear your cream silk and lace. It looks beautiful on you."

"Oh, that's sweet of you, Julia. I might wear it."

"Are you nervous about the dinner?" Betsy asked.

"Not really—well, maybe a little. I'm not sure how Sir Tyler is going to react to having them at the dinner table, but he seems to be looking forward to it. The girls will do fine, I'm sure of it. And they will look beautiful because of your talent. I'm very excited for them. They can't wait."

"Then why are you looking a bit stressed?"

"I—" There was no reason to deny that she was. "Sir Tyler told me he'd like me to stay on."

"Not go back to teaching, you mean?" Julia asked.

"Yes. And, well, I am teaching his girls, so it's not as if I'm not doing what I've been trained to do and in a much easier way. And he gave me a raise."

"Georgia, that's wonderful! He is already paying you very well," Betsy said.

"I know. Much more than I'd make in a school."

"Then why are you so hesitant about saying you'll stay?"

"I…" Georgia shook her head.

"Oh, I see. You're beginning to care too much for him, to your way of thinking, anyway," Julia said.

"Possibly."

"Georgia, you aren't still determined never to fall in love again, are you?"

"Betsy, even if I wasn't, Sir Tyler would never consider me as wife material. He's a baronet. I'm an employee working for him, no less!"

"But—"

"No. Losing my heart to him would only bring me more pain and I don't want to go through that ever again."

"But how can you keep that from happening when you see him every day? Are you that strong?" Julia asked.

"I have to be. I already care about his daughters

so much that I almost feel I must stay for their sakes. But even then, if—when—he decides to marry again, I'd have to leave."

"Not necessarily," Betsy said. "The girls will be needing a nanny for a good while yet, and if he should remarry, she might not…"

"Might not want to take on the role of mother to another woman's children?"

"Well, many women marry for more than love, sometimes even instead of love," Julia said.

"That's what I'm afraid of. I'd hate to leave them if she didn't care for them."

Betsy raised an eyebrow at her. "If that were the case, then you might have already made your decision."

It was a good thing they'd reached the Ladies' Mile, for Georgia didn't know what to say. Had she made a decision? And if so, was it the right one? *Dear Lord, please help me to know.*

On Sunday after service, the girls ran up to Georgia to tell her they couldn't wait until the next day, and their hugs warmed her heart. Sir Tyler had hurried them along, and they'd waved to her as they left church.

Georgia had come to care so much for them that she was beginning to feel as if she was deserting them on the weekends. But at the same time, as her feelings for them and their father seemed to grow each day, she clung to weekends as though they were the only thing keeping her from losing her heart altogether. But the deep-down truth was that she couldn't wait until the next day, either.

But by evening, Georgia still didn't know what to do and tried to put it out of her mind as the group decided to go for ice cream after Sunday night supper. It was usually a lighter meal than the noon one, to make it easier on Gretchen and Maida, and they had it a bit earlier.

But her thoughts turned to Sir Tyler and his daughters as soon as they passed the Walker home. What were they doing? Amelia might be getting the girls ready for bed. It was getting near that time, although a little earlier than usual. And what would Sir Tyler be doing after he heard their prayers and tucked them in? Maybe he had work to do on a case, or perhaps he'd choose a book from the many on the shelves in his study. Either way, he was alone.

"Georgia, you're awfully quiet," Julia said. "Are you feeling all right?"

No. Her heart hurt just thinking about how lonely Sir Tyler might be. "I'm just woolgathering."

"Well, snap out of it. We're almost at the ice-cream parlor. What are you going to have?"

"Depends on if we're staying or walking home."

"I vote for staying," Emily said from up front.

"Me, too," Stephen added.

"Then I'm going to have a sundae," Georgia said. That was one decision that was easy to make.

They all came to a stop just as the door to the shop opened.

"Miss Georgia!" Lilly hurried through the door opening. "I didn't know we'd see you here!"

"I didn't know I'd see you here, either! It seems you talked your papa into the ice cream."

"We did," Polly said. "And not just tonight, but

last night, too. Papa said we could stay up a little longer once in a while to get used to having dinner later with him."

Georgia glanced at Sir Tyler. "What a good idea. And how is it going?"

"Fine. Amelia gave them their baths early and all they have to do when we get home is get into their nightclothes and get into bed. Then I'll listen to their prayers and tuck them in," he said. "I decided it might be a nice change for them."

Georgia couldn't help but grin at him. He was taking the initiative of changing his schedule, and theirs, to accommodate them. And he was taking them out on his own. She wondered if he realized just how much progress he was making in truly being a part of their lives, extending his own time with them? She was very proud of him.

"Well, it looks as if they think so, too."

"Oh, we do!" Lilly said before yawning.

Her yawn seemed to be contagious, as her older sister covered a large yawn of her own.

"I don't think it will take them long to go to sleep tonight."

"I believe you're right."

"Come on, girls, we'd best get home before I have to carry you both there."

"Night, Miss Georgia," they said together.

"See you tomorrow," Sir Tyler said.

"Good night to you all. See you in the morning."

They took off down the street and Georgia smiled as she headed inside the ice-cream shop. Somehow that chance meeting had rallied her spirits in a way nothing else could have.

* * *

The week seemed to have flown by to Tyler as he sat at the Wellingtons' dinner table on Friday evening and wished he hadn't accepted their invitation. They were very cordial, and so were the other guests, for that matter. But once again, he felt as if he'd been invited simply because he was a new eligible male in the city.

The Wellingtons had two daughters, and he'd been seated between them, which gave him little chance to converse with the men at the table. While he did need to make more contacts in the city, surely he could do it in ways other than these social dinners. While he might have met some of the guests through his in-laws at one time, he knew none of the people being talked about. Between that and the young women on each side of him, it'd been all he could do to keep up with the conversations.

Once dinner was over, the women went through to the parlor while the men stayed in the dining room. Several of them had an after-dinner drink, but Tyler stuck with coffee. If any of them thought he was odd, he didn't much care.

But at last, he did get to converse with several of the men and was pleased that he was able to give out his cards to them. But he'd never been more relieved to call an end to an evening than he was now.

As graciously as he could, he excused himself as soon as the men got up to join the women, and he caught a hack for home. The Wellingtons' daughters seemed very nice, but he was not interested in any matchmaking schemes that included him and felt no need to encourage them. Not even if it meant he might lose some business.

Besides, it'd been difficult to divide his attention between the two young women when his mind was on his own girls and how excited they were about having dinner with him the next night. It was all they'd talked about when he'd tucked them in.

Instead of having the hack drop him off at home, he had the driver stop at the Gramercy Park gate. He'd begun to carry one of his keys with him so that anytime he wanted to enter the park he could. Tyler paid the man and unlocked the gate.

He meandered around the small park, looking up at the houses around it until he came upon the bench he considered "his" and sat down. He had a good view of his home and Heaton House, where a light was still on in the parlor.

It was Friday night, after all, and the boarders were probably enjoying each other's company. But as he watched, the light went on in one of the upstairs rooms and then another. Was one of those Miss Georgia's room? He wondered what she'd done that evening. And then his thoughts turned to what it'd be like to have her next to him at dinner, and Tyler was certain he'd enjoy her company much more than those he'd spent the evening with tonight.

Hopefully once his in-laws were back in the city, his social life would consist of going to their home occasionally. Surely they wouldn't be trying to set him up with anyone and would continue to help him get to know future clients.

Tyler wasn't sure what Ivy's parents' reaction to Georgia would be, but he wouldn't allow them to have any say about whom he hired or the decisions she and he had made with the girls. And he was sure that Ivy would approve.

Ivy. Tyler leaned his head back and looked at the star-laden sky. She'd been a lovely woman, a wonderful wife and mother, and he felt blessed he'd had her in his life.

But there was no denying that his thoughts were more often than not on the woman he'd hired as a nanny. He looked forward to seeing Georgia each morning and hated to see her leave at night. On weekends he missed her as much as his girls did. But that only added to the guilt he wrestled with daily.

What had he been thinking to ask Georgia to stay permanently? Suddenly he was thankful she hadn't given him an answer yet, and he wasn't going to bring it back up. Not now, maybe not ever. He'd come to care for her much more than he should and fought those feelings each day. And he'd continue to fight them for as long as she did stay. He had to…for his daughters' sake.

On Saturday, Georgia headed over to the Walker home to help the girls get dressed for dinner with their papa. She'd stayed up late the evening before, keeping Betsy company while she finished adding the trim to Polly's and Lilly's dinner dresses.

They were going to look adorable and Georgia didn't know how Sir Tyler couldn't be pleased. Betsy had taken the dresses over earlier so that Georgia wouldn't have to chance getting the lace of her gown pulled by the boxes she'd placed them in.

Mr. Tate let her in and she hurried upstairs, where the girls were in their robes. Amelia had given them their baths and helped them on with their under-clothes.

"Oh, Miss Georgia, you look beautiful," Polly said.

"You really do," Lilly added.

"Well, thank you both very much, but you are going to look beautiful, too."

Excitement shone from their eyes and Georgia prayed that Sir Tyler knew how important this evening was to them. All that Georgia needed to do was help them into their gowns and do their hair.

"I'll help, if you'd like me to," Amelia offered.

"I would. Thank you, Amelia," Georgia said.

Together they helped the girls get on their out-fits. Polly's was a blue-dotted Swiss with white trim, and Lilly's was the same material only pink-trimmed white. Then she and Amelia braided their hair and the maid watched as Georgia wrapped Polly's around her head and carefully pinned it. She did the same with Lilly's and did a very good job.

"Oh, my," Amelia said. "You both look beautiful. Your papa is going to be speechless."

Both girls giggled.

"Thank you, Amelia," Polly said.

Georgia led them to a full-length mirror so they could see how they looked.

They both gasped and put their hands over their mouths as if they wanted to say something but didn't know what. Then they looked at each other and grinned.

"Thank you, Miss Georgia. For teaching us man-ners so we could be ready to have dinner with Papa tonight," Polly said.

"And for getting Miss Betsy to make our outfits!"

Lilly exclaimed. "I hope we don't spill anything on them!"

"You'll do fine. You both look lovely and you know what to do. I'm going to be so very proud of you. Now, are you ready?"

They nodded their heads.

"Come on, then. We don't want to keep your papa waiting."

At the top of the landing, she paused and took a hand of each girl as they started down the staircase. Sir Tyler must have heard them because suddenly he was at the bottom waiting for them. The smile on his face told them all they needed to know and Georgia began to relax.

"How lovely you all look. I'm honored to be dining with you this evening."

Mr. Tate came up behind Sir Tyler just then, and when Georgia and the girls got to the bottom, he said, "Miss Polly, Miss Lilly, may I escort you to the dining room?"

"Of course you may," Polly said while Lilly seemed to be at a loss for words and only grinned and nodded.

Sir Tyler turned to Georgia and crooked his arm. "May I have the pleasure of seating you, Miss Marshall?"

Like Lilly, Georgia only nodded and put her hand through his arm to rest on his forearm. Her pulse had begun to race the moment Sir Tyler's eyes had met hers, when he'd told them all they looked lovely. And now just looking at him had her feeling all aflutter. He looked all she'd ever thought an English baronet might look like and more. So very handsome and debonair.

There was no way to ignore the fact that his daughters kept looking back at them, their smiles warming her heart.

Once in the dining room, he pulled out her chair for her and slid her toward the table, while Mr. Tate did the same for his daughters. Then Sir Tyler took his seat at the other end of the table. The leaves had been taken out for this evening and it felt cozy and more like a small family dining room. She was thankful that Mr. Tate had suggested it.

The table had been set and the centerpiece was a low bowl of flowers so that the girls could see each other across the table. Candles were placed so that they didn't interfere with Polly's and Lilly's views, too. She would have to thank Mr. Tate for thinking of everything before she went home this evening.

Georgia was glad she'd let Mrs. Biddle decide on the menu and knew the girls well enough to know that she'd prepared some of their favorites.

The first course was vegetable soup and she was pleased to see that the girls' bowls weren't too full. Later they'd learn to serve themselves from the dishes Mr. Tate brought to her and their papa. But for now, she didn't want them to be any more nervous than they already were, and they'd decided it might be best for Mr. Tate to bring their courses to them.

Once Mr. Tate left the room, they looked at their papa for guidance.

"Let us pray before we eat," he said and they bowed their heads.

Georgia did the same as he began.

"Dear Lord, we thank You for this day and I thank You for the opportunity to have dinner with my daughters and Miss Georgia tonight. Thank You for letting her suggest it and prepare them. And thank You for the food we are about to eat. In Jesus's name, amen."

He raised his head and smiled as he lifted his spoon and dipped it into his soup. Georgia nodded to his daughters and they easily picked the right one and did the same, along with her.

"Oh, I really like this soup. We haven't had it in a while," Polly said.

"It's one of my favorites, too, Polly," Sir Tyler said.

"I do like it, but I like chicken soup best," Lilly said.

Sir Tyler chuckled and Georgia relaxed. It appeared he was going to enjoy his daughters in a way he never had before.

She was more than proud of them as they were served the next courses of veal cutlets and macaroni and cheese. They knew exactly which eating utensil to use and their manners were excellent. And Sir Tyler seemed quite impressed as he led the conversation—mostly about them and their day—and they conversed quite easily with him.

From the smile Mr. Tate gave her from behind the baronet, she knew that he was as proud of Polly and Lilly as she was.

They'd purposely planned that the meal wouldn't last overly long, and they'd just finished their dessert of strawberries and cream when Lilly began to yawn and her eyes grew heavy.

"I believe it's time for bed."

"I'll be up shortly to hear their prayers. I don't think they'll make it much longer than that," Sir Tyler said. "I enjoyed the evening immensely and look forward to the next dinner with you all."

"So did we, Papa," Polly said.

"Uh-huh," Lilly added. "Thank you, Papa."

Georgia took their hands and led them back up to their room, where Amelia waited to hang up their new outfits, while they hurried to the bathroom. Then Georgia and the maid helped them on with their night-clothes.

"How did we do, Miss Georgia?" Polly asked.

"You did very well. I could tell your papa was proud of you."

"Was he really?" Lilly asked.

"Oh, I believe so. I certainly was pleased with you both."

The smiles on the girls' faces told her they were very happy it'd gone so well.

Sir Tyler came up just as they were ready for bed and Georgia kissed them both good-night before heading out of the room.

"Miss Marshall, this won't take long—Lilly is almost out now. I'd like to speak to you before you leave. Would you mind waiting in my study for me?"

"Not at all. I'll see you there." Georgia couldn't help but wonder what he wanted to talk to her about, but in the meantime, she went downstairs in search of Mrs. Biddle and Mr. Tate. They were both in the kitchen having a much-deserved cup of tea.

"Miss Georgia! Come in. Would you like a cup?"

"No, thank you, Mrs. Biddle. I just wanted to thank you both for making sure everything went so smoothly. I believe that Sir Tyler was quite pleased."

"Oh, yes, he was," Mr. Tate said. "And we were both very happy to help. We're just as proud of the girls as you are."

"I'm so glad. I'm supposed to wait in Sir Tyler's study. There's something he wants to speak to me about."

Mr. Tate started to get up.

"Please, enjoy your tea, Mr. Tate. I know my way."

"I believe I will, Miss Georgia. Thank you."

Georgia headed back upstairs to the study, hoping that Mr. Tate was right and that Sir Tyler truly was pleased with how things went. But if so, what could he want to speak to her about?

She hoped he didn't ask for her answer about staying on, for she still didn't know what to do. She felt she knew what she should do, but it wasn't what she wanted to do and she felt more confused than ever.

Chapter Sixteen

Tyler headed back downstairs with a smile on his face. He'd looked back at Lilly after he listened to Polly's prayers and she was already sound asleep. By the time he'd reached the door, he was confident Polly would be, too.

But, oh, he was glad he'd agreed to Georgia's plan. He could tell they were a bit nervous at the beginning and his first instinct had been to put them at ease. These were his daughters— the only children he'd ever have. And he'd been so very proud of them tonight.

Tyler entered his study to find Georgia—he had to stop thinking of her by her given name. *Miss Marshall* was looking at some of the books on his shelves and he took a moment to gaze at her. She'd taken his breath away when he looked up and saw her bringing his daughters down. She was dressed in a cream-colored silk-and-lace gown that made her dark brown hair seem darker, her eyes greener. She was a beautiful woman. But not just outside—she was beautiful inside, too. She loved his daughters, he had no doubt of it, and she was bringing them through this difficult time for them with care and compassion.

She turned just then and put a hand over her chest. "Oh, I didn't hear you come in, Sir Tyler."

"I just got here. Are you looking for anything special?"

"Oh, I hope it's all right that I—"

"Of course it is. You can borrow any books you choose to. Can I help you find anything in particular? They are arranged alphabetically by author."

"I was just browsing to see if there might be something the girls might enjoy. I found a few that I might want to use."

"You can come down anytime." The light from his desk cast a glow on her hair and her eyes seemed to sparkle. Tyler wanted to tell her how lovely she looked, but he'd be crossing the bounds of propriety if he did. He was her employer not her suitor.

He motioned to the small table by the window. "Please take a seat."

Once she sat down, Tyler took the seat across from her. "You've done a wonderful job teaching the girls their table manners—all their manners, really. I've noticed that they've learned some new ones from you and I appreciate your—"

Tate entered the room just then with a tray and two cups.

"You must have read my mind, Tate," Tyler said.

"I thought you might be wanting a cup. And I just wanted to say that I was more than pleased at Miss Polly and Miss Lilly's deportment at dinner. They made us all proud and—" his butler turned to Georgia "—if I may, I'd like to commend you on how well you trained them, Miss Georgia."

Her smile lit up her eyes. "Thank you, Mr. Tate. I couldn't have done any of it without your and Mrs. Biddle's help. And we do still have a way to go, so I hope you'll be on board to keep helping as the lessons continue."

"Of course we will." Tate poured their tea and then left the room.

"Tate has had nothing but good things to say for the way you take care of my daughters."

"I don't know what I would do without him to guide me and help along the way. Both he and Mrs. Biddle have gone out of their way to make it easy for me." Georgia stirred some sugar into her tea and took a sip, before continuing. "I do hope you enjoyed your first meal with the girls."

Tyler grinned. "So much more than I've enjoyed those recent dinner engagements out. And I must apologize for not being on board with your idea right away. I should never have had to think about it."

"I'm glad you've enjoyed it. And there's no reason to apologize. I suggested something that is out of the norm, even to many in this country and certainly in England."

"But my daughters will be more than ready to enter high society, if that is what they wish, when the time comes. And I will be closer to them at that time because of you. For that, I will never be able to thank you enough."

"Oh, Sir Tyler. I can't take all the credit. Your daughters are very quick learners and they would have learned table manners the normal way, I'm sure. But

I do believe that the time they get to spend with you matters a great deal."

"I know it means more to me than I ever realized it would." He wanted to say so much more. This woman had come at a time when he felt lost as to how to raise his children. Without the family support from back home and then his in-laws taking off—

His in-laws. Tyler remembered the reason why he'd asked to speak to her after putting the girls down. "I meant to tell you before now that the girls' grandparents, Ivy's parents, will be back in the city week after next. I thought you should know."

"Oh, thank you for telling me. Will you be needing me while they're here for their visit?"

Did he need her? More each day. "Of course I will. They have a home in the city and the country, and might decide to call to see the girls at an inopportune time. It's possible they might interrupt your schedule, but if it gets to be too much, please let me know and I will take care of it. Or if it is at a really bad time, you can have Tate telephone me at the office and I'll come home."

"I'm sure we'll be able to work around them, Sir Tyler. It will be good for the girls to have their grandparents in their lives."

"Yes, it will. But they can be a bit…demanding at times. Just remember that you don't answer to them, but only to me."

"Yes, sir."

She looked a bit apprehensive and he hurried to reassure her. "I'm sure everything will be all right. But I haven't seen them since a few days after we got moved in and I don't know how they'll react to seeing a new nanny in charge."

"You didn't let them know?"

"I saw no need to while they were gone. They took Ivy's death very hard. She was their only child, and even though it's been almost a year and a half..." What could he say? He'd still been grieving when he moved to the city, too.

"I understand. Or at least I believe I do," Georgia said. "Everyone goes through grief at their own pace and in their own way. And they might resent that your daughters—"

"Care very much about you. That's it. They do, you know. And I'm just not sure how their grandparents will react to the relationship you have with each other."

"I appreciate you telling me all of this, Sir Tyler. And I believe it will all work out fine. I think this may be a case of your girls and their grandparents needing to forge a relationship of their own, and I hope to help that along in any way I can."

Of course she would. That was the kind of person Georgia Marshall was. "I know you will. But if anything comes up that you think I should know, please do not hesitate in coming to me."

"Yes, sir."

Tyler would have liked nothing more than to keep talking to her, to spend the rest of the evening with her, but it was her time off and he had to let her have it. He stood and reached for her hand. "I suppose I should let you get back to your weekend after the wonderful evening you gave us."

He helped Georgia to her feet and in one instant

the nearness of her had him longing to pull her into his arms and kiss her.

She pulled her hand away—did she sense what he was thinking? Surely not. He walked with her to the foyer and then to the front door.

"I hope the rest of your evening goes well."

"Thank you. I'll see you all at church tomorrow."

"You will."

"Good night, Sir Tyler."

"Good night, Miss Marshall."

Tyler closed the door behind her and leaned back against it. *Oh, dear Lord, please help me not to fall in love with my daughters' nanny.*

Georgia worried off and on about the pending arrival of Sir Tyler's in-laws for the rest of the weekend. Even with all her assurances to Sir Tyler, deep down she was very nervous about meeting them.

But she would do her best to help Polly and Lilly develop a good relationship with their grandparents. And they probably needed Sir Tyler in their lives, too. She was sure they could all be a great comfort to each other.

Still, she prayed that all would go well and that Sir Tyler's wife's family would realize all she wanted to do was help.

No. She wasn't being totally truthful with herself. She did want to help Sir Tyler and his daughters and had from the very beginning. But as for her... Oh, she didn't dare even put it into words. All she knew was that for one brief moment last night, when he'd helped her to her feet, she'd thought he might take her in his arms. That he might kiss her. And there was no way to deny that she'd wanted him to do exactly that.

Oh, dear Lord, what am I going to do? I'm afraid I'm losing my heart to Sir Tyler and I'm not sure what to do about it. One minute I think I should give notice and the next I believe I should stay—they do need me. But the truth also is that I don't want to leave. I can't wait to get there on Monday mornings, and now I hope we can keep having our dinners on Saturdays so that I don't go two whole days without seeing them. Please help me, Lord, to know what to do and what not to do, for I truly don't know. In Jesus's name, I pray. Amen.

Now, as she let herself in the Walker home on Monday, she resolved to keep her feelings for her employer from growing and to get on about doing the job she was hired to do. To take care of his daughters.

Georgia hurried upstairs to find them grinning from ear to ear when she got to their room.

"Miss Georgia, guess what?" Lilly asked.

"What?" She smiled back at them.

"Our grandpapa and grandmama will be back from their voyage soon!" Polly said.

"I can tell you're very excited."

"Oh, yes, we are. We weren't here very long before they left, but Papa says they love us and we'll love them, too," Polly said.

"Oh, I'm sure that is true. They're your mother's parents, after all, and they will have all kinds of stories to tell you about when she was your age and—"

"Papa says they still miss her very much and being around us will help to make them not miss her quite so much," Lilly added.

"I believe he's right." She prayed he was. But what

touched her heart most was realizing how Sir Tyler was already trying to prepare the tone for his daughters' relationship with their grandparents. He'd come a long way in a short amount of time.

"He says we might get to have a formal dinner with them before too long, but that we need a little more practice with just him and you before then," Polly said.

"We had such a good time having dinner with Papa and you," Lilly said. "I can't wait to do it again."

"You made me very proud and Mr. Tate and Mrs. Biddle, too. And I know your papa was very happy at how well you did. But, yes, we do need more practice before you have dinner with your grandparents."

"And we like the practice!" Lilly said.

Georgia laughed. "So do I. But we'd better get down to breakfast so your papa can tell you goodbye before he leaves for the office."

"He took us to see it yesterday afternoon," Polly said as they left the room.

"He did?" Georgia's heart flooded with joy that he was finding ways to spend time with them when she wasn't there.

"Uh-huh. It's very pretty and way up high in the building," Lilly said. "We looked down from his windows and I almost got dizzy!"

They headed down the staircase to the breakfast room.

"And now you'll know where he's at when he's working."

"That's what Papa said."

"What did I say?" Sir Tyler was sitting at the breakfast table and it looked as if a place had been set for him.

"We were telling Miss Georgia about you taking us to see your office yesterday. Are you going to eat with us, Papa?" Polly asked.

Georgia held her breath as she waited for his answer. "I thought I might. We don't have company and there's no sense in me eating in the other room all by myself. Besides, it seems a bit large to start the day with, don't you think?"

"It is large," Lilly said, plopping down in her chair.

"And this is cozy first thing in the morning," Polly said.

"I agree. And I even got Mr. Tate's permission."

"Well, that is good."

"Yes, it is. I wouldn't want to be on his bad side," Sir Tyler said as he stood and pulled out Georgia's chair for her, sending her pulse on a rapid race around and about to her heart.

He'd just sat back down when Mr. Tate came in from the butler's pantry with a tray holding juice and milk for the girls and a coffeepot. He set down the girls' drinks first and then poured coffee for Sir Tyler and Georgia.

"Mr. Tate, did you say Papa could eat with us?" Lilly asked.

Georgia had to hide her own smile as she watched Mr. Tate battle with his. "Why, your papa doesn't need my permission, Miss Lilly. But I did tell him I thought it a good idea."

"I do, too!" Lilly said.

"Me, too!" Polly added.

"Well, very good. We're all of the same mind," Mr. Tate said. "I'll have your breakfast up here in a few minutes."

"Will you eat with us every morning, Papa?"

"I believe I will, Lilly. Unless I have an early meeting or something comes up that I need to leave early. That is, unless Miss Marshall has any objections."

His gaze caught hers and for a moment Georgia lost all ability to speak. She shook her head while she gathered herself. "Of course not. Besides, like Mr. Tate said, you don't need my permission."

"But you're their nanny, and in this case I wouldn't want to upset you or your schedule."

"Your presence doesn't upset anything, Sir Tyler." Except, perhaps, for her heartbeat. It seemed to be all over the place.

"It's settled, then. I will have breakfast with my daughters."

Huge smiles lit up both the girls' faces and their eyes sparkled with happiness. If Georgia felt a bit uncomfortable with the situation, she would hide it as best she could. It was worth a little awkwardness to give this small family more time together.

"Now, what about the next dinner? Tuesday or Thursday?" Sir Tyler said.

"Tuesday is closer," Lilly said.

"Will tomorrow evening work for you, Miss Marshall?"

"I believe it will."

"It's settled, then. You and Mrs. Biddle can decide on the menu."

"Yes, sir. We will." It couldn't be more obvious that Sir Tyler enjoyed having meals with his girls and she couldn't be happier.

Sir Tyler started the day with a prayer and then the butler entered the room, setting the small bowls of toasted wheat with sugar and cream in front of the girls. Then he brought in regular bowls for Sir Tyler and Georgia.

Once they were finished, he brought in small plates with scrambled eggs with sautéed potatoes and small griddle cakes. The girls didn't have to be reminded of what utensils to use and Georgia couldn't be prouder of them, as Mr. Tate put a plate of the same in front of her. He then refilled hers and Sir Tyler's cups with more coffee.

Georgia stole a glance at her employer to find his gaze on her and something in his expression seemed to squeeze her heart. He quickly turned his attention to Lilly and asked, "How are your lessons going?"

"I believe good, Papa, but shouldn't you be asking Miss Georgia? She knows better than I do."

Georgia couldn't contain her chuckle. Lilly was nothing if not direct. "They're both doing very well with their numbers and letters."

"I'm glad to hear it."

"And we're learning history, too. Miss Georgia reads to us and then asks questions," Polly informed him.

"She's going to start reading us stories just for fun soon, too, aren't you, Miss Georgia?" Lilly asked.

"I am. We can't have all work and no fun, can we?"

"I hope not!" Lilly said.

Sir Tyler laughed. "I think Miss Georgia makes sure you have more fun than not."

Polly and Lilly both grinned and nodded.

"She does," Lilly admitted.

"She makes learning fun, too," Polly said.

Georgia couldn't have had a better report on her

teaching abilities. "Thank you. That's what I hope to do."

"And you do it excellently." Sir Tyler smiled at her and sent her pulse zipping through her body once more.

Georgia tore her gaze away from him and looked at his girls to see them grinning while looking from their papa to her and back again, and then to each other. She glanced at Sir Tyler to find that same expression in his eyes. What was he thinking? It was time to bring breakfast to a close. Now.

Chapter Seventeen

The next evening, Georgia went home a little early so that she could dress for dinner, while Amelia supervised the girls' baths and got them dressed.

But as she began getting ready she wondered just how smart it'd been of her to suggest dinner a couple of nights a week. Of course, at the time, she wasn't even thinking about joining Sir Tyler and his daughters at any meal.

Now, including breakfast, it appeared she'd be sharing at least six or seven meals with them each week. Not that she was complaining, not really. She'd enjoyed watching Sir Tyler interact with his daughters on Saturday evening and then again at breakfast the past two days—and she wouldn't trade those moments for anything.

But it did come at a price, for Georgia could no longer deny that her feelings were growing for Sir Tyler. She loved his girls as if they were her own, worried about them when she wasn't with them and couldn't wait to see them again.

As for their papa, he was the most honorable, caring man she'd ever met. He loved his girls with all his heart and she was sure he'd loved his wife the same way. To be loved by a man like him would be all any woman could ever want.

But it was something that would never happen for her. They were from two different worlds. He was an English baronet and she was only the nanny to his girls. And their grandparents were all wealthy. They'd never approve, even if he felt the same way—and she had no reason to believe he did.

No, she'd got herself into this…predicament she found herself in and she could blame no one but herself. She'd taken the position, and his having dinner a few nights a week with his girls was her idea. She hadn't suggested anything about the breakfasts, but she certainly hadn't spoken up when he'd asked if she had any objections, either. How could she when she enjoyed his company more each day?

Georgia huffed out a deep breath as she put the finishing touches on her hair. She should have given notice. The first week. The first day. She just shouldn't have taken the position at all.

But she had and now…how could she resign? But how could she keep working there, knowing she'd never have what she longed for?

Georgia stepped into a gown a little less dressy than the one she'd worn on the weekend and hoped it was stylish enough for a weeknight dinner at a baronet's.

A light knock sounded on the bathroom door. "Come in."

"I just wanted to see if you needed any help, Georgia."

"That's nice of you, Betsy, but I think I'm ready."

"You look very nice."

"Thank you. I almost feel more nervous tonight than I did Saturday evening."

"Why? There's no reason to feel that way. You've taught Polly and Lilly very well and they won't embarrass you in any way."

"I know."

"Georgia…is it being around Sir Tyler that has you so nervous?"

Georgia began to shake her head. "No. I— It could be."

"Hmm, I wondered. He's a very handsome man. And very nice, too."

"Yes, he is. He's also a widower who might still be grieving over his wife, not to mention that he's a baronet and all the other reasons that would make it imposs—" Georgia gasped and stopped herself short. Betsy hadn't asked if she'd fallen in love and she'd said much more than she needed to.

"Don't underestimate yourself, Georgia Marshall. You're a wonderful person and a beautiful woman. Sir Tyler's children love you and, well, I've seen the way he looks at you."

Hope rose and fell within a second. Just because Sir Tyler might think she was pretty didn't mean… anything. "Thank you for trying to buoy up my spirits, Betsy. You're a good friend."

"I'm telling the truth."

Georgia smiled. "So am I. I'd better get going. See you later."

She hurried downstairs and waved to everyone in the parlor waiting to be called to dinner. Then Georgia let herself out and hurried to the house next door.

Once they were all seated, Tyler glanced around the table. "Thank you for joining me for dinner once more, ladies. You all look quite lovely," Tyler said.

His daughters giggled and he could see a delicate color steal up Georgia's cheeks. She'd never looked prettier to him than tonight, and that should be a warning signal for him. He was coming to care too much for his daughters' nanny. But how could he not? She was a wonderful woman, loved his girls and—

No. There were no *ands*. He was not going to fall in love with her. Not going to let his feelings continue to grow. He couldn't. It wouldn't be fair to her, to his girls or even to him. All it would do was make him long for something he didn't dare reach for.

Tyler was relieved when Mr. Tate brought in their first course of potato soup—one of the girls' favorites. Everything was going quite smoothly until Lilly reached for her water glass and knocked it over.

"Oh! Papa, I'm sorry. I—"

Tyler could see tears pooling in his youngest daughter's eyes. He looked at Georgia, and they both hurried around the table in a flash. Lilly blinked just as he got to her and plopped those tears right out of her eyes. How did she do that?

He gathered her into his arms and patted her on the back while Georgia grabbed her napkin and dabbed at the spreading wet spot on the tablecloth.

"There, there, Lilly," he said. "It's just water. It's

nothing to cry about. It even happens at some of the fancy dinner parties I've gone to."

"It does?"

"Yes, it does. And see? Miss Georgia already has most of it mopped up."

Lilly sniffed. "Thank you, Miss Georgia."

"You're welcome, Lilly."

Mr. Tate entered the room just then. "Oh, my! What happened?"

"Oh, Mr. Tate. I'm so sorry! I knocked over my water glass."

The butler hurried over to her. "Miss Lilly, there's nothing to be sorry about. I believe it was my fault—I did fill your glass a tad too full, I'm sure. Don't worry about it for a moment."

A folded-up cloth was put under the tablecloth to keep the table from being harmed, and Mr. Tate moved Lilly's setting down away from the spot before refilling her glass.

"Are you upset with me, Miss Georgia?" Lilly popped one more tear out as Sir Tyler sat her down in her chair.

"Not at all, Lilly." Georgia knelt down and hugged her small charge. "These things happen, and not just to children. I've done it myself."

"You have?"

"Oh, yes. And one of the boarders at Heaton House dumped a whole glass in her lap just the other day. If it happens when you're with other people, just say, 'Oh, I am so sorry.' You don't have to elaborate. Mop it up best you can with your napkin until one of the servers comes to help."

The child let out a huge sigh of relief and smiled

at Georgia. "I am so sorry. And I hope it never happens again."

"It'll probably happen to me next," Polly said. "But I'll do what Miss Georgia said to do. See, this was a lesson night."

They all managed to laugh as they put the accident behind them and began eating their soup. But Tyler knew he'd never forget how Georgia had hurried to comfort his daughter.

The fine dinner Mrs. Biddle had prepared passed without any more accidents and went very well, in fact. He was quite pleased that his daughters could carry on a conversation with him and Georgia. They didn't interrupt, and if they had a question, they were very polite and waited for a lull before asking.

He was quite certain they would be fine at a dinner with Ivy's parents. He just wasn't sure his in-laws were ready for such an adventure.

By the time dessert had been consumed, Lilly's eyelids were getting heavy again, and he carried her up the stairs while Georgia took hold of Polly's hand.

Amelia was waiting to help get them ready for bed and hurried them into the bathroom to do so.

Much as Tyler wanted to ask Georgia to stay and have a cup of tea, he didn't. He had to protect his heart the best he could, and if he were truthful, he knew he should be looking for a new nanny. Should put an advertisement in the paper first thing tomorrow.

But his heart twisted at the very thought and he knew he wouldn't. Couldn't. His girls loved her and she loved them. He had to keep his feelings to himself.

"Looks as if I'd better just wait here so I can tuck them in and hear their prayers, if they last that long."

"Probably a good idea," Georgia said before join-ing Amelia and his daughters in the bathroom.

He could hear Lilly telling the maid about her ac-cident and had to smile when she said, "And no one was mad at me!"

In only a few minutes they were back and Geor-gia helped them both into bed. She gave them each a kiss and then said, "You did very well tonight and I'm proud of you. Sleep well and I'll see you both in the morning."

"Good night, Miss Georgia," his daughters said in unison.

"Good night."

"Thank you for dining with us, Miss Marshall." Tyler hated to see her go, wanted to stop her. But he couldn't. He had to accept…so much he didn't want to. "We'll see you in the morning. Thank you for ev-erything."

"You're welcome, Sir Tyler. Good night."

Loneliness washed over him as he watched her walk out of the room. *Dear Lord, please help me here. I'm quite sure she took a part of my heart with her.*

Georgia kept hoping Sir Tyler would call her back and ask if she wanted some tea, coffee, anything, be-fore she went home as he'd done the first night. But he didn't. She felt something was wrong. He'd been fine at dinner. But then suddenly he'd seemed distant. Had she done anything wrong?

Perhaps she shouldn't have been so quick to hurry to Lilly. But that'd been an instinctive reaction, one she hadn't even thought about. Still, Sir Tyler was their father and she was only the nanny. He had every right to be upset with her.

She almost expected Mr. Tate to be waiting for her at the bottom of the staircase. But he wasn't there—probably having a well-deserved cup of tea with Mrs. Biddle. She should probably thank them before leaving…but she'd do it in the morning. She let herself out and took a deep breath. It was a beautiful night, all starry and bright, but even that didn't settle her insides.

If Sir Tyler was feeling he should distance himself from her, he was right. He was her employer, after all. He probably could tell that she'd taken his compliment to her and the girls too much to heart.

And his timing was perfect—especially with his late wife's parents coming back soon. Georgia had a feeling they weren't going to like the way she was taking care of their grandchildren. And from talking to Elizabeth, she'd realized that perhaps she wasn't quite as strict as many English nannies—or those of the wealthy here in the States should be. But then again, Sir Tyler knew she was a teacher and had never been trained as a nanny. And, well, if he or his in-laws thought she should go, they could tell her!

Regardless of all that, Sir Tyler was perfectly right in…not asking her to stay. It would make it easier for her to distance herself from him. And she needed to do that. Starting tomorrow.

She let out a big breath on the steps of Heaton House and made herself smile as she opened the door and went in.

"Georgia? Is that you?" Emily said from the parlor. "Do you want to go get ice cream with us? We're just about to leave."

She might as well. It sure would beat going up to her room and moping. Besides, it was dark out and by the time they got to the ice-cream shop or, at the least, back home, hopefully she'd be able to deal with the reality of her life.

"Sure, I'll go. Let me run up and change. I promise to hurry."

"Good. We don't mind waiting," Betsy said. "We were hoping you'd get here in time to go with us."

Dear Betsy. Georgia hurried up and quickly took off her outfit, laying it on the bed to hang up later. Then she put on the skirt and shirtwaist she'd worn earlier in the day. She certainly wasn't trying to impress anyone at the ice-cream parlor.

She rushed back downstairs and said, "Let's go!"

Georgia hurried outside and stood at the bottom of the stoop to wait for them. She could feel the tears building behind her eyes and she didn't want anyone seeing them. *Dear Lord, please, help me to get my feelings under control by the time we get there.*

Betsy was the first one out the door and she hurried down to walk with Georgia. She never asked a question, never mentioned the dinner. Betsy just walked beside her and kept conversation going so that Georgia didn't have to say anything at all. Finally, Georgia could feel herself begin to relax. The Lord had answered her prayers with the help of a friend.

Chapter Eighteen

It'd been a longer-than-normal few days for Tyler, and as he left work he was glad it was Friday. He'd worked late on Wednesday and Thursday, barely getting home in time to tuck in his daughters and hear their prayers. And he couldn't deny he'd done it on purpose.

Breakfasts had felt a bit strained the past few days and he couldn't tell if it was his mood that served as the catalyst for it or the fact that Georgia didn't seem herself, either. Whatever it was, the distance seemed to be growing between them faster than he wanted it to.

After this evening he'd have the weekend to try to get in a better disposition before Monday, when his in-laws got back. He'd received a telegram from his father-in-law asking him and the girls to meet them. And their coming home now was part of his problem. He feared they were going to be critical of the decisions he'd made in regard to raising his girls. That they'd think he was being too…indulgent with them and that Georgia—Miss Marshall—wasn't strict enough with them.

Well, they could think what they wanted. He liked the relationship he had with his daughters, loved spending more time with them, although in the span of a day, it truly wasn't that much. Still, he knew his parents hadn't spent even that much time with him and his brother. And he didn't think Ivy's parents had spent all that much time with her when she was Polly's and Lilly's ages, either.

Still, he didn't want his in-laws disparaging their nanny, and especially not in front of them. Perhaps he was borrowing trouble where none existed, and he prayed that was the case. He wanted his girls and their grandparents to have a close relationship. They all needed each other. But Polly and Lilly needed Georgia, too.

As soon as Tyler's foot hit the top of the stoop, Tate opened the door as always. "Good afternoon, sir."

"Good afternoon, Tate. I hope it has been. Anything out of the ordinary happen?"

"No, sir. Not that I know of. I believe everything has gone smoothly. Miss Georgia will be leaving in a little while to go get dressed for dinner, and Amelia will be getting Miss Polly and Miss Lilly ready. I have your things laid out and Mrs. Biddle is making the meal as we speak."

Dinner. What he'd both dreaded and looked forward to all day. More time to spend with his girls. And time with Miss Georgia that he couldn't let himself enjoy too much. He only hoped that, somehow, this evening would end on a better note than Tuesday had.

"I'll go look at the mail and then go up and get dressed. I wouldn't want to be late for dinner with my girls."

He went to his study and looked over the day's correspondence. Two more dinner invitations that he had no intention of accepting at the moment, and one lunch invitation that he would. A letter from home, which he read quickly. His father was a man of few words. Then Tyler leaned his head back against his chair, and only after he heard Georgia in the foyer telling Tate she'd be back soon did he get up and go upstairs. He paused at the landing and smiled as he heard his daughters giggling from their bathroom. He loved the sound of their laughter and the very fact that it seemed they laughed more each day.

By the time he went back downstairs, he wondered if Geor—if Miss Marshall was there yet. He had to quit thinking of her as Georgia in any way. If he slipped and called her anything but Miss Marshall while his in-laws were there, he could only imagine their response.

He'd almost be glad for Monday to get there so that he didn't have to dread finding out how they were going to react to all the changes he'd made in his household since they'd left.

He'd been downstairs only a few minutes before he heard his girls at the top of the stairs. At breakfast this morning, they'd been so excited about this evening and it appeared that hadn't changed. And then he heard Georgia's voice asking if they were ready to go down, and his pulse galloped through his veins so fast it seemed to turn his heart upside down.

And suddenly he knew he could try to distance

himself from Georgia all he wanted, but she'd found a place deep inside his heart and he had a feeling that spot could only be filled by her.

He tried to fight the urge to go to the bottom of the staircase to watch them come down, but it was a losing battle. And so was his plan to only look at his girls. Pretty as they were, his gaze landed on their nanny, beautiful in a rose-colored gown that made her brown hair darker and her eyes a deeper green. Tyler's heart expanded as he acknowledged that, futile as a future was with this woman, he could not stop his love for her from growing.

Georgia's heart flooded with warmth for the man at the bottom of the stairs. Much as she tried to deny it, hopeless as it was, she feared she was falling in love with the baronet and there seemed to be nothing she could do about it.

She let his daughters hurry down in front of her and watched him give them each a hug as his gaze held hers while she made her way to them.

"You all look beautiful tonight. I'm honored to be dining with you."

Lilly giggled. "Oh, Papa. You are very handsome and we like dining with you, too!"

Georgia was in total agreement with the four-year-old. He was quite handsome. And there seemed to be something different about him tonight, although she didn't know what. She only knew that instead of fighting how she felt, she was going to enjoy the evening. With the girls' grandparents coming back, Georgia had a feeling that the cozy dinners might come to an end or at least be put off for a week or so. She could be wrong and hoped she was, but right or wrong, she was going to make sure the girls enjoyed this evening.

Mr. Tate showed up just then to seat Polly and Lilly, and Sir Tyler held out his arm for her to take. Georgia hesitated only a second before slipping her hand through to rest it on his forearm. He smiled down at her and her world seemed to turn right side up—at least from where it was after Tuesday night. She didn't quite know why. All she really knew was that the vise that seemed to be squeezing her heart for the past few days loosened just enough that she felt she could finally breathe easy.

After everyone was seated, Sir Tyler said the prayer, asking for safe travel for his in-laws, for them to like the changes he'd made while they were gone and for a happy reunion for them all.

Georgia couldn't help but wonder if one of the changes he was referring to was her and her way of doing things—and his, in taking some of her suggestions. If so, she hoped that they wouldn't interfere and make him second-guess his decisions where his girls were concerned. Especially not when they were growing closer by the day.

Mr. Tate brought in the first course and began to serve them. The whole meal went beautifully, with Sir Tyler's girls conversing quite comfortably with him and Georgia. The butler made sure not to fill Lilly's and Polly's glasses too full and, with Lilly being extra careful, there were no accidents.

"What time will Grandmama and Grandpapa be getting here, Papa?" Polly asked in her most grown-up manner.

"Their ship arrives midafternoon on Monday.

They want me to bring you with me to pick them up. Then we'll take them home and they'll come back over later for dinner with me."

"But not with us?" Polly said.

"I'm not sure they're ready for that, Polly. But they will be soon, I'm sure."

"Will Miss Georgia be going with us to pick them up?" Lilly asked. "And she'll have supper with me and Polly?"

"Oh, no. I won't be going with you but I will be having supper with you. And I do hope to meet your grandparents in the coming days," Georgia said, before their father had a chance to answer. If she wasn't mistaken, the look he flashed her was one of relief.

"You will certainly meet them soon," Sir Tyler said. "And I hope you will not mind having dinner with the girls—"

"Of course not. It's what I do."

"Thank you."

"Will we still be having *our* dinners together? Us and you and Miss Georgia?" Lilly asked.

"Of course. But we may have to change the days or put them off for a week or so until your grandparents go to their country home."

That they had two homes, one here in the city and a country one, told Georgia they were wealthier than she'd thought.

"I remember it," Polly said. "Grandmama said maybe we could come stay for a week or so when they got back."

"Well, we'll see about that. I'm not sure—"

"You would come with us, wouldn't you, Papa? Or Miss Georgia would?" Lilly asked.

Georgia looked at Sir Tyler to find his eyes on her. Of course a nanny would go with them, to help them dress and take care of them when they weren't spending time with their grandparents. But—

"I don't think you'll be going for a visit right away. Perhaps later in the summer, and I am sure I'd go with you then, but we'll see how things go."

Georgia had to admire the way he'd taken care of the question without actually answering it where she was concerned. But what did that mean? Would he want her to go or would she even be their nanny by then?

She wasn't prepared for the stab of pain she felt at the very thought that she might not be. Suddenly she dreaded meeting Polly and Lilly's grandparents. She had a feeling they weren't going to approve of her at all.

When Tyler came home early to pick up his daughters to take them to meet their grandparents on Monday, it was to find Georgia had dressed them in some of their newer outfits. They looked very nice and he was thankful that they wouldn't be seeing their grandparents in the same outgrown clothes they'd been wearing when Georgia became their nanny.

"You both look quite fashionable," Tyler said to his daughters. Then he turned to Georgia. "Thank you for seeing to it that they have new clothes, Miss Marshall. If not for you, I fear their grandmother would take me to task for not paying attention to their needs."

"You're welcome, but I'm sure you would have noticed on your own. And besides, I wouldn't want their grandparents to think I wasn't doing my job."

She seemed a bit tense and he had a feeling she was very nervous about meeting his in-laws. "I have no complaints at all with the way you do your job. Feel free to take some time off while we're gone."

She gave a little nod. "All right. I might run over to Heaton House. If I'm not here when you return, just have Mr. Tate telephone to let me know when you get back."

"I will."

"The hack is here, Sir Tyler," Mr. Tate said.

"Come on, girls. Let's go welcome your grandparents home." His daughters followed him outside and he helped them into the hack. They did seem excited and he had Georgia to thank for it. She'd been talking about how nice it would be for them and he'd have to remember to thank her when his girls weren't around. They really didn't know this set of grandparents that well, and yet, because of their nanny, they were excited about seeing them.

Dear Lord, please let Ivy's parents be as excited about developing a relationship with Polly and Lilly as they are with the prospect. He looked at them and remembered how they'd tried to run off their nanny before Georgia came into their lives. She'd helped them to be happy again and he'd be beholden to her from now on.

The girls whispered between themselves as they did so often and he smiled watching Polly and Lilly together. He noticed so much more now that he was spending extra time with them.

He and his daughters watched the passengers disembark until they spotted Ivy's parents in line. Tyler let out a sigh of relief when his in-laws saw him and the girls. Their smiles were all he'd hoped they'd be.

As the Altmans hurried over to them, Tyler was

pleased to see his daughters' response. Peter and Margaret hugged them both and then Margaret hugged him and Peter held out his hand. Tyler shook it and they all got back into the hack.

"Oh, my, how the girls have grown! Much too fast, I might add," Margaret said. "They're beautiful. They remind me so much of Ivy when she was their age."

Tyler could see the tears in his mother-in-law's eyes and his heart went out to her. He couldn't imagine life without his daughters, and he did hope that having them near would help Ivy's parents with their grief.

"You are expecting us for dinner tonight, aren't you? If so, we'd like to come a bit early so that we can visit with the girls before they go to bed."

"Of course. Mrs. Biddle has been planning it for days. And you're welcome anytime."

"And you can meet Miss Georgia, Grandmama," Polly said.

"Miss Georgia?" Margaret looked at Tyler. "Who is she?"

"She's our new nanny, Grandmama," Lilly informed her. "Our old nanny got homesick and went back and then we didn't like the new one and—"

"Miss Marshall came to our aid." Tyler didn't want to get into how they'd run off the last nanny. "And the girls are quite fond of her."

"I see. I look forward to meeting her," Margaret said.

But the tone in her voice didn't ring quite true and Tyler prayed it would change once she actually met Georgia.

"You'll love her, Grandmama!" Lilly said. "She's

been teaching us table manners and the history of 'merica and numbers and letters and—"

"Is she a nanny or a governess?" Peter asked.

"Actually, she's acting as both. She's a teacher who moved to the city in the middle of the school year and hadn't been able to find a job. She kindly stepped in when I went to Mrs. Heaton to ask if she knew of anyone and—"

"Mrs. Heaton? That name sounds familiar," Margaret said.

"She's my next-door neighbor who runs a very nice boardinghouse, remember? And you might know her from charity events. She's very active with the ladies' aid society."

"Oh, yes, I do remember her now. But, Tyler, you could have asked any of our friends for advice on nannies, you know."

"But I actually know Mrs. Heaton better than I do your friends, Margaret. And I feel blessed that Miss Marshall was available at the time."

"But you need our friends to help get your business going, Tyler," Peter said.

"I do. And I have accepted a couple of invitations from them in the last few weeks. But you know Ivy and I were not into the social scene that much in England, and I don't see that changing for me that much."

Both of his in-laws looked disappointed, but he shrugged it off and told them the truth. "I am hoping to make more contacts through you, of course, and I thank you for any help you can give me. However, I'd prefer to develop those relationships by having dinner with you and your friends and not so much at their invitations. They all seem to have young daughters of marriageable age and I don't want to give any of them the wrong impression."

"That's understandable, I suppose." Peter surprised him by agreeing with him.

Thankfully, the hack pulled up at their mansion before his mother-in-law could give an opinion, and Tyler breathed a sigh of relief. Their luggage had been sent out in a different hack, and with no invitation to stay for tea, there was nothing to do but let them out.

Peter and Margaret hugged the girls.

"We'll be over as soon as we freshen up." Margaret smiled at the girls. "I can't wait to see how you've settled in."

"We'll see you soon," Tyler said.

The Altmans waved and headed inside, while Tyler told the hack driver to take them home. Relief for the moment turned to concern for later. He'd better let Georgia know to be prepared for inspection.

Chapter Nineteen

When they arrived home, Tyler sent his daughters upstairs to their playroom and told them Miss Marshall would be there shortly. Then he turned to Tate. "Would you telephone Heaton House and let Miss Marshall know we're back?"

"There's no need, sir. Miss Georgia came back a short time ago and is in the library trying to find a new book to read to the girls."

"Good, I want to speak to her before the Altmans arrive." Tyler turned and hurried to his study. But when he got there it was to find Georgia Marshall just coming down from the sliding ladder to his bookshelves. "Did you find something?"

"Oh! I didn't hear you." Georgia turned with a hand to her chest and let out a big breath.

"I'm sorry. I didn't mean to frighten you."

"I'm fine. I did find a short one for now. I'll look longer when they're down for their rest tomorrow. I hope everything went well with the girls' grandparents."

"It seemed to."

"I'd better go see to them." She started out of the room.

Tyler stopped her with a touch on her arm—a touch that shocked electric sparks through his pulse and he quickly dropped his hand. "I'd like to speak to you before you do."

"Certainly. What about?"

"My in-laws will be here before you leave. The girls want them to meet you." Georgia visibly paled and he rushed to reassure her. "As I said earlier, I want you to remember whom you work for. That is me. They have no bearing at all on your employment. But that does not mean they won't irritate you. Or that they might suggest you should do something different than what you've been doing."

Fire flashed in her eyes for a moment, which told Tyler something he was already pretty certain of. His in-laws wouldn't easily intimidate Georgia. Which was good. "You are to do things exactly as you have been or as you decide to do. If there is something you think you need permission on, you come to me as always."

He could see her shoulders begin to relax and color return to her face as she smiled and nodded. "Yes, Sir Tyler."

"And if they upset things in any way, I want you to come to me."

She nodded. "I will."

"Good. *Now* you may go see to my daughters."

"I'm on my way. And thank you."

"No, Georgia. Thank you."

She dipped her head and hurried out of the room.

Tyler took a seat in his favorite chair and leaned his head back. The urge to make sure Ivy's parents didn't upset her, or that she was as prepared to meet them as she could be, told him his feelings had grown into something he couldn't deny.

Nor could he act on them, hard as it would be to see her every day knowing that he couldn't bear the thought of her leaving. His girls needed her in their lives and so did he—even if it was only as their nanny. As long as she stayed, he would hide his true feelings for her. He simply had no other choice.

When Tyler went up to change, he couldn't resist peeking into the girls' playroom, where Georgia was reading from the book she'd picked out. They were paying rapt attention to every word as they sat on the sofa, one on each side of her. He was tempted to join them, but then Georgia closed the book. Besides, he could only imagine what the Altmans' reaction would be to find them all cuddled up on the couch listening to Georgia read.

He didn't want Ivy's parents hurt, either. He did care about them and wanted his daughters to love them and have a good relationship with them. But he wanted no interference from them on how to raise his girls. He wouldn't want it from his own parents if he still lived in England.

He and Ivy had talked about what they wanted for their children and he believed she would approve of the changes that'd been made since they'd come here. And her parents would have to accept that he knew how their daughter wanted her girls raised better than they did. He just had to find a way to explain it all to them so that they didn't think he didn't care about what they thought. *Dear Lord, please guide me through all of this. And if I'm wrong in believing they are going to be disapproving, please help me to know.*

"All right, girls," he heard Georgia say. "It's time for your supper. We don't want Mrs. Biddle waiting on us."

Tyler quickly moved away from the door and headed to his room instead. Hopefully they'd be through eating before his in-laws got there. When he finished dressing, he went down to check on their progress. It appeared they were just beginning to eat their dessert when he looked in on them to hear Lilly talking about the ships they'd seen at the harbor that day.

"They were so big, Miss Georgia! Even bigger than the one we came over on."

"Really?"

"No," Polly said. "It was the same size, I'm sure."

"I believe Polly is right, Lilly," Tyler said, coming into the room.

"Papa! When will Grandmama and Grandpapa be here?"

"Anytime now, I'm sure."

The doorbell rang and Tyler's stomach sank. "I think that may be them now. Miss Marshall, please bring the girls to the parlor when they've finished with their meal."

"Yes, sir."

Tyler turned to go greet his in-laws, but before he could take more than a step, they were barging into the breakfast room, with Tate close behind.

"Mr. and Mrs. Altman insisted, sir."

"It's fine, Tate."

"I'm sorry, Tyler. Margaret wanted to—"

"I understand. But the girls are just finishing up their meal. Let's go to the parlor and Miss Marshall will bring them in as soon as they are finished."

He took hold of his mother-in-law's arm and gave her no choice but to follow him. Once they were safely in the parlor, Tyler let go of her arm.

Margaret gave a little huff and sat down on the sofa. "Really, Tyler—they have supper in the breakfast room?"

"Yes," Tyler said. "It's easier for Mr. Tate to set up dinner for them there, now that they are using proper dishes and utensils."

"But aren't they a little young—"

"Margaret—" Peter put a hand on his wife's elbow "—why don't we let Tyler decide what is best for his girls?"

"I am not trying to interfere, Peter. But they are young and I know it wouldn't be done in England or even here among our social set."

Tyler clenched his jaw, trying not to alienate Ivy's mother on her first night back in the country. He was ready for this day to come to a close. It'd been much too long already.

Georgia's heart went out to Sir Tyler as he led his in-laws out of the room. He looked as apprehensive as she felt. And why? He'd made a few changes to the way his children learned things and didn't have a typical nanny for them, but he loved them immensely and had only their best interests at heart. Surely they would see all of that.

The girls finished their dessert in record time and then Polly wiped the corners of her mouth with her napkin and asked, "May we go to the parlor now, Miss Georgia?"

"Yes, we'll go in now."

She helped Lilly down from her chair and made sure they had no spots or crumbs on their clothing. Then she took hold of both girls' hands and led them to the parlor.

"There they are," their grandfather said, opening his arms wide.

Lilly looked up at Georgia as if asking if it was all right to run to him, and at her nod the child did just that. Polly was right behind her and then they hurried over to their grandmother.

Then Lilly ran back and caught Georgia's hand in hers and led her over to her grandparents. "This is Miss Georgia! She's our nanny."

"And our teacher," Polly said.

Tyler stood. "Peter, Margaret, this is Miss Georgia Marshall, as the girls said, their nanny and teacher. Miss Marshall, this is Mr. and Mrs. Peter Altman, Polly and Lilly's grandparents."

For a moment Georgia wondered if she should curtsy, but good sense prevailed. The Altmans weren't royalty and this was America. She didn't curtsy to Sir Tyler and she wasn't going to curtsy to them. But she would mind her manners—she had to set an example for the girls, after all.

"I'm pleased to meet you both," Georgia said. "Polly and Lilly have been very excited about your return."

"We're glad to be back. And we're pleased to meet you, too, Miss Marshall," Tyler's father-in-law said. "We heard a great deal about you today, didn't we, dear?"

"We did. The girls seem to be quite happy with you."

Tyler's mother-in-law seemed to be saying all the right words, but there was a tightness around her mouth that told Georgia she had reservations about her son-in-law's hiring her.

"They are a pleasure to take care of."

"I'm sure they are. You may leave them with us for a while," Mrs. Altman said.

Feeling dismissed, Georgia looked at Sir Tyler for confirmation.

"It's all right, Miss Marshall. I'll send them up shortly. But you have time for a cup of tea, if you'd like."

"Yes, sir. I'll go lay out their night things and then go to the kitchen." She smiled at the Altmans. "Good evening."

"Good evening, Miss Marshall," Mr. Altman said.

Mrs. Altman seemed preoccupied with the girls and Georgia had the distinct feeling she just wanted her to leave the room. No matter. She had work to do.

She hurried upstairs and found that Amelia had already been up to turn down the girls' beds. They'd taken their baths earlier, since they'd be visiting with their grandparents, and all that was left to do would be to help them change into their nightclothes and put them to bed.

"So, what are the grandparents like?" Amelia asked from the bathroom, where she was straightening up.

Georgia peeked around the door and shrugged her shoulders. "I don't really know. They do seem glad to see the girls, but—"

"I'm sure they are for the little time they'll spend with them. It was the same back in England. We've all been very surprised at the change in Sir Tyler and his relationship with his daughters. In a good way, of course. It's just very different but we can see the change in the three of them."

Georgia's mood lifted immediately. The changes had been for the good of Sir Tyler and his daughters. And if his servants saw it, she could only pray that their grandparents would, too.

She smiled as she laid the girls' nightclothes out on their beds, but with nothing more to do until they came up, she hurried down to the kitchen to make herself a cup of tea.

Mrs. Biddle and Mr. Tate were getting things ready for Sir Tyler's dinner with his in-laws.

"Miss Georgia, is there anything we can get you?"

"Oh, no, Mrs. Biddle. I'm just going to make myself a cup and go back to wait on the girls. I don't want to get in your way."

"You never get in our way," Mr. Tate said. "How do you think things are going?"

"I don't know. Mrs. Altman asked me to leave and Sir Tyler said he'd bring them up shortly. So, I'd better get back upstairs."

Mr. Tate rubbed the side of his cheek. "Don't let them upset you."

"I won't."

"And just so you know, Sir Tyler has asked me to let him know if they do upset things around here in any way. Although, he didn't need to ask—I would anyway."

"Thank you, Mr. Tate. I hope all goes well with

dinner." Georgia left the kitchen to head back up-stairs, feeling as if she'd been totally accepted by the staff.

And her heart soared at the knowledge that Sir Tyler seemed to want to protect her. Then it dipped to the pit of her stomach. If he thought he needed to, he must believe there might be problems.

Dear Lord, please let things go smoothly for him. I don't want his life or the girls' lives upset because their grandparents might not approve of me. Please help me to know how to meet this challenge in a way that doesn't create a problem where there might not be one.

She made it back to the girls' room and enjoyed her tea as she thought about some of the books she might choose for them from their papa's collection. She'd just taken the last sip when she heard them coming upstairs.

"Miss Georgia! Papa said to tell you he'd be right up. But guess what?"

"What is it, Lilly? From the way your eyes are shining, it must be good." Georgia helped her get ready for bed, while Amelia came in and helped Polly.

Lilly raised her arms to slip into her gown. "Grand-mama and Grandpapa want us to come to lunch to-morrow!"

"Oh, how nice. I'm sure you'll enjoy that."

"We will," Polly added. "And they're going to pick us up and bring us back before our nap time."

Both girls got into bed just as their papa came into the room.

"Will I need to accompany the girls?"

"Not this time," Sir Tyler said. "They want to have

their 'own' time with them. So you're free to have
lunch at Heaton House or wherever you'd like tomorrow. Just please be back before their rest time."

He seemed out of sorts, but she didn't think it was
with her. She'd done nothing to bring it about. "Yes,
sir. I'll be here."

She gave the girls a hug. "Good night. I'll see you
in the morning."

"Good night," the girls chorused.

"I'll be right back, girls. Miss Marshall, may I have
a word with you?"

"Of course." They stepped out into the hall.

"I hope this doesn't upset you—that they want the
girls to themselves."

"No. I understand."

"I suppose I do, too, but I'm not sure I like it. Still,
they are their grandparents."

"I'm sure everything will be all right. Are we…?
Did you want to put off having dinner with the girls?
Or what night would you want to have that?"

"Let's do it Thursday evening. My in-laws have already suggested a dinner party at their home on both
Friday and Saturday evenings this week. I didn't feel I
should refuse, as they're trying to help me make new
contacts for my business."

"Then Thursday evening sounds fine. I'll let Mrs.
Biddle know on my way out."

"Good. I'd best get the girls tucked in. Good night,
Miss Marshall."

"Good night, Sir Tyler."

Georgia headed down to the kitchen. The girls
would be disappointed about the weekend, but at least
their papa was trying to make sure he had a dinner

with them. With the Altmans in town their routines were bound to occasionally change, but she'd try to help them understand. And she had a feeling that Sir Tyler didn't like it any more than they would.

Chapter Twenty

The Altmans did bring Polly and Lilly back in time for their midafternoon rest, but it took Georgia a while to get them settled down.

"Oh, Miss Georgia, Grandmama and Grandpapa have photographs of our mama all over their house! She said she would bring us some soon," Lilly said.

"Oh, I'm glad." But she wished their grandmother had given them a few to bring home.

"She told us lots about Mama and asked us all kinds of questions, too," Polly said. "And we do look like Mama when she was our age! I thought Grandmama was going to cry when she showed the photos to us."

In that instant, Georgia's heart went out to the woman. She'd lost her only daughter, after all. And seeing how much the girls looked like her must have brought back many memories.

"But then Grandpapa said lunch was ready," Lilly continued. "I think they were surprised that we knew which utensils to use."

"Grandmama said it was just lunch and we didn't have that many servings, but she seemed happy," Polly said.

"And we didn't spill a thing, Miss Georgia!"

"I didn't think you would. And I'm glad they got to see how well you are doing."

"Me, too!" Lilly said.

Polly chuckled. "Me, too!"

Finally, they quieted down enough that Georgia decided to go to Sir Tyler's study to find more books. His daughters loved their reading time.

She went downstairs feeling a sense of pride in knowing that the girls had carried off lunch with their grandparents quite well. Hopefully that would go a long way in convincing them that Sir Tyler was raising his daughters in a manner that would do them proud, too.

Georgia entered the study and began searching the shelves once more. She'd been surprised that Sir Tyler had such a nice selection of children's stories—even if they were older books. But she hadn't had enough time to really look through his collection the other day. Now she slid the ladder over to the spot where she thought she'd seen some of them and climbed up.

Her eyes skimmed the upper shelves to find even more than she thought. As they were all shelved alphabetically, they were scattered throughout. So many classics the girls would love. *Robinson Crusoe, Gulliver's Travels* and *The Tales of Mother Goose*. She pulled that one off the shelf and bent over to put it on a lower one that she could reach from the floor.

Then she spotted one of her favorites, *The Swiss Family Robinson*. Oh, how she loved that story. It was on a shelf almost an arm's length away, and rather than get down and move the ladder, Georgia reached out, leaning out so far she began to lose her balance. Then she began to fall. *Oh, please, Lord, don't let me break anything!*

Her breath left her as strong arms broke her fall and she looked up to see Sir Tyler letting his own breath out in a whoosh! Held tight against him, Georgia looked into his eyes and her heart slammed against her chest as her hands rested on his shoulders.

"You nearly fell! What in the world were you reaching out so far for? I didn't think I was going to make it in time!"

"I…" She tried to find her breath. "I'm sorry. I wasn't thinking… Thank you for catching me."

The expression in his eyes seemed to change as he held her, doing nothing to quiet her heartbeat. "Sir Tyler…"

Only then did he seem to realize he still had her in his arms. He gently set her feet on the ground, but his hands rested on her upper arms as his gaze locked with hers.

"I really thought you were going to crash to the floor before I could get to you."

"I'm glad you were able to." The look in his eyes had her heart beating so hard she could feel it in her fingertips resting on his shoulders.

"Yes, so am I." He lowered his head and tipped her face up to his. "I don't want anything to happen to you, Georgia."

She caught her breath as his lips captured hers and for a moment time seemed to stand still. Georgia didn't even know if she was breathing, but she did know that she had to respond. And she did.

Then suddenly Sir Tyler broke the kiss and pulled away. "I'm sorry. I should never have— I don't know what came over me, Miss Marshall."

Georgia's heart broke right then and there for the second time in her life. Only this was much worse.

"I understand. I'm sorry. Do you want my resignation? I—"

"No! The last thing I want is for you to resign. I want your forgiveness and I promise it will never happen again."

Oh, dear Lord, please don't let me cry. I don't want his apology for kissing me. I—

"Georgia, please don't leave us. The girls need you and I never intended to put your position here in jeopardy."

She didn't know what to say. She didn't want to resign but how could she stay on? At the moment all she wanted to do was go back to her room at Heaton House and cry like a baby.

"Please think things over, Georgia. And please forgive me."

"There's nothing to forgive, Sir Tyler. You saved me from falling and that is all." How could she forgive him for giving her a memory that would last a lifetime? At least she would have that. And perhaps it was best this way.

At least now she knew to stop weaving dreams over a kiss and her misread instincts where he might be concerned. She gathered up the books that she'd dropped and held them close to her chest. Her heart constricted so that she could barely breathe, much less talk. "I'd better see about the girls."

"No, please wait, Georgia. I don't think you do see. Don't blame yourself for this. It's entirely my fault and I—"

Sir Tyler put a hand on her arm and that was almost her undoing. Georgia shook her head and rushed out of the room.

Tyler watched Georgia hurry out of the room and then dropped down into his chair. From the hurt in her eyes, Tyler knew he'd said all the wrong things. But he didn't know how to take them back. And he didn't know what to do next.

What had he done? Georgia was his daughters' nanny. How could he have overstepped the bounds of proper behavior with an employee?

He hadn't been thinking about any of that while he'd held her in his arms. He'd only thought about how afraid he'd been when he came into the study and found her leaning over in such a precarious way. He'd been afraid to say anything in case it caused her to lose her balance while he started toward her before she did.

Then all he could do was pray that he got there in time. He hadn't expected how right it felt to hold her in his arms. But he had imagined what it would be like to kiss her—a thought he'd fought for weeks now. And then he simply couldn't resist the urge to find out. And now…he'd never forget it. Didn't even want to.

But he had to. The reality of what he'd done hit him full force. Even if he hadn't crossed the line with an employee, and even if Georgia cared about him in the way he now knew he cared about her, he couldn't—wouldn't—ask her to be his wife.

Oh, dear Lord, what have I done? My girls need her and so do I—even if only as their nanny. I need to see her, to have her help in raising my daughters. But I know that isn't fair to her. She did respond to that kiss in a way that I'll never forget and never expected. I don't think she would have kissed me back if she didn't care, too, and how unfair of me is it to want her to stay on? I don't know what to do. Please guide me, Lord.

"Sir Tyler," Tate said from the doorway. "I must have been downstairs. I didn't expect you home early."

"I wanted to see how the girls' visit with their grandparents went, but it's still their nap time. I'll check on them in a bit." If he could deal with seeing Georgia again so soon.

"Would you like some tea, sir?"

"Yes, thank you." He needed to pull himself together—before he went up to see Polly and Lilly and Georgia.

Would she stay on or would she leave? And what would he do if she left? His heart twisted at the thought. Oh, why hadn't he just set her on her feet and let go of her?

He needed to speak to her again. Apologize again. Say anything to get rid of the ache in his heart. Tyler got up and started out of the room, then turned around and went back to his chair. He couldn't talk to her about any of this in front of the girls.

And she might not talk to him anyway. Maybe

it'd be better to wait until she was ready to go home for the evening. Would she come back tomorrow? Tyler sighed deeply, closed his eyes and leaned back against his chair.

"Your tea, Sir Tyler," Tate said from beside him. He poured the tea and then paused before leaving the room. "Are you all right, sir? Is there anything I can do for you?"

"I only wish it was that easy, Tate. But thank you for your concern."

Instead of going up before the girls came down for their supper, Tyler waited until they'd come down and then went up to change for his dinner. Then he waited until he knew Georgia had them ready for bed before he went to their room. But he almost bumped into her as he entered.

"Oh, I was just coming to let you know they're ready to be tucked in."

"Thank you."

"I'll be on my way now."

"Will you be here tomorrow?"

"I've told them I would see them in the morning—unless you don't want—"

"I want you to continue on as you always have. Please don't leave."

"I will try. For now."

"I can't ask for more." If only he could. For after today, there was no denying that Georgia Marshall was in full possession of his heart.

She gave a little nod and turned. "Good night, Sir Tyler."

"Good night, Georgia."

She paused but never turned around, only continued down the stairs.

Tyler took a deep breath and forced himself to smile before he went to hear his daughters' prayers and tuck them in.

Mrs. Heaton was just leaving the parlor when Georgia came in. "My dear, what is wrong? You don't look like yourself. Has something happened?"

"No. Yes." Georgia looked over at the parlor. She could hear voices in there, but there was no way she could join them all.

Mrs. Heaton took her by the arm. "Georgia, dear, come to my study. I'll get us a pot of tea and we can talk privately there."

Her landlady whisked her down the hall before anyone even knew she'd come home. Mrs. Heaton was like a mother to her and she'd never needed to speak to someone she could trust more than now.

In only moments Mrs. Heaton was pouring them tea. She handed Georgia her cup and then leaned back in her chair. "Tell me how I can help."

"Oh, Mrs. Heaton, I'm not sure you or anyone can."

"What's happened?"

"I'm in love with Sir Tyler."

"Oh, Georgia. I feel this is my fault. I should never have encouraged you to help him out. Has he—"

"He's done nothing. Except he kissed me today."

"Oh, my, I—"

"He wasn't treating me in a compromising way. He'd just kept me from falling off a ladder and, well, it just happened. And I kissed him back."

"What did he do?"

Tears gathered in Georgia's eyes. "He took the blame and apologized."

"Well, at least he did that."

"But that's the problem. I didn't want him to say he was sorry about kissing me!"

Tears began to flow down her cheeks and Mrs. Heaton patted her on the hand while handing her a kerchief. "I understand. I'm sure he didn't mean he was sorry about kissing you. Just that he did it when he didn't have the right. He's probably worried you'll resign."

"He is. But because of his girls or—" Georgia shook her head. "I should never have kissed him back. Now he must know I care and—"

"Georgia. He is your employer. He overstepped the bounds and he should have apologized. But he's also a man and, well, I'd been meaning to ask. I've seen the way he looks at you at church. He admires you a great deal."

"But admiration isn't love, Mrs. Heaton."

"No. It isn't. And if you don't want to go back, there is no reason you should. I will support you in whatever you decide to do."

"But his girls need me. At least until they get used to having their grandparents around."

"That would probably be best for them, unless Sir Tyler makes you feel too uncomfortable to stay. And then you assure them that they can come see you anytime."

"I could do that, couldn't I? Oh, Mrs. Heaton, I don't know what to do."

"I can only advise you to pray about it all. And

don't rush to a decision unless you're forced to. But if Sir Tyler makes you feel at all uncomfortable, don't hesitate to give your resignation."

Georgia couldn't bear the thought of doing that. "Thank you for listening to me. I do feel better now."

"I'm glad. I do feel responsible for your unhappiness now. I should never have—"

"Oh, Mrs. Heaton. I've loved being at Walker House. I love the girls and I feel I've been able to help them and Sir Tyler have a closer relationship. When I do leave, and I know I'll have to at some point, I'll know that they will be all right."

"You're a wonderful woman, Georgia. And Sir Tyler would be a blessed man to have you as a wife."

"But there are too many problems. We aren't in the same social class, I think he's still grieving over the loss of his wife and, well, I don't think his family or his in-laws would ever approve."

"My dear. Do not underestimate yourself."

"Thank you, Mrs. Heaton. I think I'll go up now and hope I don't run into any of the other boarders."

"I'll look out and make sure you have a clear path. And, Georgia, you're like a daughter to me and I'm glad you came to me tonight."

Georgia kissed her on the cheek. "So am I."

Mrs. Heaton looked into the hall and motioned Georgia to the door. Then she went to the bottom of the stairs and looked around, motioning a clear path for her to make her way to her room.

"Good night," she whispered.

"Good night, Mrs. Heaton." Georgia hurried upstairs and into her room. She did feel better and thought she could face the next day and seeing Sir Tyler again.

Until she went to bed. And then she remembered how it felt to be held in his arms and kissed by him, and Georgia turned over and sobbed into her pillow.

When Georgia brought the girls down to breakfast the next morning, Tyler was waiting for them and speaking to Mrs. Biddle about their family dinner.

One look at Georgia, and he was sure she'd been hoping he'd left for work earlier so that she didn't even have to see him, much less speak to him.

But he had to see her. Had to see what her reaction was after that kiss that'd kept him up most of the night.

"Are you sure it won't be too much trouble?" he asked his cook.

"Of course not, Sir Tyler. Two more for dinner is no problem at all."

"Thank you, Mrs. Biddle." Then he turned to his daughters and their nanny. "Good morning!"

"Good morning, Papa!" Lilly said.

"Who is coming to dinner, Papa?" Polly asked.

"Your grandparents telephoned first thing this morning and asked if they could join us for our family dinner this week."

He looked at Georgia, but could tell nothing about how she felt about having dinner with his in-laws. She busied herself with getting Lilly seated while he did the same for Polly.

"Really?" the girls asked.

"Yes, really. Unless Miss Marshall doesn't think you're ready yet."

"Of course they're ready," Georgia said.

"That's what I thought."

"But you don't need me to be there—"

"Oh, yes, we do, Miss Georgia," Lilly said. "What if I spill water again?"

"You'll do fine."

"But we need you there, Miss Georgia," Polly insisted. "It was a little scary just having lunch with them yesterday. I don't think their butler was happy about it."

"But Mr. Tate is. And—"

"Please have dinner with us Geor—Miss Marshall," Tyler said. "The girls will feel more comfortable if you are. And actually, so will I."

His gaze caught hers and his heart seemed to stop beating. There was still a world of hurt in her eyes and he didn't know what to do about it.

"Please, Miss Georgia!" the girls said, bringing her attention back to where it should be. On them.

"All right. I'll be here."

The two girls smiled at each other and Tyler breathed a sigh of relief.

"I appreciate it, as I know the girls do."

Mrs. Biddle came in with their breakfasts just then and Tyler could almost see the relief in Georgia's eyes that she wouldn't have to converse with him. Would they…could they ever get back to the kind of relationship they had before?

When he caught her glancing at him, she quickly looked away. It didn't appear so.

Tyler's chest tightened with remorse. Actions certainly had consequences, and after giving in to the longing to kiss her, he knew he'd be suffering from it for a very long time.

Chapter Twenty-One

The next few evenings Georgia made sure to leave Walker House as quickly as she could. It hurt too much to be around while Sir Tyler listened to his girls' prayers and tucked them in. Besides, she was afraid he might ask to speak to her and she wasn't ready to talk about what happened. And she was even more confused than ever. But she'd agreed to have dinner with them, and she wouldn't break her word. After that, however, she wasn't sure what to do.

As she went back to Heaton House after dressing for dinner on Thursday, she prayed, *Dear Lord, please help me. I don't know how much longer I can continue working here, sharing breakfasts and some dinners with him and the girls. And yet I can't leave them. Not yet.*

Mr. Tate opened the door for her and bent near her ear. "The Altmans showed up early and are in the parlor with Sir Tyler."

"Thank you for letting me know, Mr. Tate. I'll go

up and help the girls get ready. Will we be having our dinner at the regular time?"

"We will."

"Good." She wanted this evening over with. And she prayed it all went well and the Altmans would have nothing to complain about in the way she'd taught the girls or in how Sir Tyler was raising them.

She was glad to see that Amelia had already given them their baths and started on Polly's hair. Georgia set to work on Lilly's and in no time they both looked beautiful.

Then they helped them into their prettiest outfits and helped them on with their shoes. Their grandparents couldn't have anything but good to say about the way they looked.

"You both look lovely."

"So do you, Miss Georgia!"

She wore a gown she'd never worn before. It was a green-and-white dotted Swiss, with green trim and a green lace insert in the bodice. At least she felt she wouldn't bring embarrassment to Sir Tyler or his household.

"Are you ready?"

"We are!"

Georgia took their hands and they went downstairs to find Sir Tyler and their grandparents coming out of the parlor. Mrs. Altman had on a blue gown one could tell was quite expensive, but Betsy's creation held up well against it.

"May I escort my granddaughters to dinner?" Mr. Altman asked.

"You may," Lilly said, taking hold of his left arm while Polly took hold of his right.

Sir Tyler held out an arm to his mother-in-law and gave a nod to Mr. Tate, who held his arm out to Georgia. At least she didn't have to seat herself. Mr. Altman took one end of the table and Sir Tyler the other, after seating Mrs. Altman beside Lilly. Mr. Tate seated Georgia beside Polly.

"Thank you, Mr. Tate."

"You're welcome. And you will do just fine," he whispered.

The butler's kindness and expectation went far to help her shore up all the confidence she could muster, as Sir Tyler said the blessing and Mr. Tate began to serve the meal.

All through the first course of cream-of-celery soup, through the next courses of roast beef and Franconia potatoes, macaroni with cheese and a tomato-and-lettuce salad, the girls' manners were impeccable. They never interrupted a conversation, but waited for a lull to say anything, and Georgia had never been prouder of them. By the time the dessert of chocolate cream came, she could tell their grandparents were quite impressed and had enjoyed the meal a great deal.

As Mr. Tate poured coffee for the adults, Mrs. Altman looked at her from across the table. "Miss Marshall, I must say you have done an excellent job teaching the girls in every way."

Her compliment came as such a surprise, it took Georgia a moment to answer. "Why, thank you, Mrs. Altman. It's been a pleasure to see how quickly they've learned and how well they've done. I'm quite proud of them."

"As you should be," Mr. Altman said.

"Thank you, sir."

Georgia felt herself relax for the first time that eve-ning. It had gone well. They wouldn't need her at the table the next time they visited. It was time she began thinking about what she was going to do.

Lilly hid a yawn behind her napkin and Georgia excused herself. "I believe it's time to take the girls up."

"Of course," Mrs. Altman said. "It's time for us to let their papa tuck them in. He's told us that it's one of his favorite times with them, so we won't hold him up long."

"Night, Grandmama and Grandpapa," Polly said.

"Yes…" Lilly yawned again. "Thank you for com-ing."

The adults chuckled as Georgia took them by the hand.

"Good night, my dears," their grandmother said.

Georgia led them upstairs to get them ready for bed. They'd just jumped under the covers when their papa came up.

"I was so very proud of you two this evening. And so were your grandparents." Sir Tyler kissed each one and then turned to Georgia. "I need to speak to you, Miss Marshall. Will you wait in the study for me?"

Georgia's stomach clenched. She wasn't ready to speak to him—especially not alone. But he was her employer and she couldn't just say no. "Yes, of course. Good night, girls. See you tomorrow."

"Night, Miss Georgia."

She headed down the stairs wondering what it was he had to say. Would he still want her to stay or did he want her to go?

* * *

Tyler listened to his daughters' sweet prayers and kissed them good-night before heading down to his study. He wasn't looking forward to this talk. But he had to be truthful with her.

The evening before he'd heard laughter in front of his home and went to look out. As he expected, it was the group from Heaton House and Georgia was with them. They'd gone to the ice-cream parlor as they did many nights. He knew because he waited until he heard them come back and saw the near-finished cones in their hands. And he'd seen Georgia listening to something one of the men leaned over to say to her.

Oh, dear Lord, how he loved that woman. Sharp pain dug into his heart at the admission. Even deeper because she could never be his and he realized there were men in the group who might claim her. But he couldn't marry her. And he had to tell her why. Tonight.

She was pacing back and forth when he entered his study. She'd never looked lovelier than she did this evening, and he wanted nothing more than to take her in his arms and tell her so. But he couldn't let himself give in to that longing.

"I'm sorry to keep you waiting. I know you're probably tired and ready to go home. But I— Please sit down." Tyler motioned to the chair adjacent to his favorite one. Once she was seated, he sat down and put both arms on his knees, clasping his hands in the middle.

"Georgia, I feel I must apologize once more for the other night." The pain in her eyes spurred him to reach out and take her hands in his.

"Not because I kissed you. I'd do it again in a heartbeat. But because I don't have the right to. And I never can have that right, no matter how much I might want to."

Georgia tried to pull her hands from his but he grasped them firmly.

"Georgia, please hear me out. After my wife died, I vowed not to fall in love or ever marry again. You see, Ivy died trying to give me the son she thought I wanted. And I—"

"I'm so very sorry for your loss, Sir Tyler. It must have been devastating for you. But from all I've heard about your Ivy, I'm sure that she wouldn't want you to feel guilty about her death in any way. And that she would want you to eventually remarry and she'd want the girls to have a mother in their life. I understand that it wouldn't be me. I'm only an employee and you're—"

"That has nothing to do with it." Tyler looked down and shook his head before gazing into her eyes. "I can't risk ever losing another woman I love. I can't go through that kind of pain again and I can't put her in that kind of danger."

Tyler pinched the bridge of his nose to hold back the sudden sting of tears behind his eyes. He didn't want to lose *this* woman. She was the woman he loved now. But he had no choice. "I understand that you might want to hand in your resignation after what happened. It was entirely my fault. But I do ask if you will continue to help out until I can find someone to replace you—and until we feel the girls can handle your leaving." An impossible task, as there was no way he could replace Georgia in his girls' lives—or his. "They love you, you know."

He heard her shaky breath. "And I love them and I— But I understand that you wouldn't want me to stay."

Tyler ran his fingers through his hair and groaned. "Oh, Georgia. You don't understand at all. Nothing could be further from the truth. It's not that I *don't* want you to stay. It's that I *do*."

The silence in the room was deafening and Tyler was at a loss for words, but he began, "Will you think about staying until—"

"I will. I'll pray about it and give you an answer tomorrow."

"That's all I can ask."

Georgia nodded and stood. "I'll be leaving now. But I will be here in the morning. What…when will you tell the girls?"

"Not yet. I'd like to wait until next week if that's agreeable to you?" By then he might be able to accept that Georgia would be leaving. Until he could, he didn't see how he could help his girls accept it.

Tyler saw her to the door, his heart seeming to crack with each step he took. He let her out and leaned back against the door. *Please help me here, Lord. You got me through losing Ivy. Please show me the way through this pain I've brought on myself.*

Georgia had never been more relieved to have a day over with than she was the next evening. It'd been all she could do to go to work that morning.

Her heart had broken last night—not just for her, but for Sir Tyler and his daughters, too. He needed a wife and they needed a mother. She might not be the one, and much as she'd dreamed about it, she knew that it would be highly unlikely that Sir Tyler would ever care about her the way she did him. And the thought of him loving someone else shot pain through her heart to the pit of her stomach. But she loved him, loved his girls and wanted the best for them, even if it didn't include her.

But how could she continue to work for him, loving him as she did? Part of her said yes, she could. However, she knew deep down that only being a nanny would never be enough. She wanted to be a wife to him and a mother to his girls.

The thought that he'd be living in that large home, raising his girls all alone, made her want to cry all over again. She wasn't even sure whom she hurt more for. Sir Tyler or herself.

Somehow she managed to get through the day without letting the girls see how miserable she was. It'd helped that Sir Tyler had gone in to work early—because of an early appointment, Mr. Tate had said. At any rate, she'd been relieved that she didn't have to see him so quickly after last night. And when Mrs. Biddle had remarked that she didn't seem herself at teatime, Georgia had simply stated the truth. She wasn't feeling well.

The cook had quickly alerted Mr. Tate and he in turn requested that Amelia take over so that she could leave early, saying he'd explain things to Sir Tyler when he got home. The girls were concerned and told her to get some rest and feel better by Monday.

She'd been relieved when she got back to Heaton House to find that Mrs. Heaton was having tea out and the coast was clear to make it to her room. Or so she thought. Maida was just coming out of the bathroom after placing fresh towels in it.

"Are you all right, Miss Georgia? Would you like some tea?"

"I'm not feeling very well, Maida, and no tea right now, but thank you for your concern."

"Well, you just rest. I'll check on you later." With that, the maid left her room and Georgia flung herself down on the bed. How could the life she'd enjoyed so much just a few days ago have changed so much from one wonderful kiss?

Sir Tyler cared about her; she knew he did. That kiss had told her he did, and if it hadn't, she'd seen it in his eyes the night before. She'd never expected to fall in love like this—never expected to want his happiness over hers. This was nothing like the feelings she'd had for Phillip. She hadn't thought of him in ages. But now she realized what she'd once felt for him wasn't love.

And poor Sir Tyler, blaming himself for his wife's death. It couldn't have been his fault that she'd passed away during childbirth—she'd given birth to two very healthy girls.

But he felt responsible and had made up his mind never to remarry. Heartache engulfed her, and all she could do was hug her pillow and pray. *Dear Lord, I know You will get me through this, but it hurts so much. Please help me to be strong and to know what You would have me do.*

Chapter Twenty-Two

Tyler had been more miserable the past few days than he could remember since Ivy died. Maybe even more so. He'd had no choice in the matter then and couldn't bring her back. But everything in him shouted that he should run to Georgia, declare his love and ask her to marry him. But then…what if the same thing happened to her?

He couldn't—wouldn't—let himself chance losing her. The Lord had helped him through Ivy's passing and Tyler knew He would help him through this. But seeing Georgia… Even if she resigned, she'd still be next door, and just knowing that she was… Tyler groaned. He saw no way around the heartache. He'd be seeing her pass by his window with other boarders, possibly having a suitor accompanying her at some point. He would have to depend on the Lord to get him through the pain.

He'd made himself go to his in-laws to dinner on Friday evening and even they could tell something was wrong. But how did he tell them what it was?

When he'd arrived home that evening, he'd looked in on his daughters. They were going to be distraught if Georgia left—even knowing that she might one day. They loved her. He loved her. *Dear Lord, if there is a way, please show me.*

On Saturday night, when he left for dinner with his in-laws again, his mood was no better, although he'd managed to hide it from his daughters. And somehow he managed to be pleasant to the guests his in-laws had invited for his benefit.

He'd made new contacts both nights, even some appointments with potential clients, and for that he was thankful. But after two nights in a row away from the girls, he decided he wasn't going to tie up every weekend evening away from them again.

He'd mentioned that he might leave early to his father-in-law but Peter had asked him to stay, saying that he and Margaret needed to speak to him. So he'd tamped down his desire to run and stayed until the last guest left.

Then the Altmans asked for coffee to be brought to the library and the three of them headed that way. Once they were settled, his mother-in-law looked at him and asked, "Tyler, dear, I haven't seen you like this since Ivy passed away. Please tell us what is wrong."

He shook his head. This was nothing he could share with the mother of his deceased wife. He didn't even know whom he could talk to about any of it, but certainly not her parents.

"You know, when the girls were here for lunch the other day, they told us how you'd put your photograph of Ivy in their room and how Miss Marshall had gotten them to talk about her and their memories of her. How she'd said we would love them and—" His mother-in-law paused and sniffed.

Tyler could tell she was holding back tears but she gathered herself together and went on. "And that we all needed each other. They opened up to us a great deal, showing us that they did need us in their lives, thank the Lord."

"They also told us they wished they had a mother," his father-in-law added. "And that they wished it could be Miss Marshall."

"They told you all of that?" Why had they never said anything to him about it?

"They did. More even, but I'll not give away all their secrets," Margaret said. "I'm only telling you this now because I believe you care a great deal for Georgia Marshall. At first I was…upset at how you went on and on about her, and then the girls, too. It was as if she was trying to take Ivy's place."

"She's never tried to do that." Although, she had taken her place in his heart—but without trying to.

"I know that now. I also know she's in love with you and with our granddaughters. It's in her eyes for anyone to see."

"Margaret, I—"

"Tyler, dear. You are a young man in your prime and the girls are young. You do need a wife. Peter and I—"

"I can't take a wife, Margaret! I—" He jumped up and began to pace the room.

"What are you talking about, Tyler? Of course you can," Peter said. "And you should."

"How can you say that after Ivy died during childbirth? How could I ever put anyone else through that—take a chance on losing someone I loved ever again?"

"Tyler, none of that was your fault," his father-in-law said.

"But it was."

"No, son. Ivy knew she was ill long before she conceived. She didn't want you to know and—" Peter looked at his wife. "Margaret?"

"Ivy left us both a letter," his mother-in-law said. "She sent yours to me. They were only to be opened in case something happened and I was too concerned with my own grief to give you yours. I'm sorry."

The butler came in just then with coffee, and Margaret poured for them all. Then she stood and went to her writing desk and pulled a letter out of one of the drawers. She brought it over and handed it to Tyler.

"I believe I know a lot of what it says, but I didn't open it. However, Peter and I want you to know that should you decide to ever remarry, you will have our blessing. We like Georgia a great deal and we would welcome her into the family, should you change your mind about things."

Tyler turned the letter over and over in his hands. But he didn't want to read it here. He slipped it into the inside pocket of his jacket and stood. "I thank you for your concern. I don't know if anything can change my mind, but I thank you for your support. It means more to me than I can say."

"You mean a great deal to us, Tyler," Margaret said. "You made our Ivy very happy and you're the father of our only grandchildren. We love you and want you to be happy."

Tyler inhaled sharply and bent down to hug his

mother-in-law. "I love you both, too. I'll read this at home and take all you've said into consideration. And I'll pray about it all."

"That's all we can ask," Peter said.

By the time Tyler got home, a tiny bud of hope had taken root in his heart and he went to his study, where he slit open the letter his wife had left for him. He sat down and exhaled a shaky breath.

My dearest Tyler,

If you should get this, it will mean that I did not make it through childbirth, and possibly that the baby didn't, either. I should have let you know that the doctor advised against my having another child after Lilly was born, but you know I've never liked advice. He said my heart wasn't strong enough, and if you are reading this, I must admit that he was right. I do so want to give you a son, my love. But I've not been feeling well lately and I know that might not happen.

Please don't even think about blaming yourself. My illness is not your fault. I kept it from you and I decided to ignore the warnings the doctor gave me. There's no one to blame but me.

I want you to find someone to love, who loves you and our daughters as much as I do. I want them to have a mother and I want you to have a fulfilling, happy life, my love. Please grant me this one last wish.

Your loving wife,

Ivy

Tyler ran his hand over her script as tears escaped. His Ivy. Freeing him—to love again, to have a life. He read and reread the letter and spent most of the night praying, thanking the Lord for the letter she'd left and asking for guidance on what to do. Finally, after giving it all over to Him, he drifted into a deep sleep.

The next morning, he overslept but woke with a plan in mind—one he needed his girls' help with. He felt like taking the stairs two at a time down to breakfast, but if Mr. Tate saw him, he'd be appalled. Not to mention it wouldn't be a good example for his daughters.

He entered the breakfast room with a smile and kissed his girls, who were already dressed for church, before taking his own seat.

"You're late, Papa," Lilly said.

"I know. I'm sorry. But your grandparents wanted to speak to me after everyone else left last night. They had some things to tell me. Some of which you haven't told me."

Lilly gasped and glanced over at her sister, who bit her bottom lip and stared back. Then they both looked back at him.

"What did they say? Are we in trouble?" Polly asked.

"No, you are not in trouble of any kind, but I need to know—did you tell your grandparents that you wished Miss Georgia could be your mother?"

The girls looked at each other and back at him. They both nodded at the same time, their expressions earnest.

"Can you tell me why?"

"We love her!" they said in unison.

"And she loves us," Lilly said.

"How do you know this?"

"From the way she treats us and looks at us and she just does," Polly said.

"I do believe she does."

"She loves you, too, Papa," Lilly added.

"And you love her," Polly added.

"Now, girls, how can you possibly know that?"

"We see how you look at each other and how you are happy around each other," Polly said.

Out of the mouths of babes. "Why didn't you tell me how you felt?"

"You didn't ask, Papa," Lilly said.

"And Grandmama kind of did. She asked if we wanted you to marry again and we told her the truth," Polly said.

"And that we wanted it to be Miss Marshall," Lilly added.

"We talked about a lot of things," Polly admitted.

"Hmm, well, rest assured your grandmother did not tell me everything. And you are right. I do love Miss Georgia, but I'm not sure how she feels about me. I might need your help to find out."

"We can ask her!" Lilly said.

"No, but I do have a plan in mind. Will you help me?"

"Of course we will, Papa! What do you want us to do?"

Georgia's heart twisted when she saw Sir Tyler and the girls at church on Sunday. Her heart had ached more each day, and much as she realized she should resign immediately, she knew she would stay until Sir Tyler could find someone to replace her.

By then maybe she could come to terms with the reality of her life. She would either be their nanny until they were too old for one, or she would make sure they knew they could come to her at any time—as long as their papa allowed her to keep seeing them.

Georgia tried to keep her thoughts on the sermon. It was about new beginnings and how to embrace change. But she didn't want to embrace the changes that were coming. And yet she wanted to accept the Lord's will in her life. She prayed for His guidance now, knowing He would get her through this time in her life, this day and the next, no matter what might come her way. The only way to get through it all was to lean on Him.

When the service was over, the girls ran to her as usual and she hugged them. "Have you had a nice weekend?"

"We have. Are you feeling better?" Polly asked.

Georgia didn't dare look at Sir Tyler. "I believe so."

"And you'll come tomorrow?"

"I'll be there."

"Papa—" Polly nudged her father.

He nodded. "Miss Marshall, the girls and I were wondering if you might come to our home for Sunday night supper?"

"I—" She couldn't ignore the pleading look in his daughters' eyes.

"Please, Miss Georgia! We missed you this weekend!"

It'd really been only one whole day so far, but she'd felt as if it'd been a week. Still, after their talk the other night, she couldn't figure out why Sir Tyler would be asking her to supper.

"Please."

His gaze met hers and her heart did a double somersault. How could she say no? "What time?"

"Around six. You don't need to dress up more than you are now."

Georgia gave a little nod. "I'll see you then."

The girls grinned and clapped and whispered to each other. Was this their idea?

"Georgia, are you coming?" Julia asked.

"I am. See you all later," she said to Sir Tyler and his daughters. Then she turned and walked away, trembling all the way. Something had changed since Thursday night, but what?

By the time Georgia left Heaton House to go over to Sir Tyler's she felt as if a hundred butterflies had been let loose in her stomach. But she had to find out what this was all about.

Mr. Tate must have been waiting for her, for the door opened before she could ring the bell. "Miss Georgia, it's good to see you. I trust you've had a good weekend?"

It'd been anything but, with the heartache over Sir Tyler, but she couldn't say that to him. Trying to sidestep an answer, she said, "The weather has been very nice, hasn't it?"

"It has. Please, come this way. Sir Tyler is waiting for you." He led her to the study, where the small table had been set for two, with a candle in the middle.

"That will be all, Tate. You may begin serving whenever Mrs. Biddle is ready," Sir Tyler said, coming forward to greet her.

"Thank you for coming, Georgia. I wasn't sure you would." He took hold of her arm and had her seated before she could speak.

"What is this, Sir Tyler? Where are the girls? I thought we were having dinner with them."

"I must admit to pulling a bit of a trick on you. I wasn't sure you'd come if I asked you to have dinner with just me."

"And you pulled your daughters into it?"

"I confess I did. But they were happy to ask you for me. And if you remember, they asked if you'd come to 'our home.' They didn't exactly say dinner with *them*."

"Sir Tyler—"

Mr. Tate arrived just then with their supper. Georgia was relieved to see that it wasn't much different from one of Mrs. Heaton's Sunday night suppers. There was vegetable soup and roast-beef sandwiches. He also brought in peach cobbler in bowls. Not his usual course serving, but it had to make his job easier tonight, and for that, Georgia was pleased.

"That will be all for now, Tate. Thank you."

"You're welcome, sir." He quietly left the room, shutting the door behind him.

"Please tell me what this is all about."

"I will over our dinner. But I need to say grace first. Please bow with me."

Georgia bowed her head and Sir Tyler began to pray.

"Dear Lord, I thank You for this day. I ask that You

bless this food we are about to eat and that Georgia would hear me out when I explain why I've asked her here. And that Your will be the outcome. In Jesus's name, amen."

He dipped a spoon in his soup and took a sip, then put it down and gazed at Georgia. "I had a talk with my in-laws after their dinner last night and one with Polly and Lilly this morning." He dipped into his soup once more.

Apparently, he was going to draw this out. Well, so could she. Georgia brought a spoon of soup to her lips and waited.

"Have the girls ever mentioned that they'd like me to remarry?"

Georgia nearly choked on the soup she'd just put in her mouth. Then she took a sip of water. "No. Never."

"Nor me. But they told their grandparents when they went to lunch that day. I had no idea."

Georgia's heart began to beat—what was all of this leading to? He'd said he'd never get married again, so why even bring it up?

"And…Margaret gave me a letter."

"A letter? Why would she give you something she could say to you in person?"

"It was from Ivy."

Georgia put down her spoon. "Sir Tyler, please tell me what this is all about."

Tyler's gaze held hers as he reached for her hands. "Ivy had a heart problem and had been advised not to have more children after Lilly was born. But she never told me. The letter was to be given to me only if she didn't make it through the birth."

"And your mother-in-law just now gave it to you?"

"I don't think she could bear the thought of my carrying out Ivy's wishes. But after speaking to the girls, she had a change of heart."

"What were Ivy's wishes?"

"Never to blame myself. And to find someone who loves the girls and me as much as she did. To find someone I loved the same way. Her letter freed me to do what I've longed for weeks to do."

Hope filled Georgia's heart to almost bursting as Tyler came around the table and got down on one knee. "I know I may be presumptuous, but I have to ask. Georgia, do you—could you love me and my girls with—"

"All my heart." She reached out and cupped his jaw in her hand. "I do love you. I have for weeks now."

Tyler took her hand in his and brought it to his lips. "I love you with all that I am. Will you marry me? Become the wife I long for and the mother my girls need?"

Tears of pure joy slipped down Georgia's cheeks. "Oh, Tyler, yes. Yes, I will marry you!"

Tyler stood, pulled her to her feet and into his arms. "I love you, Georgia Marshall, and I thank the Lord above for bringing you into our lives. You've made us come alive again, laugh again and given me no choice but to fall in love again."

He tipped her face up to his. And then he did what she'd been holding her breath for. He kissed her, claimed her as his, and she kissed him back in the same way—until they were suddenly jerked apart by the sound of the study door opening.

The girls burst in with Mr. Tate right behind them.

"Papa, did you ask?" Polly asked. "We've been waiting and waiting to hear!"

"I'm sorry, sir! I tried to tell the girls that you would ring for me to bring them to you, but they caught me with my back turned and made a run for it."

Georgia couldn't help but giggle at the look on the butler's face, but the hesitation she saw in Polly's and Lilly's eyes shot to her heart. She smiled at them and they rushed over to her and their papa.

"Did Papa ask you to marry him yet, Miss Georgia?" Polly asked.

Georgia glanced at her new fiancé and back at his daughters. "He did."

"And what did you say?"

"She said yes!" Tyler answered for her. "She will marry me and become my wife and your new mother."

"If that is all right with you two," Georgia added.

"It's what we've been praying for, Miss Georgia!" Lilly said.

Polly nodded. "Every night, after Papa hears our prayers and leaves the room!"

Georgia blinked back tears as Tyler grasped her hand and they both knelt on the floor, their arms open for a group hug with his daughters. The joy in his— soon to be *their*—daughters' expressions filled Georgia's heart to overflowing. She'd never felt more loved, or more needed, than at this moment.

Overwhelmed with happiness, Georgia sent up a silent prayer. *Thank You, dear Lord, for giving me a future I've been afraid to dream of and one I thought*

I'd never have. Please help me to be the best wife and mother I can be to these three I love so dearly. In Jesus's name, amen.

* * * * *

Dear Reader,

I hope you enjoyed reading Georgia and Sir Tyler's story as much as I enjoyed writing it. It was a little different having much of the story take place somewhere other than Heaton House this time, but Mrs. Heaton's boarders tend to fall in love quite often, necessitating bringing in new ones to take their places. With her neighbor's house being sold in the last story, I thought it would be fun to write about Sir Tyler, the widower with two children who moved in. He needed help badly and Georgia seemed the perfect one to come to his aid.

I had so much fun writing about her and Sir Tyler, Polly and Lilly, and seeing how Georgia helped them through their grief. Everyone has different ways of dealing with the loss of a loved one and Georgia's heart went out to Sir Tyler and his girls.

With both Georgia and Sir Tyler determined never to love again, it was a challenge to get them to change their minds. They both fought their growing feelings for each other—to no avail, for the Lord had plans of His own. And with them both looking to Him to guide them, to let His will be done, it was a joy to see them finally admit their love for one another.

Please let me know what you thought of this story and feel free to connect with me at my website at: janetleebarton.com. I'd love it if you'd sign up for my newsletter there. You can also email me at janetb writes@cox.net.

Blessings,
Janet Lee Barton

STAND-IN RANCHER DADDY
Lone Star Cowboy League: The Founding Years
by Renee Ryan

CJ Thorn's unprepared to raise his twin nieces. But when his brother abandons them to his care, he has to learn quickly. And with the help of Molly Carson—their late mother's best friend— he might just become the stand-in father the little girls need.

LAWMAN IN DISGUISE
Brides of Simpson Creek
by Laurie Kingery

Wounded during a bank robbery, undercover lawman Thorn Dawson is nursed back to health by widow Dalsy Henderson and her son. Can he return the favor by healing Daisy's shattered heart?

THE NANNY SOLUTION
by Barbara Phinney

Penniless socialite Victoria Templeton agrees to work as a nanny for widowed rancher Mitch MacLeod as he transports his family to Colorado. But she isn't quite prepared to handle the children...or their handsome single father.

COUNTERFEIT COURTSHIP
by Christina Miller

Former Confederate officer Graham Talbot must support his stepmother and orphaned niece...so he can't afford to marry any of the women swarming to court him. And Ellie Anderson— the woman he once loved—has a plan to stop their advances: a fake courtship.

———————

LIHCNM0616

REQUEST YOUR FREE BOOKS!

2 FREE INSPIRATIONAL NOVELS
PLUS 2 *FREE* MYSTERY GIFTS

Love Inspired® HISTORICAL

SPECIAL EXCERPT FROM

Love Inspired HISTORICAL

*When a bachelor rancher abruptly gains custody
of his twin nieces, he needs all the help he can get.
But as he starts to fall for the girls' widowed caretaker,
can love blossom for this unexpected family?*

Read on for a sneak preview of
STAND-IN RANCHER DADDY,
the heartwarming beginning of the series
LONE STAR COWBOY LEAGUE:
THE FOUNDING YEARS

At last, CJ thought. Help was on the way.

With each step Molly took in his direction, he felt the tension draining out of him. She was a calming influence and the stability they all needed—not just Sarah and Anna, but CJ, too.

If she ever left him…

Not the point, he told himself.

She looked uncommonly beautiful this morning in a blue cotton dress with a white lace collar and long sleeves. The cut of the garment emphasized her tiny waist and petite frame.

He attempted to swallow past the lump in his throat without much success. Molly took his breath away.

If he were from a different family…

"Miss Molly," Anna called out. "Miss Molly, over here! We're over here."

Sarah wasn't content with merely waving. She pulled her hand free of CJ's and raced to meet Molly across the small expanse of grass. Anna followed hard on her sister's heels.

Molly greeted both girls with a hug and a kiss on the top of their heads.

"Well, look who it is." She stepped back and smiled down

at the twins. "My two favorite girls in all of Little Horn, Texas. And don't you look especially pretty this morning."

"Unca Corny picked out our dresses," Sarah told her.

"He tried to make breakfast." Anna swayed her shoulders back and forth with little-girl pride. "He didn't do so good. He burned the oatmeal and Cookie had to make more."

Molly's compassionate gaze met his. "Sounds like you had an…interesting morning."

CJ chuckled softly. "Though I wouldn't want to repeat the experience anytime soon, we survived well enough."

"Miss Molly, look. I'm wearing my favorite pink ribbon." Sarah touched the floppy bow with reverent fingers. "I tied it all by myself."

"You did a lovely job." Under the guise of inspecting the ribbon, Molly retied the bow, then moved it around until it sat straight on the child's head. "Pink is my favorite color."

"It's Pa's favorite, too." Sarah's gaze skittered toward the crowded tent. "I wore it just for him."

The wistful note in her voice broke CJ's heart. He shared a tortured look with Molly.

Her ragged sigh told him she was thinking along the same lines as he was. His brother always made it to church, a fact the twins had reminded him of this morning.

"Pa says Sunday is the most important day of the week," Sarah had told him, while Anna had added, "And we're never supposed to miss Sunday service. Not ever."

Somewhere along the way, the two had gotten it into their heads that Ned would show up at church today. CJ wasn't anywhere near as confident. If Ned didn't make an appearance, the twins would know that their father was truly gone.

Don't miss
STAND-IN RANCHER DADDY
by Renee Ryan, available July 2016 wherever
Love Inspired® Historical books and ebooks are sold.

www.LoveInspired.com

SPECIAL EXCERPT FROM

Love Inspired®

*When Lauren McCauley comes home to Montana after
her father's death, will she decide to sell the ranch to
handsome rancher Vic Moore?*

Read on for a sneak preview of
TRUSTING THE COWBOY,
the second book in Carolyne Aarsen's romantic trilogy
BIG SKY COWBOYS.

"So you didn't like it here?" Vic asked. "Coming every
summer?"

"I missed my friends back home, but there were parts
I liked."

"I remember seeing you girls in church on Sunday."

"Part of the deal," Lauren said, a faint smile teasing her
mouth. "And I didn't mind that part, either. The message
was always good, once I started really listening. I can't
remember who the pastor was, but what he said resonated
with me."

"Jodie and Erin would attend some of the youth events,
didn't they?"

"Erin more than any of us."

"I remember my brother Dean talking about her," Vic
said. "I think he had a secret crush on her."

"He was impetuous, wasn't he?"

"That's being kind. But he's settled now."

Thoughts of Dean brought up the same problem that
had brought him to the ranch.

His deal with Lauren's father.

"So, I hate to be a broken record," he continued, "but

I was wondering if I could come by the house tomorrow. To go through your father's papers."

Lauren sighed.

Vic tamped down his immediate apology. He had nothing to feel bad about. He was just looking out for his brother's interests.

"Yes. Of course. Though—" She stopped herself there. "Sorry. You probably know better what you're looking for."

Vic shot her a glance across the cab of the truck. "I'm not trying to jeopardize your deal. When I first leased the ranch from your father, it was so that my brother could have his own place. And I'm hoping to protect that promise I made him. Especially now. After his accident."

"I understand," Lauren said, her smile apologetic. "I know what it's like to protect siblings."

"Are you the oldest?"

"Erin and I are twins, but I'm older by twenty minutes."

Lauren smiled at him. And as their eyes held, he felt it again. An unexpected rush of attraction. When her eyes grew ever so slightly wider, he wondered if she felt it, too.

He dragged his attention back to the road.

You're no judge of your feelings, he reminded himself, his hands tightening on the steering wheel as if reining in his attraction to this enigmatic woman.

He'd made mistakes in the past, falling for the wrong person. He couldn't do it again. He couldn't afford to.

Especially not with Lauren.

Don't miss
TRUSTING THE COWBOY
by Carolyne Aarsen, available July 2016 wherever
Love Inspired® books and ebooks are sold.

www.LoveInspired.com